MELHARA

A Novel

By
Jocelyn Tollefson

Lost Girl Creations
Edmonton, Alberta

Copyright © 2016 Jocelyn Lewis

All rights reserved. The use of any part of this publication reproduced, transmitted in any form or by any means, electronic, mechanical, photocopying, recording, or otherwise, or stored in a retrieval system, without prior written consent from the publisher is an infringement of copyright law.

This book is a work of fiction. Names, characters, places, and incidents either are the product of the author's imagination or are used fictitiously. Any resemblance to actual persons, living or dead, events, or locales is entirely coincidental.

Library and Archives Canada Cataloguing in Publication
Tollefson, Jocelyn, 1982-, author
Melhara / a novel by Jocelyn Tollefson.
ISBN 978-0-9953086-1-9 (paperback)
I. Title.
PS8639.O444M45 2017 C813'.6 C2016-906257-0

Edited by: Vanessa Ricci-Thode and Marg Gilks, Scripta Word Services

Cover art by: Chris Moet, chrismoet.com

Lost Girl Creations
4811 31 ave, NW
Edmonton, Alberta T6L 4H8

Dedication

For all the women who have felt lost as they fought their demons, struggled with destiny and creating their own path.

MELHARA

A Novel

by
Jocelyn Tollefson

Prologue

The Year 2000

Kyra dashed down the dark hall on the balls of her feet, running from the demon. As she neared the open doorway of the bathroom, a sensation of anxiety rushed over her, but too late—she turned the corner and her momentum carried her into the room.

She stopped.

Something was wrong.

Someone was in here.

Panic rose from her stomach and clenched in her chest. Her eyes struggled to adjust in the dimness. Slowly, she made out a dark figure on one side of the tiny room. It stood up.

Holding her breath, Kyra fumbled for the light switch, flicked it on. Light flooded the tiny room, temporarily blinding her.

"What the hell!" demanded her sister Hailey, looking startled before her expression grew puzzled. "Why are you naked? Just because it's your birthday doesn't mean you can run around in your birthday suit," she teased. "Get a freaking towel." She grabbed a towel off the shelf and tossed it at Kyra without unfolding it.

Kyra felt her cheeks heat up. She caught the towel and wrapped herself up.

"Yeah, that was pretty cheesy."

"So was saying *cheesy*." Hailey smirked.

"Sorry I barged in on you. I-I couldn't sleep so I was going to take a shower and get ready. I didn't think anyone else was awake yet," Kyra stammered. *Idiot.* Foolishly panicking over a mystery shadow. Of course it was her sister in the bathroom—what did she expect, the monster from her nightmare to be in there, waiting to pounce? That's just silly.

"What's wrong?" Hailey asked, looking closely at Kyra's face. "You look like you've seen a ghost—well, like a normal person would look like, if they saw a ghost." Giggling, Hailey faced the mirror and turned on the tap.

Kyra peered into the hallway before focusing back on her sister.

"You have to promise not to say anything," she whispered.

Hailey tipped her head toward her, her soapy hands poised over the sink. "Oh my God, did you see a ghost again?"

"No, but—" Kyra recoiled, flooded by memories of psychiatrists and countless prescription drugs. She lurched forward, commanding her memories to recede back to where they belonged, buried in the past. "You can't say anything, no matter what," she said, her voice sounding more desperate than she intended.

"I won't," Hailey said, and bit her bottom lip.

Kyra nodded, just once, and drew a deep breath. "I had another dream about that demon, but this time, it actually freaked *me* out."

"You're still having nightmares about demons and angels?" Hailey rinsed her hands in the warm water. "I thought they had stopped."

"They did," Kyra lied, wanting to vanish from the room and reappear in her bed—and she could—but then Hailey would know that secret too, and that might be too much for her to keep to herself. It was too late to escape, and besides, it might help her nerves if she told someone, and there was no one else she could talk to. "Or I thought they had, until last night. I saw the same demon that I always see." She realized she was nervously scrunching her towel tighter between her hands, and willed herself to stop. "But this time, it felt different." She dropped her voice. "I think it's after me."

"What are you talking about?" Hailey asked. "Why would a demon be after you?" She reached around Kyra and pulled the hand towel off the bar hanging on the wall.

"Before, my dreams were always like watching a movie," Kyra explained. "But this time, it knew I was watching, and it spoke to me."

"What do you mean?" Hailey grimaced. "Tell me exactly what happened."

"It wasn't doing anything, just lying in a cave, then it sat up and looked at me—like, *really* looked at me. And it said, 'Soon you will belong to me.' Then it lunged at me and I woke up terrified."

Hailey puckered her lips a moment, then said, "It's a creepy dream, but it's still just a dream, Kyra."

Kyra sighed. "It was so real that I panicked and had to check my arm where the demon's claws had grazed me. I thought for sure there was going to be huge gashes bleeding all over the place. I swear, I felt the claws cut me."

"You're okay. It's over and nothing actually happened. It was just a dream," Hailey said, pulling her sister in for a hug. "Are you going to be okay, moving out and going off to a college where no one knows about the crazy girl?" She pulled away, met Kyra's eyes, and grinned.

"Ha-ha," Kyra drawled, then she smiled. "I'll manage. It'll be nice to have friends that aren't afraid of me."

"Happy birthday, by the way." She thrust a thumbs-up gesture into Kyra's face. "Now you can buy us beer."

Hailey spun around and dashed out of the bathroom, purposely avoiding the response.

"Um, thanks," Kyra muttered and started the shower, hoping her morning routine would help her forget the nightmare. But she couldn't purge from her mind the vision of the demon's black eyes, or the cold trickle of dread that ran down her spine as it spoke to her.

She stepped over to the tiny window, cranked it open a crack, and rested her folded arms on the windowsill. She closed her eyes and inhaled deeply of the refreshing morning air. The sun was rising, and she savored the wan warmth of it on her face as she tried to reassure herself that what she'd experienced really was nothing more than a bad dream.

The sunlight dimmed, as if clouds cast shadows over her face, then the sunlight on her eyelids disappeared. Her eyes popped open to a cluster of green leaves, and she jerked back. The Virginia Creeper vines that normally hugged the lower wall of the house jerked away from the window and hung, unsupported, the tips arcing toward the window, swaying, as if they were watching her.

How could they have climbed three feet in a couple of minutes? Squinting, she leaned in closer and the vines drifted toward her. She drew back, surprised, and then scratched her head in confusion. One of the vines on the outer edge of the cluster bent inward and vibrated, its leaves fluttering. She shifted her weight, swinging her arm down from her head.

The vines mimicked her.

Impossible. What is happening?

She flapped her hand in a shooing motion and willed the vines to return to their original state. They obeyed and shrank down below the window.

She shook her head. She didn't want to think about this right now. Not on the heels of the nightmare. Dropping her towel, she stepped into the bathtub. Taking a deep breath, she closed her eyes and plunged her face into the spray of water, washing the residual fear from her nightmare and the mystery of the freaky vines down the drain.

She kept her eyes closed and dropped her face, allowing the water to hit the back of her head, then trickle down her body. Calmer now, she breathed deeply.

The spray of water began to slow. Then the pressure of the water on the back of her head stopped. Confused, she opened her eyes and stepped back. The water from the showerhead stood still—as if time had stopped. It was as if the spray from the showerhead was frozen.

Almost frozen, she amended. It still fell, but at an impossibly slow rate; it was barely moving, like the wings of a bird taking flight in a slow motion video. The drops that had escaped the showerhead and dripped off her body clung to the point in time where they had been when it had slowed; those in the tub made their way sluggishly toward the drain. She put out her hand to touch the drops suspended in front of her. As her hand moved upward, a pool of water formed in it.

She sensed a presence approaching, and lost her concentration. The water began to flow freely again before the knock at the door startled her.

"Honey, are you almost done?" asked a muffled voice from outside the door. "I'm going to start making pancakes. Do you want chocolate chips or blueberries?"

"Um, yeah Mom, I'll be right out. Chocolate would be great. Thanks."

Her attention turned back to the showerhead and she held both her open hands toward it. Closing her eyes, she listened to the running water, the heat from the droplets relaxing her. Then she took a deep breath and opened her eyes. The water slowed almost to a halt. Gravity had stopped forcing the water to the floor, but it was more than that. The pressure from the water was barely forcing the flow out of the showerhead, too.

She stood on her tiptoes and brought her face closer to the showerhead. It was in slow motion again. And she was controlling it.

"Damn it, what's wrong with me now?" She dropped her hands and the water resumed its natural flow.

Chapter One

Present Day

Alexis Bennett scanned the parking lot, careful to ensure it was vacant of any potential witnesses. Satisfied, she turned to the SUV that was parked a foot over the yellow line of her assigned stall—probably by some drunk idiot headed to the bar down the street last night. She narrowed her eyes. The encroaching SUV slid away from her Honda Fit and into its own stall.

Kyra Parker pulled into the lot as Alexis climbed out of her car. Deciding to wait for her best friend, Alexis watched her park, but then stay in her car with the engine running, her hands clenched on the steering wheel. Sighing, Alexis approached Kyra's vehicle. As she drew closer, she could see Kyra's nails tapping against the steering wheel as she stared blankly at the wall of the bank.

She's overthinking again. She spends too much time doing that, and it's getting worse.

Moving up the driver's side of Kyra's car, Alexis made a jerky dance movement to get her attention. Kyra looked over to her side window and frowned. Alexis contorted her face, crossed her eyes, and stuck her tongue out the corner of her mouth, then made another awkward dance move. No reaction from Kyra.

Not a good sign.

Kyra took the keys out of the ignition and stepped out of her car, tucking her necklace inside her button-up blouse.

"Morning, crazy lady," said Alexis. "Whatcha daydreaming about this time?"

"Nothing," she said, too quickly. "Nothing exciting, anyway. Why do we have to be here again?"

"Um, 'cause someone has to pay the bills and we like shoes!" Alexis squealed.

"Ha! True story." Kyra smirked and her emerald eyes lit up.

They headed toward the building. Kyra sighed. "I don't know what's up with me lately. I can't seem to focus on my life." She dropped her keys into her purse and slung it over her shoulder. "I mean, I'm not sure what I'm doing anymore. I just feel... lost."

"That's depressing," Alexis replied. "If you weren't taking off after work to go on an adventure, we could go get some drinks and create some of our own excitement." She wriggled her eyebrows and winked at her friend.

Kyra groaned. "What adventure? Our camping trip?" She rolled her eyes. "Maybe if we went into the bush with nothing but a pocketknife, it would be an adventure. Our trip has turned into hotels and cabins. James wants Wi-Fi and cable, 'in case it rains.' Yeah, right, in case it rains. He'll probably spend the entire trip in the cabin."

"That's just James for you. He's never been the outdoorsy type."

"Well, we both know that I am. I feel like I'm being suffocated by the city, more now than ever. I need to be out in the wilderness, surrounded by nature."

"Yeah, your flower gardens are amazing, but they could be better if you used," Alexis dropped her voice and adopted a wheedling tone, "just a tiny bit of your powers." Kyra grimaced at her. "Oh, come on, it's so little, it wouldn't even count as using magic!"

When they reached the door, Alexis pressed her hand over the lock. Her keys were still in her purse.

"This vacation will help you reconnect with yourself and figure out the path you want to take."

Kyra placed her hand over Alexis's. When Alexis looked at her, her mouth was pinched with worry.

"I have some reservations about this whole thing," she said somberly.

"What do you mean, did you have a premonition?"

She shook her head, making the large curls of her long blonde hair bob. "I-I can't explain it."

"Neither did I, but I have a bad feeling about you going too," Alexis admitted, "and I can't pinpoint it either." *Whoa, lighten up.* She grinned. "Maybe, it's because I'm going to have to entertain myself while you're gone." She gave Kyra a playful poke. "It's probably just nerves, because you're venturing into new territory and leaving Calgary—finally," she said, trying to ease Kyra's anxiety, but she knew there was more to it. Even to her, though she couldn't identify why, it felt like a major change loomed over Kyra. "Yeah, maybe, but…" Kyra trailed off when the heavy clunk of the deadbolt unlocked the door.

Alexis pushed open the door and stepped inside. The familiar high-pitched beeping from the alarm system made Alexis oddly uneasy. She flicked her wrist at the keypad, the numbers for her code punched in, and the alarm fell silent.

"If it's meant to be, it will be," Alexis said, knowing Kyra was still struggling at a crossroad. "It can still be a great trip. You can go hiking with your sister, and it's a good way to start Xavier's summer vacation." She smiled reassuringly.

Kyra responded with a weak smile.

***

Seated behind her desk, her chair turned around so her back was to the door, Kyra gazed out the window, letting her irritation at the shady client dissipate faster than the stench of his cologne. Her eyes wandered the landscape outside, pausing to watch a flock of sparrows swoop in to land gracefully on the sidewalk, where they hopped around, pecking at invisible tidbits, before taking off into the sky en masse. With nothing more to distract her from her thoughts, her eyes glazed over and her daydreams took hold.

She was ripped back to reality by the ringing of her office phone. Spinning her chair around, she stared at the blinking red light, her hand hovering over the clunky receiver. She closed her eyes and tried to determine who was on the other end, but she couldn't tell. Which left only two options.

"Hmm, I wonder…"

She opened her eyes and snatched up the receiver. "Good morning, Kyra Parker speaking." She glanced through the sidelight next to her office door. The hallway outside was vacant.

"Oh, hey." She grinned. "Miss me already?"

She pushed the stack of paperwork and file folders off to the side of her desk, then swiveled her chair to face the window again. Her fingers instinctively toyed with the chain around her neck as she listened.

"I don't want you to go."

Her smile turned into a frown. "I know. We will sort this out when I get back. I have to go. Everything is just so… so *confusing* right now. It will be okay, I promise." She sighed, staring at the walnut-colored sphere hanging from her necklace, then pulled the chain over her head and set it on her desk. "I just need some time to sort things out for my family first."

She listened to the chatter that followed, nodding along and throwing in the odd "uh-huh."

"I don't think it's a good idea. You should stay in the city and spend some time alone to figure out what you want. Take some more time off work so Alexis doesn't distract you or maybe work some extra hours to keep yourself out of the house."

"Work is actually part of the problem. I think I might quit. It's become so stale and I just don't give a crap anymore."

She heard her door close abruptly behind her, and spun around. Alexis was standing in her office, lips pursed, the harsh overhead fluorescents making the light dusting of freckles over her cheeks stand out. The effect made her look younger than her thirty-five years.

"I have to let you go," Kyra said quickly, and hung up the receiver.

Alexis marched over to Kyra. Her eyes dropped to the necklace on the desk, then drifted back to Kyra. "Sooooo, who was that?"

"Alexis, it was no one. My door was closed for a reason. It was supposed to be a private conversation," she retorted, casually swiping her necklace into the desk drawer. At times it was annoying, not being able to sense other witches—no, unfair, because even though they shouldn't be able to, somehow they could sense her. Well… in a small way, the fact they could sense her presence did help her feel more normal; more human. "How long were you eavesdropping?"

"Does that matter? Long enough," Alexis scoffed. She pulled her auburn hair over her shoulder and twisted it as if she were wringing out a towel. "Why didn't you tell me you were thinking about quitting?" she asked, sounding hurt. "I know you hate our boss as much as I do."

Kyra hesitated, realizing that Alexis thought she'd been talking to a headhunter. *Okay, that will work.*

"Sorry. I wasn't sure if you would understand and I'm not sure I'm going to leave yet."

Alexis's shoulders relaxed. "No worries. And I *do* completely understand." She flipped her hair behind her back. "Your patience with clients has diminished since Colleen took the management position. She's so uptight and a huge, ball-busting pain in the ass. I've thought about quitting because of her crap too."

"Yeah, she does have a huge stick up her ass." Kyra snickered. "And she always looks so constipated and angry."

"She probably hasn't gotten laid in thirty years."

They shared a laugh at their boss's expense. Alexis flopped down into one of the oversized armchairs facing Kyra's desk. When the giggling subsided, Alexis's expression turned serious.

"I know you've been going through some other things, even though you haven't really talked to me about it since the initial incident at the Christmas party, but I can see it on you." She held up her hand as Kyra opened her mouth to protest. "You're always daydreaming or distracted and never really here anymore." Her face softened. "I know it's hard with James being the way he is… and I sometimes really wonder why you picked him to be your husband. He's so—so *vanilla*."

Kyra chuckled, then sat back in her chair with a sigh. "James is a lot like my father was, and I love him for it, but—" she threw up her hands "—is this really all that my life was meant to be? It doesn't feel right."

"Maybe you do need a bigger change," Alexis said. "You know I love you and just want you to be happy, whatever you decide."

"Thank you."

If only she could tell Alexis everything, every detail about what she was really daydreaming about! But she didn't fully understand it herself, so how could she explain it to someone else? If Alexis only knew…

Her thought escaped unfinished. A presence was fast approaching, one she immediately recognized.

"Oh, shit." Kyra fumbled for some papers and pulled a pile in front of her as Alexis slouched down in her seat, doing the best she could to hide in her chair, and started casting.

The office door swung open and their stout manager, Colleen, stormed in before Alexis could finish her spell.

"What just happened with Mr. Rumaluck?" Colleen demanded, her pudgy face flushed red. "I could barely get him to calm down and talk to me as he rushed out of the building. You were supposed to schmooze him into being a client, not alienate him... and *you*." Her head rotated to Alexis. "What are you doing in here? This is not a coffee break or social hour. Get back to work. I wonder how either of you could possibly have the numbers that you do, with all of the clients that walk out on you two."

Alexis offered a tight smile. She glanced sympathetically at Kyra before leaving the office.

Colleen stepped forward and braced her hands on Kyra's desk. "Keira, this is getting ridiculous."

Kyra unclenched her teeth. "It's K-eye-ra, like Tyra or Myra. We've had this conversation before."

"Oh, yes. Well, the spelling suggests it should sound like Keira." She shrugged. "Now what happened with Mr. Rumaluck?"

Rumaluck. He'd given off a vibe that made her uncomfortable. She was convinced he was involved in some sort of criminal activity, although she had failed to uncover any evidence. She knew she was right, though—her intuition was seldom wrong.

"He's not looking to move his accounts at this time," she lied. "I've no idea why he'd have been upset when he left."

"I'm sure," Colleen said bitterly. "Well, you have another new client after lunch, and you'd better get the account. No excuses. If you don't snag this one, I'll be talking with my superiors about your lack of performance."

Their eyes locked as Colleen leaned over the desk, bringing her pudgy, red-mottled face closer to Kyra's. Kyra refused to sit back, even when she could smell the onions on Colleen's breath. She forced a smile.

With a soft huff of displeasure Colleen pushed back from the desk and turned to leave. She paused in the doorway. "Good luck, Keira." She disappeared into the hall.

Chapter Two

The sun was a burning orange orb as it set behind them, casting a revitalizing glow over the landscape as James guided the car through the hills. Kyra opened her window a crack, allowing the sweet smell of summer to flow into the car. There were few signs of civilization out in this open space, just the odd car on the narrow highway bordered by farmer's fields and fences, and the occasional house.

Kyra peered into the backseat at her son. Xavier was playing his video games, completely unaware of the passing beauty outside. With the exception of his mother's bright emerald eyes, he was the spitting image of his father.

Kyra's little sister, Hailey and her husband, Nick Miller, had recently become the proud owners of a beach house, which Hailey had found a way to work into every conversation with her since the fall, until this had become the compromise for a camping trip. Kyra was no longer sure how camping in a tent out in the bush had turned into a two-day drive to an oceanfront beach house for a week's vacation.

She looked at James and slowly smiled. With one hand draped over the wheel and his other arm resting on the door beside him, he looked relaxed and content. And classically handsome, with his normally clean-shaven face now sporting a five o'clock shadow. At this moment she found him very tantalizing. Her smile turned into a grin.

He caught her gaze and turned serious brown eyes her way before he returned the smile. "What's that look for?" he asked.

"Oh, nothing. Just thinking about the things we can do while we're on vacation."

"Oh? Please do elaborate."

"Can't, honey. We're not the only ones in the car. But I can show you tomorrow," she said with a wink. "We could go for a walk along the beach while Xavier stays with my sister."

"I like that idea," James said, smiling. He returned his attention to the road. "But it is a public beach, and I'm not so keen on rolling around, getting sand in places where sand shouldn't be."

She sighed. "It's been a while since we've actually spent any time together, just us." She paused. "I miss us. The way we used to be."

"What are you going on about? We spend time together every day."

"Lying in bed for an hour with laptops and books before we go to sleep doesn't count as spending time together."

"We're taking two days to drive out to the ocean instead of flying so we could spend time together, aren't we? Or what's the point of this waste of time?" he said, his tone defensive.

"Yes, but—"

James cut her off. "We could have flown there, which would have been more cost-effective and saved us four days of driving and two hotel nights, never mind the mileage on the car."

She sighed. "I just miss the way we were when being together and in love was more important than getting to work on time. We were an hour late for dinner reservations more than once, because we couldn't seem to keep our hands off each other. And we put the effort into timing our schedules so we could spend our lunch hours together, talking our heads off. That sort of thing used to be important to us."

"Well, sweetheart, things change. We couldn't stay like that forever. We both have more demands on us now, with our careers, and Xavier's activities that you insist on him being in; they take up a huge chunk of time, money, and energy. Between that and taking care of the house, there isn't much time left for us to act like newlyweds."

"True story, but... there should be," she grumbled. "Don't you think that's important?"

She sighed when she realized he wasn't going to say what she wanted him to say—that she was more important than everything else. She turned away from him and looked out her window.

"We can hire a housekeeper and a gardener or some other help, if you like," he said after a moment.

"I'm in my garden because I like to be there. You're missing the point. It's not the busy schedule so much as the priorities we give to everything."

"I don't know what else you want me to say. You've been bugging me to go on a work-free family vacation, so that's what we're doing—even though I'm going to have a ton of catching up to do when we get home. I'm hoping this will bring you back from whatever midlife crisis you seem to be going through. Your head has been in the clouds for a while now, and I—"

"Hey, look at that," she blurted, pointing to an old motel on the horizon, the two-story wooden structure was lit up by the final rays of the setting sun so that it stood out from the shadowy hills around it, drawing the eye, demanding attention like a highlighter over ink. "It's a very cute motel. Can we stop?" She whipped her head around to face him. "I want to stay there."

She sat forward and squinted to read the distant sign. Her heart raced when she hit the last word: VACANCY.

"Oh, look! It says vacancy!" she squealed in a little-girl voice. "Please, James."

Xavier looked up from his game and took part in the conversation for the first time since they left the city limits. "Hey, that's kinda cool," he said, his eyes on the motel. Saloon doors had been painted on the real doors, and bales of straw marked both approaches to the service road, supporting arrow signs. "It looks like a motel from cowboy movies," he added.

"It's not where we planned on staying tonight. Besides, it looks cheap and dirty. We only have an hour to go to get to our planned hotel," James argued as he drove past.

Kyra looked to him with the biggest pouty face she could muster. "Please, James. I keep saying that I want us to be more spontaneous. This is something we never do, so let's do it—*now!*" Kyra pleaded, filled with a desperate excitement.

"Gee, you're a little intense. What's all this about?" asked James.

"I don't know. I just really have an impulse to stop here."

"I like it too, Dad." Xavier popped his head up between the two front seats.

"All right. Two against one. We can stay at the shady motel in the middle of nowhere, but only because I love you guys so much," James said. "But, if we end up with hepatitis, I'm going to say I told you so."

"What's hepatitis?"

"Nothing. Your father's just being silly."

James slowed the car and reluctantly pulled onto the service road, then headed toward the motel. He drove into the small parking lot and parked a few spaces from the office attached to the motel rooms. The drapes were drawn but lights within illuminated them, and an oval neon sign hanging in the window glowed with the word *OPEN* in red. Murals of cowboys, Native Americans, horses, cattle, and tumbleweeds sprawled across the walls. A picture of a sheriff had been painted on the door. Above his head were the words *Sheriff's Office*.

James frowned. "Are you guys sure you want to stay here? This place is creepy enough to belong in a horror movie. We might find questionable stains on the carpets."

Kyra and Xavier exchanged looks before nodding in unison, smiles on their faces.

"Okay, then. Wait here and I'll check us in."

Kyra rolled her window all the way down and watched James as he headed for the office. As he pushed open the door, he collided with two men trying to exit.

"Hey man, watch it."

"Sorry, I didn't see you," James said quickly.

"You better open your eyes or you might get your ass beat," the older man warned as he pushed his way past James, nudging him in the ribs.

The second man glared at James, then pursed his lips to kiss the air in front of his face as he passed. Momentarily stunned, James stood holding the door open for a moment, then went inside.

Kyra's anxiety began to build the moment James stepped through that door and the two scruffy-looking men stepped out. They made her uneasy. Her impulse to leave this place grew as they wandered closer to her.

The younger man was around her age and passed by without a glance, but the older one, mostly bald beneath the greasy mesh trucker hat he wore, stopped in front of the car to stare at her. He turned his head to the side, looking perplexed. Kyra's tension escalated as he stood watching her.

The first man, once he realized his companion was not listening to what he was saying, stopped walking and turned around. He hurried back to the man—at least twenty years his senior, though there was not enough of a resemblance that he might be his father—and followed his gaze to the car. His jaw dropped, then he smacked his friend in the arm and said something, his expression enthusiastic.

James stepped out of the office with a key in his hand. He stopped short and locked eyes with the men when their heads swiveled toward him. They turned away and continued down the wooden sidewalk before James reached the car.

"Are you okay?" he asked, pulling the door open. "Did they say anything to you?"

"No, they were just staring at me. It was really creepy. I-I don't know if this was such a good idea after all; maybe we should keep driving to the city."

"I bumped into them in the lobby, if you can call it that, and irritated them a bit more than I thought, I guess." He frowned and reached for Kyra's hand. "Don't worry, we'll go unwind in our room and have a few drinks. We can just relax and get some sleep before we finish our long drive to the coast tomorrow."

"I don't know. I have a bad feeling about this place now. I think we should go."

"Kyra. What is going on with you? You wanted to stop here so badly, even though we'd already booked a five star hotel. Nooo, you wanted this crap-hole instead—and now you don't. I will gladly keep driving for another hour to stay in a nice, safe, clean hotel."

Xavier's head bobbed between the seats, looking first to his father, then to his mother. "No way. This is where we're supposed to stop. It's fate."

"Xavier, there's no such thing as fate. Life is choices," James said, annoyed.

"I'm sorry. You're right. I'm a—I'm just being silly." Kyra took a deep breath and slowly exhaled. "I don't know what's wrong with me. It's like I'm being pulled in different directions. I just feel... I don't know. Never mind, it'll be fine."

As soon as they walked through the door of their room on the second level, James turned on the TV. Kyra rummaged in the suitcases for sleepwear.

She washed the dirt and worries from her face in the small sink as James flicked through the channels. Xavier, already in his pajamas, sat next to his father, watching the channels flick by.

Kyra watched her boys from the bathroom doorway. They're such a pair, those two, solely focused on their own worlds—oblivious and isolated from the reality of the world around them—like father, like son. Except, Xavier won't always be just like his father. One day, he will change to be more like his mother.

James settled on the news channel and moved to get more comfortable on the bed. Xavier lost interest in his father's choice of entertainment and hopped over to the other bed. He pushed aside the open suitcases, clothes spilling out onto the blankets.

"Mom, could you tell me one of your angel stories? A good one about battles and fighting and stuff."

She looked at her son and smiled. "Sure, baby, but you have to clean up that mess on your bed first."

"But I didn't make it," he whined.

"I know, but I made it looking for your jammies—and I asked you to. Besides, I can't tell you a story if I have nowhere to sit."

Xavier started to push the clothes off the bed onto the floor. Kyra looked down at him. "If you do that, then there will be no story at all. Do it the right way."

"Argh! Fine."

Xavier gathered up the pile of clothes and stuffed them into the suitcase before zipping it shut. He struggled to tug it off the bed until Kyra grabbed the handle and lifted it to the floor for him. Then she plopped down beside him and smiled.

"So, any particular story you want to hear?"

He snuggled under her arm. "Just one that is from a super long time ago and has people fighting the bad guys, too."

She thought for a moment. "Once upon a time in a land far away—way, way back in the old world—there lived a young girl. She had vibrant, fiery red, curly hair."

"Was she pretty?"

"Beautiful. And all the boys loved her and wanted to be her boyfriend."

"Like all the girls love Axel?"

She laughed. "Yes, just like that, but she was different from regular girls. When she was twenty years old, an evil sorceress summoned a dark entity."

"The demon," he breathed.

"The sorceress knew the demon was searching for the beautiful enchantress. When he came to the girl's small seaside village, the sorceress took him to the girl. The evil demon killed the girl's parents and her little brothers. He took the redheaded beauty and tortured her. She fought him with all of her strength and refused to join him in his evil ways, for a long time."

"Then what?"

"And then the angels came to save her and they won. The end."

"Come on, Mom, the angels didn't save her."

"Why would you say that?" she asked quickly, a quaver in her voice.

A stunned look swept over his face. "Um, you told me before."

"No, I didn't. How do you know that I changed the ending?" She pressed, trying to hide the panic in her voice.

"I-I just guessed."

"Just guessed?" Her eyes skimmed over the room.

"Well, the angels can't win all the time. Sometimes the demons win, and sometimes the humans have to win without the angels helping."

She sighed. "That depends on what you consider winning. All the sides still lose something when they cross each other's paths."

"Why are they always fighting, anyway?"

"I don't really know. They've always been in a battle with each other."

"Why can't the angels just get rid of the demons? Then they won't have to fight anymore."

"Because they just can't."

"So, what about the rest of the story? What happened to the girl?"

"She spent many years with the demon before she gave in to him and became evil. When they started to ravage the country, the people who loved her tried to save her." She eyed her son. "And then they did."

He looked up at her, confused. She cringed.

"They tried to save her, but she was evil now. She struck down many of the people she loved in a frenzy of madness. Eventually, one man was able to get close enough to her. He stabbed her in the heart with a dagger even though he loved her, because he had to stop the evil from spreading any further."

"Yeah, he had to stop her," Xavier whispered, looking down at his feet.

"The demon attacked him and he perished before the evil presence vanished from this world. He sacrificed his life to save the rest of the world."

James cleared his throat. "Is that really an appropriate story for an eight-year-old?"

"Story is over." She attacked her son with tickles. "It's time for bed anyway."

He rolled around in a fit of giggles, squirming to escape his mother's reach.

Chapter Three

Kyra grabbed the ice bucket off the table and stood in front of the TV, facing the boys. "I'm going to grab some ice from that grungy-looking machine we walked by on the way here." She shifted her weight to better block the TV from their view. "Did you bring the Hennessey in from the car?"

"Yes, yes. It's right there." James peered around her, pointing to a bag next to his suitcase.

"Okay, I'll be right back," she said and headed out the door.

She made her way toward the ice machine, trailing her fingers along the raw wooden banister that stretched the length of the walkway. Pausing halfway along, she slowly inhaled the crisp evening breeze, letting the fresh air fill her lungs. Night had found its way to the countryside; the highway was hidden in the dark distance. Here, outside of the smothering street lamps of the city, the moon and the stars shone brightly.

She leaned over the handrail to peer down on the parking lot. It appeared everyone had called it a night. The lights in all the suites were off, except for their room. Even the manager had turned off the *Open* sign and all of the office lights. She continued to the ice machine, the dim overhead bulbs gently illuminating her path. She found this place calming, yet it was also energizing, being out of the hustle and bustle of the city and the pressures that went with it.

Kyra placed the ice bucket under the dispenser and pushed the button. It made an awful grinding sound as it sputtered out shavings of ice. A loud bang ended the machine's struggle.

"Great," she muttered to herself.

A familiar eerie feeling rushed over her. She released the handle of the ice bucket, flexed her shoulders back, and stretched her neck from side to side in preparation for what was about to begin.

"Hey, pretty lady, do you need some help with that ice machine?" a voice cooed from the darkness. The speaker cautiously approached her. "Sorry about before. You look a lot like my sister; coulda been twins, you two."

"That's fine. I don't need any help. Please keep your distance." She turned to face the older of the two men. When he had leered at her from the sidewalk she knew, without a doubt, that he was a tainted soul with malicious intent.

"Name's Derek. And you are?" He continued toward her, slowly closing the gap between them. "No need to be afraid. I can help you," he assured her. "Or I can leave you be, but I have to pass you to get to my room."

Kyra could feel his lies deep within her. There was something else happening... she felt another presence. The thought swiftly entered her mind—

Decoy.

She spun around. The other man, within steps of her, gripped a needle-tipped syringe. Shock flooded his face before he stumbled back. She glared into his eyes and he froze.

"What is this? What do you think you're up to tonight, boys?" she challenged, turning back and forth between them as she spoke. "This is not a wise decision for either of you. Maybe you should reconsider and try behaving."

They both stood still. They exchanged baffled glances, then the younger one broke the silence. "She must be the right one, or she would be afraid of us."

"Grab her, Jed! What are you waiting for?" Derek shouted.

"You grab her," Jed retorted.

Kyra fixed her scowl on Jed and the syringe. "I am giving you your last warning. Piss off or things are going to end badly."

"Yeah, for you, sweetheart." He lunged at her with the syringe held high.

She raised her arm to block his strike as the needle swooped down on her. Jed's other hand clenched around her throat when she moved too slowly to block it. She quickly twisted her arm and grabbed hold of his wrist before he could stab her. Derek rushed up behind her and wrapped his arms around her waist, lifting her off her feet, and Jed's fingers slipped off her throat. Jerking her hair from behind, he pushed her to the floor. Jed tried to scoop up her thrashing legs.

Her anger flashed. *Enough.*

Time slowed as she fell. She repositioned herself on her feet and removed her hair from Derek's grasp, slipping away from them with ease. Plucking the syringe from Jed's fingers, she tossed it over the balcony. She stepped back to survey the two immobilized men, still standing hunched over where she'd been. She sensed the darkness in them and knew they'd done horrific things and would continue to do so, if she didn't put an end to it.

She would teach them a lesson they wouldn't soon forget.

Kyra casually waved her hand and both men collapsed onto the wooden walkway. Confused and disoriented, they scrambled around on the floor for a few seconds until they saw her.

"That was tricky, you clever girl, you," Derek hissed.

She focused on his eyes. Mesmerized, he couldn't look away, even when the pain in his head became intolerable. He screamed as blood seeped from his ears. His hands maneuvered to touch his face as his eyes and nose began to bleed.

Jed looked on, horrified. "She's just like him," he mumbled, backing away, preparing to run. Kyra's gaze fixed on him. "Please," he whispered.

He dropped to his knees and started to bleed. Invisible claws ripped through the air, cutting into his flesh. Both men rolled around on the floorboards, screaming in horror and pain.

"We're sorry! Please," Derek choked, "we weren't going to hurt you."

"Please, oh God, please," Jed begged, blinking, trying to see through the blood streaming from his eyes. "Please don't kill us."

Furious and focused, she ignored their pleas for mercy. They had attacked her and she was determined to show them that they had messed with the wrong woman.

***

The commotion brought James out into the walkway.

"Kyra! Kyra!" James rushed down the hall to his wife's side. "What happened; are you okay? What—what's going on?"

As her face became clearer in the dim lighting, he saw a look of pure anger and nothing else. He had seen her furious before, but this face was unrecognizable. He looked down at the men rolling around on the planking, wailing away for no apparent reason. Were they having some kind of seizure? He looked back at Kyra. Why was she just standing there, not trying to help? She seemed unaware of his presence. Shock. She must be in shock.

He moved directly into her line of sight, trying to break her out of whatever trance she was in. She seemed to look right through him. Holding her shoulders, he shook gently and her eyes rolled to the back of her head, then refocused on him. She took a deep breath and as she released the air from her lungs, she collapsed into his arms.

The two men on the walkway went silent. Gathering their wits, they climbed to their feet and ran their hands over themselves, searching for nonexistent injuries. Their expressions confused, they surveyed the dry floorboards under their feet before they noticed James and Kyra.

"Stop," the older man said sternly. "She's coming with us."

"Yeah, I don't think so. You need to back off." James picked up Kyra. "I'm calling the police if you come near any of us again." He turned away and started back to the room.

Xavier poked his head out from the room. "Dad, look out!" he shouted, startling James.

He started to turn, but the younger man grabbed his shirt collar and jerked him backward. He stumbled and almost dropped Kyra. The older man jumped in front of him and pulled Kyra from his arms. He threw her over his shoulder and started carrying her to the end of the walkway. Before James could go after them the younger man was in front of him, throwing punches. Kyra disappeared down the stairs with her abductor while James was fending off blows and throwing a few of his own. Xavier, crouched in the doorway, began to cry.

James wrestled with Jed and they fell to the floorboards, rolling around in their struggle to overcome the other. Punches landed repeatedly, eliciting grunts and groans.

A cry of relief drew James's eye to Xavier, then beyond him to Kyra, who came strutting back up the stairs alone. She planted her feet shoulder width apart and balled her hands into fists. A vindictive grin split her face, and her eyes narrowed. Seconds later Jed and James burst apart, flung aside by some invisible force between them.

James lifted his head to see Kyra still standing defiantly near the doorway where Xavier crouched. He rolled over to his stomach, pushed himself up, and started toward Kyra, but the look on her face stopped him. Quickly following her stare, he turned around in time to see the attacker go flying off the edge of the balcony.

A strong gust of wind—a really strong wind? That only affected him? Maybe he tripped... upward over the railing. Or he jumped. Nothing made sense, and it frightened James not to have an answer—so he pushed the questions out of his consciousness.

"We have to get out of here right now," Kyra said calmly.

"What? What are you talking about? Do you know those men?" James asked, pushing himself to his feet.

"Get in the car now!"

James swung his head back and forth between the last point where he'd seen the younger attacker and his wife. "Kyra, what is going on? We can't just run away and leave our stuff. Let's call the police and report the attackers."

"James, we have to go *now!*" She grabbed Xavier's hand and pulled him toward the stairs. "I'll explain later. Just trust me now."

Kyra ushered Xavier into the backseat before she jumped in behind the wheel. James climbed into the passenger seat, not quite as panicked as his wife seemed to be. The car peeled out of the parking lot and headed for the exit to the freeway, whipping past the two men as they climbed into an old rusty pickup truck. Its engine roared to life as they shot onto the highway. The tires squealed when she pressed down on the accelerator.

"There's a town only a few miles ahead. Maybe we can find the police station," James suggested.

"Or maybe we can lose them," Kyra said through clenched teeth. "Those men are damned. I should've killed them."

James gaped at her. "What's going on, Kyra? I feel like we're in the twilight zone."

"It's a long, complicated story. I'll explain later."

She kept her foot on the accelerator as she guided the car toward the dimly lit town ahead. James looked away from the speedometer. He had never seen her this way in the fifteen years he'd known her.

"What just happened back there? Did you do that to them? Are you some kind of spy or secret government agent, living a double life?"

"James, please, I am none of those things. Well, maybe the double life is *partly* accurate. There is a wide range of things I am able to do that are supposed to be impossible. I can feel the evil surrounding certain people and I've had dreams about angels and demons fighting for as long as I can remember." She paused and glanced at him. "The stories I tell Xavier about angels and demons are a positive spin on my dreams."

"Kyra, dreams are just your subconscious working through things that you experience when you're awake."

She snorted. "Fucking typical."

"What is typical? What is your problem?"

"You are. You always do this."

"Do what?"

"There are realities in this world that you can't fathom but trust me, they still exist, nonetheless."

Headlights glared through the car's rear window; the pickup truck was gaining on them. They sped into the small town. She jammed on the brakes, whipped the car around a corner, and made another turn at the end of the block, losing their pursuers. The car screeched to a stop and she cut the engine.

"Get out. We don't have much time."

Xavier and James obeyed even though James could barely keep up with everything that was going on.

Kyra took several agitated steps forward, then whirled to face James and her son. "Look. They're after me. You guys go to the police and I'll call you after I lose them," she instructed.

James shook his head and took a step toward her. "No. No way. What makes you think you can lose them? What if you can't?"

"Um… what you witnessed at the motel is kind of minor compared to other things I can do."

"I don't know what I 'witnessed' at the motel."

"I can take care of myself, but I might not be able to protect you both." Her eyes searched the streets. "We don't have time for this."

She put her hand on James's arm and their eyes met. His tension and confusion gave way to trust. He didn't understand why, but he knew he had to let her go.

"Okay. Be careful." James grabbed Xavier's hand, and headed down the sidewalk. "We'll have to finish this later. I'll need a better explanation then about 'I have a double life,'" he called back to her.

James tugged Xavier along, the boy glancing frequently back to his mother with worried eyes. They paused at the entrance to an alley and took one last look at Kyra. She gave them a reassuring smile before they ducked into the alley.

***

Kyra turned away and waited.

The old truck squealed around the corner onto her street. Now she could lead them away while her family escaped. And prevent them from witnessing any more of her powers that she didn't want to explain.

She bolted in the opposite direction. The headlights skimmed over her as she darted across the street and fled through a grassy field filled with children's playground equipment. She fell to her knees at the edge of the park, just short of inadvertently launching herself down a steep hill that was only dimly revealed by the moonlight. She crouched, catching her breath, and watched the truck turn off the road, bounce up over the boulevard, and head across the grass toward her.

She shook her head and tried to focus. She had to slow them down, or use her powers on them again. Her eyes drifted back to the steep embankment. It descended into hiking trails through a forest. They wouldn't be able to drive down there; that would slow them down enough.

Using the tree trunk in front of her for support, she pulled herself to her feet and clambered down into the woods. Cold, damp grass whipped her ankles as she abandoned the path; branches scratched her legs and arms as she stumbled her way toward the moon hanging above the trees. Her mind raced, trying to figure out how to escape these men but still keep them from turning back to look for her family. Weakened from her first encounter with them, she now wished she had built up her endurance in using her powers.

She heard voices, and snapping twigs and the thrash of leafy branches as they charged clumsily after her. They were far enough away that they couldn't see her in the darkness, but she figured they could hear her as clearly as she heard them. And they were gaining on her; soon they would spot her. She's wasn't going to make it. She had to try something before they caught up.

Ducking behind a large tree, she pressed her fingers into its bark, not knowing if it would work. Calming her breathing, she melted into the tree, becoming silent and invisible.

Jed rushed past her, unaware of her presence. His arms flailed wildly in front of him as he chased shadows through the dark forest.

She waited silently.

Now Jed was at least fifty feet ahead of her. Derek had still not appeared. She closed her eyes and searched for his presence. She released her breath when she couldn't sense anyone in the vicinity—Jed had disappeared from her sight and was now off her supernatural radar. Where was Derek? He might have run out of energy and returned to get the truck to try to cut off her exit from the trees.

She peered carefully around her tree.

Silent darkness.

She shifted to peer around the other side of the tree. When she still saw nothing out of the ordinary she stepped away from her hiding place and ran off to her left, not wanting to run into either of them.

She'd taken fewer than ten steps when she felt a sharp pain in her butt. She must have been stabbed by a thorn or a sharp twig, she assumed, reaching back to pull it from her flesh. *Crap. Not a twig,* she thought, staring at the small tranquilizer dart with its red fluff end. She started to feel muzzy as she stared down at the dart. She lifted her eyes and looked around and the movement made her head spin.

"I got her, Jed!" she heard Derek yell. "Get back here!"

She dropped to her knees as the fog settled in. Her vision faded away, though her eyes were still open. She could feel her body going limp and tried vainly to get back on her feet. She toppled over. Dragging her numb hands out from under her, she pushed her torso back up, bracing her hands on the ground as she struggled to wobble onto her knees. She could hear footsteps drawing closer.

This can't be happening, she thought. How could a couple of hillbillies have outsmarted her? Probably going to die and be cut up into tiny pieces. Why did they have to stop at that crappy motel; was it fate? Maybe that was what all her dreams of being chased by evil were trying to warn her about—how she was going to die.

One of the men grabbed her arm. She jerked it away and let out a final shriek of defiance, until all the air had left her lungs. Then she collapsed onto the soil.

Chapter Four

Kyra stirred. Damp, stale air and the metallic tang of blood invaded her nostrils. She opened her mouth to lick dry, chapped lips, struggling to muster up enough saliva to swallow. Her eyelids fluttered and it felt like grains of sand were scraping across her eyeballs. She opened them and her eyes slowly adjusted to the light, but she could only make out blurry shapes around the room. She tried to bring her hand to her face but her wrist caught on something. Her other wrist. Her wrists were tied together behind her back.

What the—

She was sitting slumped on an uncomfortable wooden chair with her arms tied behind her back. She twisted her wrists and her skin burned as it rubbed against the thick rope binding them together. She stopped and sagged in the chair. Her elbows ached from the unnatural position of her arms. Her vision slowly came into focus.

She remembered the attack at the motel.

James.

Xavier.

They were safe, she reassured herself. The two thugs had pursued her into the park. The police were probably out searching for her right now. James would never give up on finding her.

"Hey, she's awake," a male voice yelled.

A man crouched down in front of her to look up at her face. She moved away from him and sat upright, resting her back against the chair. It relieved the strain on her arms. She looked at him, puzzled. She didn't recognize him. He was not one of the ones from the motel.

Another man looked up from her cell phone—another unfamiliar face—and smugly smiled at her before turning his attention back to searching through her iPhone.

One lightbulb dangled from a cord in the center of the small room, hovering over a metal floor drain. The concrete floor felt cold under her bare feet. It sloped slightly toward the drain, pocked in spots where time had worn away the surface and chunks had been chipped out, revealing the roughness of gravel that had been combined with the cement. Across the room, a rickety table was pushed against the wall near the door.

Kyra focused on the man closest to her, squinted her eyes and blinked once. Nothing. She twitched her eyes at him a few times and still nothing. Eyes closed, she took a couple deep breaths, exhaling the air slowly through her nose before she opened her eyes again. Still nothing. She couldn't do it—she needed her hands.

"Would ya look at 'er. She be tryin' to put da mojo on us." He grabbed her chin with his grubby hand. "Won't work, darlin'. Da boss man has some stuff to block your trouble makin'."

"I guess I'll have to take you out the old-fashioned way," she said.

He slapped her across the face. "Not likely. On account of ya been tied up and powerless. And soon enough, bloody."

"What do you want?" she demanded, ignoring her stinging cheek. "Where am I?"

"We are here on orders to *break* you in. So that's what we're gonna do."

"Touch me and I'll kill you." She glowered at him.

He smiled a toothless grin—absolutely toothless; nothing but gooey pink gums sprawled across his mouth. He stood over her with clenched fists. Then he punched her in the face. "You're in for a lotta long days of whippings. Eventually you'll break. They all do."

He hit her again. And again.

That was it, she decided. He would be the first one to die.

Once again she faded into unconsciousness.

***

The senseless beatings went on for days without questions or explanations. Different faces came and went, taking turns with their methods of torture. She would often wake to find her bruises had inexplicably vanished while she was unconscious, but the bloodstains remained. The days blurred together, unchanging, nothing to distinguish them until the day when she woke to find a familiar man sitting a few feet away, directly in front of her.

He looked out of place, dressed as if on his way to a black tie event. He sat with perfect posture, his hands on his knees, and flashed an attractive grin accompanied by one eloquently raised eyebrow.

Must be another part of the psycho kidnapper crew, she thought, before unease washed over her. Her stomach twisted in knots. Evil radiated in the room around her, denser than she had ever felt it, and it made her nauseous. She feared him, but at the same time she was drawn to him. His broad shoulders and rugged features made him very attractive, but it was something else—something similar to her own alluring anomalies. She had always been on the receiving end of the admiration, not the one who was mesmerized by it. It felt strange to want him to kiss her and want to run from him in the same moment.

Then a fragment from her dreams flashed before her eyes and she recognized him as the man she'd been fantasizing about for months—or maybe it was her mind playing tricks on her. Either way, he was not like the others here. No matter what he wanted, she had to fight it. Whatever the cost.

"Hello, Kyra." He dragged his chair closer to her, the legs scraping over the concrete, making her cringe. "My name is Alastor. I have been waiting for you for a long time."

"What?" she whispered, confused. She looked at the floor. "Why am I here and why have these guys been torturing me?" She stole a glance into his eyes and quickly looked away.

"You know me, though this face is not the real me. Open your eyes." He cupped her chin and tilted her head to look at his face. "Look beyond this shell and see me," he urged, his dark eyes intense.

"See you? See what? What are you talking about?" She pulled away from his hand.

"Search your soul and your mind for the knowledge of your destiny."

Her breath caught in her throat. "It's not possible," she whispered, her voice trembling. "They were only nightmares. You can't be real." She studied his face. "Are you a—I can't even say it out loud. It just sounds crazy. You're evil, pure evil."

He smiled. "You know it to be true." He leaned forward and slid his hands up her thighs. She flinched under his touch. "You were extremely difficult to find," he continued. "It has taken me over a decade longer than it should have. And you *will* be mine."

"This can't be real. Why do you look like a man?" She squirmed, trying to shake his hands off her legs. "I've always seen you as a monster."

"I am not a monster. I am a demon. This is my camouflaged form."

"What are you doing here, on Earth? You don't belong here, do you?"

"Enough! No more questions." He jerked his hands away. "You will understand everything as soon as you say yes, and join me." He rose from his chair and circled behind her.

Her eyes followed him. "Join you? Join you in what? What do you want from me?" She turned her head forward again. "I-I can't join you." Then cautiously she whispered, "I won't."

She felt his hands slide into her hair and begin massaging her scalp. "You have no idea what I am capable of, my darling. I can be quite persuasive." He jerked her hair and pulled her head back until he could look down on her face.

She knew her fear was apparent on her face. He grinned, and she wished she had hidden it better. He leaned in and nuzzled her neck. A surge of panic made her heartbeat skyrocket as he drew closer. He kissed her neck and she gasped. To her surprise, she enjoyed the rush of his touch.

No. Stop.

"*No!* Get away from me!" She bent her neck away from his mouth.

He stood upright and rested his hands on the back of the chair. She turned her head to glare at him. "I will never do anything you want. You can go fuck your hat."

Alastor moved around in front of her, bent down, and gently kissed her on the forehead. He drew back and slapped her hard across her face, looking pleased by the shock on Kyra's face before he balled up his fist and drilled her. Her head flew back, then snapped forward, her split lip stinging. Her fear fizzled into anger, giving her the strength to fight through the pain.

He relentlessly continued, raining blows on her abdomen and chest, breaking bones. Pain stabbed through her chest. Determined not to give in, she tried to focus her thoughts on her realization that he was the evil from her dreams. She choked on her blood with every gasp for breath.

The savage beating stopped only when Kyra was barely conscious, and incoherent. He stood over her, smugly admiring his work. Blood saturated her clothes and she could feel it making a sticky mat of her hair. She suspected the throbbing lump on her forehead felt larger than it was.

Alastor walked over to the table near the door and grabbed a bottle of water. He twisted the cap off and held it out toward her. His anger ignited when she turned her head away. Clenching his teeth, he threw the bottle against the wall. It bounced off, leaving a trail of water behind its final resting place on the floor.

"Does it hurt? Shall I take your pain away?" he asked with genuine concern.

She opened her lips; thick red blood drooled out instead of words.

He put both his hands on her face, lifting her head until she looked in his eyes. The bruises stopped hurting, the blood stopped flowing, and the pain melted away as she held his innate stare.

"See, darling? I can be generous. I have the ability to mend people as well. We can do it together—punish the wicked and heal the worthy." He stroked her cheek, then moved his hands from her face.

She looked up at him, puzzled. She doubted there was anything noble in his soul—if there was, she couldn't sense it. Now she was sure he was the demon from her nightmares. She had seen him do terrible things. They must have been real, if he was real. Either way, she was getting whiplash from the Dr. Jekyll/Mr. Hyde game.

"Will you accept my offer?" He pulled his chair close to her and sat down. "Rule the world by my side, and you will be able to do as you wish, to change the way things are into the way you would have them."

"You're insane," she said dryly. "Never going to happen. You might as well just kill me now, because we won't be doing anything together, now or ever." She leaned closer to him. "I know exactly what you are, *demon*. No matter what you do to me, I will die and go to Heaven, but you will go back where you belong!" As she spouted the words she wondered how long she would have to live like this, hoping it wouldn't be years, or even months. Alexis—Alexis and Axel would find her if the police failed.

"Is that what you believe?" He stood up, towering above her. "Your beliefs are incorrect."

She pressed her back against the chair and looked up at him. "I know you. I've seen you countless times and I know that I can beat you. And I absolutely will."

"It is destiny. We are meant to be together, forever." He slapped her hard, as though it would make her believe the words that he spouted.

She stretched her jaw, taking the edge off the sting before turning her head back to him. He pulled an ancient looking dagger from his belt and twirled the curved blade around his fingers. The handle was made out of bone—a black bone. He touched her face with the tip of the blade and slowly ran the knife down her cheek, gently enough not to cut her. Her fear grew when he placed it across her neck. Panic washed over her as he slowly increased the pressure. She was careful to remain still and not slice open her own throat. Drawing a slow breath, she regained her composure before looking him in the eye. He brushed his free hand through her hair as he pulled the knife away from her neck. There was a strange flash in his eyes, then he plunged the dagger into her thigh. A cry escaped her throat and she tossed her head back in pain.

Alastor jerked her head by her hair until she faced him. He held her stare as he slowly pulled the dagger from her body. She grimaced as she felt the blade move inside her leg and her breath hitched, but she stifled any sound; she wouldn't give him the satisfaction of hearing her cry out in pain again, though in her head she screamed.

Alastor wiped the blood off his blade on Kyra's pants and sheathed it on his belt before he began to beat her again. Taking blows to her face and body, she remained as silent as she could.

The dreams that she had tried to block out and forget came flooding back to her. Dreams of angels, demons, magic, war, blood, death—and the fear and hope that accompanied them.

When her body was broken and bruised, the beating stopped. Only her restrained wrists held her in the chair, her head hanging. She registered only that there were no new blows, until Alastor tapped her foot with his. She was too weak to react. He kicked her, hard. She looked up. His smile made her stomach turn—or maybe it was the smell of her blood or the fact that she had inadvertently swallowed quite a bit of it.

"Have you had enough? Do you wish to stop and heal your wounds?" He surveyed her expressionless face for a moment, then sighed. "All you have to do is say yes. Say you will be mine and you'll see everything clearly." He placed his hands on her face and tilted her head up to look at him. "Limitless," he whispered. "That is what we would be together, you and I. It is so simple, just say yes."

"Never," she rasped.

"Boys," he called out. "It is time to show Kyra to the guest chambers." He glanced at Toothless and the quiet one as they entered the room, then leaned close to Kyra. "Perhaps you will reconsider my offer and do the noble thing for everyone," he whispered, his lips grazing her ear.

Alastor cut the rope that tied her hands together with the dagger from his belt. Her arms fell limply to her side. He stepped back with the rope dangling from his hand, eyeing her.

She made no motion to escape or even stand. He stepped backward, watching her face, then turned and left the room.

The men came forward and lifted her by her upper arms and dragged her out into the hall. Her head slumped forward, her dirty, sweat-soaked hair obstructing her view—not that she was paying much attention to what was going on. Her feet dragged behind her, scraping dirt from the floor, and she made no attempt to pull them under her body. They dragged her into another windowless room lit by softly buzzing fluorescent lights. The floor was the same as the other room she had been in, there was just more of it. She was aware of the presence of others at the far end of the room, though her dirty hair blocked her view. The two men slammed her down into a metal chair and pushed the back of her head until she was bent double at the waist, her chin above her knees. One of them pulled her hands behind her back and the other handcuffed them together. Then they sat her upright. Her hair fell away from her face.

The room was four times larger than the previous room, but it still had only one exit. To one side of her, ten feet away, a steel frame supported a massive glass tank filled with water, about seven feet long by three feet wide and at least three feet deep. She couldn't imagine what the purpose of it was, and was pretty sure she didn't want to find out. In front of her, at the far end of the room, several people huddled on the floor, bowed by exhaustion, their faces pinched with fear. She gasped. She recognized those faces.

Chapter Five

Alastor entered the room wearing a fresh white suit and silk tie. He walked behind Kyra's chair and began to stroke her hair, his fingers gently guiding the sticky strands from her face and releasing them behind her shoulders.

"You see you are not my only guest," he said. "Mind you, you are the only one of value, the only one that needs to be alive in the end." He moved his hands to rest on her shoulders, his fingers stroking her neck. "How many survive is up to you."

Several gasps escaped from the prisoners. Kyra watched the wave of fear that washed over them. She didn't flinch, simply stared at her family and friends gathered there. But her heart sank. Their fates were now tied to her own.

Her husband and son had not been able to escape after all. Both were shackled to the wall by their wrists, James straining against the restraints to wrap his arms around the shoulders of the pajama-clad boy shivering on his lap. And her mother, Iris, exhausted and fearful slumped next to Hailey—who was huddled with her husband, Nick—her clothes torn and spattered with blood. *She definitely put up a fight. Good girl.* She'd braided her hair back from her face, the braid sloppy and uneven and so dirty, it held together without the use of an elastic. Alexis was there too, with her brother, Axel. *So much for the rescue party,* Kyra thought, her hope draining away. *How had they even been caught off guard and captured?* Alexis's usual chipper vibe had been overshadowed by gloom, but she didn't appear to be overly fearful, more calm and concerned. Kyra shrugged when their eyes met.

She'd brought this on them by having them in her life, and now she didn't know if she would be able to save them.

"I'm sorry," she said, looking from face to face.

Alastor bent down and grazed over Kyra's ear with his lips. Tired, hungry, bruised, bleeding, and now holding the fate of the people she loved in her hands, she blocked out his touch with an exasperated exhale.

The wounds on her body faded away. The repetitive cycle of being beaten until her body could take no more, then being miraculously mended in the blink of an eye was relentless. Her irritation escalated and pushed her hostility over the edge. She'd had enough.

She adjusted her shoulders and flung her head backward, smashing her skull into Alastor's face. She heard the crack as his nose broke; it echoed through the cavernous room as an opaque black liquid with a consistency far thicker than human blood started dripping. He touched his face and drew his hand away to stare mystified at the viscous liquid that had dripped from his nose.

Kyra bounced from her chair, spun around, planted one foot firmly on the floor, and kicked the chair as hard as she could toward her demon. Still preoccupied with examining his bloody hands, Alastor jolted upright when the metal chair came flying at him, stumbled backward, and lost his footing. The chair landed on top of him as he slammed against the floor, his head rebounding off the concrete.

Her mother, Iris, winced and James let out a gasp, shocked.

The two henchmen rushed toward her. Kyra ran toward the quiet one, turning her back on Toothless. Just before their bodies were about to collide, she spun around and slammed into him with her back, knocking both of them to the floor. The quiet one lay there, struggling to recover his breath.

A thrilled Hailey squirmed and pulled against her chains. Alexis held her breath, glancing from Kyra to the motionless demon.

Toothless closed in on Kyra. He slowed to maneuver around Alastor and the chair, which bought her the time she needed. She wriggled her handcuffed hands under her butt, down to her knees, then quickly slipped her legs through, one at a time. She finished as Toothless dove at her; he landed on his accomplice as she rolled away. He scrambled around and grabbed for her, but his hand swept empty floor. Kyra slid away, propped herself up, and threw her weight onto his back. He struggled to hold himself off of his winded partner.

"Come on Kyra," Alexis called softly, "you've got this." Taken aback, James shot her a withering look; she looked at him, rolled her eyes, and returned her attention to Kyra.

As Toothless tried to throw her off his back, Kyra slipped her hands over his neck and pulled the small chain between the handcuffs tight against his throat. She crossed her wrists and quickly circled around his head; the chain twisted tighter as she moved around him. He flailed and scratched at her arms, desperate to throw her off of him, but he collapsed back onto his partner, starved for air. The cuffs cut into Kyra's wrists and drew blood. She put her knee on his back and pulled harder to speed up his death.

Alastor stirred. "Kyra!" Axel and Alexis called out in unison as Alastor rose the floor and brushed himself off.

"Mom, look out!" Xavier cried as Alastor moved quickly toward her.

Kyra flung a look over her shoulder, then turned back to the asphyxiating man. "Just die, already!" she screamed, fighting panic.

Alastor struck her across the head and she tumbled to the floor with her victim. He muttered something incoherent and released her wrists from the handcuffs before unwrapping them from the dead man's neck. "You." He shot a look at the quiet one on the floor. "Go get Jed and Derek in here."

The henchman shrank back, then picked himself up and hurried out of the room.

Anger darkening his face, Alastor grabbed Kyra's arm and pulled her to her feet. His eyes glazed over, engulfed in black, as if his pupils had expanded completely over his eyeballs. He pulled his lips back and growled at her, revealing his fangs. Then he dropped her arm and glared at her for a moment before driving his fist at her face. She raised her arm but was unable to block the blow in time. She heard a collective gasp from the group of spectators as her head snapped around, followed by her body. She heard Axel curse as she went down.

She lay on the dirty floor, spitting blood out of her mouth. Her body still ached from the memory of the last beating she had endured and her mind was exhausted, making it difficult to collect her thoughts and keep a clear head. She shook her head and forced herself to refocus—she had to fight through the pain and figure out a way to save everyone.

Well, not everyone. She had to find a way to kill Alastor.

"You have angered me for the last time," he growled, grabbing her hair and pulling her to her feet. Still gripping her hair, he shoved her toward the water tank, forcing her to move hunched over with her head angled to the side. "This lovely tank is called the drowned rat tank." He pressed her face against the glass. "It is time for a swim, my darling."

The quiet one walked back into the room with Jed from the motel. He saw Alastor at the tank and went directly over to a gray control panel in the corner of the room. Jed started to approach Alastor, then stopped at a quick gesture from his boss.

Kyra put her hands on the glass and pushed her face off the cool surface. "The drowned rat tank—really? That's a clever one. Did you come up with that all by yourself, or did your minions think it up for you?"

Alastor returned his attention to Kyra. He pulled her hair, turning her head to look into his angry black eyes. "Becoming a saucy bitch now, are we." He raised an admiring eyebrow at her.

"What can I say, you bring out the worst in me."

Alastor let out a frustrated noise that sounded almost like an animal growl. He jerked her around to face him, one hand on her bicep, his other hand wrapping around her thigh, squeezing her hard. Without even a grunt, he lifted her up over his head and tossed her into the water.

Water spilled out over the edges of the clear tank as she splashed into it and sank to the bottom. Her cuts stung as the water washed them clean. It was almost soothing, she thought, like going for a swim to wash off mud after a fun day of off-roading. Her butt touched down while her arms and legs remain suspended. She opened her eyes and turned to her side to find Alastor staring back at her, his face expressionless as the black retreated in his eyes, leaving golden-brown irises.

"Why are you here, Kevin? You do not look like Derek," asked Alastor without turning his head to look at the quiet guy in the corner.

"Sorry, sir," Jed answered for him. "Derek is not on the grounds. He went to town about an hour ago."

"Fine."

Kyra moved her arms in a circular motion until her feet were beneath her. When she stood up the water level was just below her waist. She stood there, dripping and calm. She and Alastor silently studied each other's face. The loud rattle of a chain quickly running through a pulley broke the trance. The sound echoed through the room.

"Look out!" James and Axel shouted.

She looked up just in time to raise her arms as the rusty steel grate came crashing down on her. It smashed her back into the water. Her forearms throbbed from the impact and she was fairly sure she had just broken her index finger. The grate stopped descending two inches from the surface of the water. Kyra slipped her fingers through the holes on the new lid of her fish tank and pulled herself up to retrieve a desperately needed burst of air. She didn't know if she had even reacted in time to hold her breath, or if the force of the impact had knocked it out of her. It didn't matter. All that mattered right now was that she needed air.

Gasping for breath, she tried to avoid sucking water into her lungs as it splashed back and forth in the tank. She could hear laughter. She took a deep breath, kept her hands on the grate, and pushed herself underwater to see who it was.

Alastor.

He had never laughed before. Disappointed that she'd amused him, she turned away and resurfaced. She calmed her breathing as she stared at the ceiling.

The chains made their frightening click-click-click again, slower this time, as the heavy grate pushed Kyra under. Pure terror made Kyra momentarily lose her composure. She flailed around for a few seconds, then stopped and swam to one side of the tank. With her feet on the bottom and her back against the grate, she pushed with all she had as she tried to stand up. When that failed, she sank down to the bottom. Alastor's expression caught her attention as a smug grin slowly worked its way across his face, revealing his perfect white teeth. She narrowed her eyes at him and clenched her teeth, kicking wildly at the glass.

Just as she ran out of breath and started to panic again, the top was lifted out of the water, a little higher this time but still within the glass structure. She gasped for air. She didn't know how long this was going to go on, but if it was anything like his other tricks, it could be a while.

"So, darling, have you reconsidered my offer, or shall I test if some of your loved ones can handle the tank as well as you have?"

"What offer?" James blurted.

Alastor turned around slowly and focused on James. "The *offer* does not concern you." He looked over the others as he spoke. "You are all irrelevant wastes of flesh. The only sound coming out of you shall be screams of agony as you are being tortured momentarily."

Gasps escaped from the group and Kyra flinched.

"Ignore him, he's a pencil-dicked shit stain, overcompensating for his pathetic excuse of an existence." She tilted her head to face them as best she could while keeping her mouth out of the water. "A vile, disgusting creature unfit for the company of cockroaches."

"What is wrong with you!" he bellowed, turning to her. "You are becoming increasingly difficult as time moves forward."

"I already told you: I will never say yes. I know what you are and I have a pretty good idea of what that would mean for the world."

Alastor wildly waved his arm. Kevin pushed a button and the grate lowered once more, pushing her back into the water, even deeper this time. She floated there, keeping her eyes on her personal demon, simmering with anger.

Alastor turned away from her to the people on the floor and she could tell he was speaking to them, but couldn't make out what was being said from underwater. She knocked on the glass. He turned around and she used her one good index finger to call him over.

A smile formed on his face and he started toward her. He stopped a few feet from the tank but Kyra wanted him closer.

She coaxed him again until he was up against the glass, his hands splayed on either side of his face. The pleased look on his face never faltered. Their faces now inches apart, separated only by glass, she smiled and pressed both of her middle fingers against the glass in her final act of defiance. Centering her face between her gesturing hands, she screamed at the top of her lungs, "Fuuuck yoooooooouu!" Her words grabbled in the water as she emptied her lungs of oxygen.

Then she had no choice but to inhale. Water filled her lungs and she wondered if she would be going to Heaven after this. Too late, it's done now. She tossed and turned around in the tank as her life slipped away.

"Get the cage up now!" Alastor bellowed.

Chapter Six

Kyra Parker's body had gone still. Alastor reached in and grabbed her when the grate was just inches out of the tank, and pulled her to the surface. The heavy lid pivoted and swung on its chains as Alastor pushed it back from the tank. Yanking her clumsily from the tank, he half lowered, half dropped her to the floor. Jed rushed to his side while the snivelling coward continued to retract the grate back to its starting position.

Alastor quickly checked for a pulse, then held his hands over Kyra. A moment later Kyra jerked forward and coughed violently, spewing water from her mouth. Relief flooded the faces of the captives. Her eyes sprang open. Alastor rolled her over and more water gushed from her mouth.

***

Her lungs ached. Still coughing hard and shaking with shock, Kyra nevertheless scanned the room, looking for a way to defeat Alastor. Her powers may not work in this place, but she was out of the tank and no longer tied up, both pluses. There had to be something she could do.

Her coughing eased, leaving her breathing hard. She pushed her chest off the floor and rested on her elbows while she tried to catch her breath. Kyra's eyes met those of her mother. Tears streamed down her face. There had to be something she could do!

Jed knelt next to her head, then sat back on his heels, and Kyra caught a glimmer in his boot. The handle of a hunting knife protruded from its sheath, tucked inside his boot. Kyra hid a smile.

"That was very foolish Kyra. I shall never let you die," Alastor said.

"That wasn't stupid," she retorted, "but this is." She snatched the knife and swung around toward Alastor.

The blade connected, slicing across his throat. She flinched as black ichor gushed from the gaping gash, splattering her already stained clothes. His pupils grew, engulfing his irises, then the whites of his eye in blackness. He fell over into the growing pool of black blood.

Jed's jaw dropped. A moment later he shook off his shock and grabbed for her. She drew back, but not fast enough; his hand wrapped around her arm and she struggled as he pulled her toward him, dragging her across the floor, unable to break free. She kicked off the floor and pushed backward, knocking him onto his back. Sliding off him, she scrambled to her feet, but Jed was rising, too. She turned and raised the knife, preparing to lunge.

He caught her wrist and laughed, holding her knife hand out to one side. "Deja vu, but I wasn't trying to kill you."

She pounded on his chest with her free hand until he caught and held that wrist, too. She glared at him for a second, then brought her knee up into his groin.

His eyes bulged and his face went red. He let out a whimper. His hands dropped to his crotch before he slumped to his knees. She thrust the knife into his throat with such force that the tip burst out the back of his neck. His wide, shocked eyes went blank and his limp body toppled to the floor, pulling the knife from her hand. She reached down, gripped the handle, and pulled, but Jed's torso lifted with it. She tugged, and his body flopped around; the blade scraped against his spine, making an eerie popping sound. Finally she braced one foot on his collarbone and jerked the blade free.

Blood spattered across her friends' horrified faces. They recoiled and cried out. Her mother and Hailey shrank away when Kyra glanced in their direction. Kyra briefly considered trying to calm them or explain, but decided against it. She couldn't allow herself to be distracted by their terror; she had to get rid of the threat first. She turned her back on them to focus on the last man standing. The quiet one. Kevin.

He cowered back into the corner. She launched herself into a hard sprint, straight for him.

Kevin dropped to the ground as she was about to strike. *Shit!* She was moving too fast to stop. Without Kevin in the corner to absorb her momentum, she'd plow right into the wall.

At the last moment, she flung her right leg forward. Her right foot connected with the wall, followed by her left foot, and she ran several paces up the vertical wall, then twisted her body to change her trajectory and transferred herself to the adjacent wall. She saw Kevin scurrying away on his hands and knees below her as she ran two more steps along the wall, sheer momentum propelling her along, then flipped around and pushed off the second wall to slam into the man trying to escape her.

Kevin collapsed beneath her weight. For a moment Kyra lay experiencing the ache from the landing before her adrenaline took over and she picked herself up. Kevin's limbs flailed around like a spider being crushed into the concrete, trying to lift himself up to his hands and knees. Kyra swung one leg over him and sat on his back, keeping him from rising further. Grunting, gasping desperately, he still tried to crawl away, but she planted her feet firmly and gripped his hair, yanking his head back as far as his neck would allow. She lifted the blade she still held in her right hand.

The blade came across, slashing into his throat, blood spurting as she pulled the blade across his neck. His mouth moved, as if belatedly begging for mercy, but blood, not words, came bubbling out. That and a burbling sound as his last breath of air escaped his lungs. She released her grip on his hair as his arms and legs buckled beneath her and he slumped silently to the floor.

She stepped over the body and started toward her friends, but hesitated after only a few steps. Something was wrong. She could feel it, but wasn't sure what it was until movement caught her eye, and she turned her head.

There, on the floor several feet away, Alastor's body stirred. Kyra held her breath. *He can't still be alive. Postmortem spasm? Yeah, must be.* Alastor's arm moved. Then his other arm, and his legs, and he rose up from the floor and stood, blocking her path to the others. Kyra found it hard to breathe. She vividly remembered how deep she'd cut into his throat.

She stood staring at him, still holding the knife that she had used to slit his throat. His wounds had vanished, although the bloodstains remained. His expression calm, he looked over the bodies and blood on the floor, then lifted his eyes—now back to golden-brown—to Kyra. His eyes narrowed. He took a step toward her.

"I cannot be killed." He took another step and slowly extended his hand, offering it to her. "I am immortal. I have existed since the beginning of time and I shall be here in the end."

The triumph she'd felt moments before faded to sadness as her eyes moved from Alastor to Alexis. She didn't know how to kill him or if it was even possible; her dreams had never shown her.

"I'm sorry," she said to Alexis and the other captives. "I tried, but I have failed you." Her eyes swept across them. "He *is* a demon, and I-I can't..." Her voice trailed to a stop for a long moment. "So many people will die." She scanned their faces, looking for encouragement, or understanding. "He's right. I can't—I can't kill him."

She looked to Alastor, then to the knife in her hand, the sharp metal shining beneath the fresh blood. She wracked her mind, searching for the answer, for the means to defeat this evil—it had to be in her dreams. She'd seen him defeated in her dreams over the years, but the method was not encouraging. If there was another way, she couldn't recall it.

She looked to her husband and her son, her heart breaking. James seemed more confused than afraid; Xavier's fear was tinged with worry. Her eyes scanned the others, and she felt an overwhelming sadness. Mom, Hailey, and Nick looked terrified and she figured they would have the hardest time understanding and accepting all that had transpired, but they would in time. Axel seemed to have regained his composure, with the exception of his clenched teeth—very little could unnerve him.

Alexis shook her head slowly and started to tear up when Kyra met her eyes. She suspected that Alexis had put everything together by now; she knew what Kyra was about to do.

"I'm so sorry, you guys. It's not what it seems." It was only a matter of time before he wore her down and she gave in to him, and she couldn't let that happen, she reasoned, trying to convince herself that she only had one option.

"You can't give him what he wants. All the world is in danger. Please remember and trust me—any deal with him is worse than any death you may face." Images of Hell, recollected from her dreams, flashed through her mind and she trembled. "Endure the pain knowing that you will enter Heaven when you die." She looked to the floor, hoping that suicide was not a damnable offense or a one-way ticket to Hell. "Living for a short while in horrendous pain is far better than giving up your soul to escape the pain and then spending the rest of eternity with more pain than you could ever imagine."

Will my sacrifice be noble enough to gain entrance to Heaven? Ridding the world of the demon should cancel out suicide, she reasoned. She shook her head. It didn't matter what happened to her, she had to stop the demon and save her loved ones.

Her eyes shot up. Alastor had moved several more steps closer to her and would soon reach her. *It has to be now.* She swept the knife up. It sliced through the air and embedded itself in her throat. The shock of it, the intensity of putting a blade in her own body made her eyes pop wide open. And then she dropped to her knees.

"Nooooooo!" Alastor lunged for her as the others cried out.

She closed her eyes and dragged the blade across her neck before Alastor could reach her. She heard the others' screams as her blood flowed out onto the floor. With it flowed her strength, her vitality. But she kept the knife deep in her neck, kept her hand on the hilt.

As soon as Alastor touched her shoulders, she yanked the blade from her body and fell to the floor. Warm blood pooled around her, yet she felt cold, so cold. Darkness was closing over her vision. The last image she saw was the horrified faces of her family, gaping at her in shock.

As she lay dying, satisfaction washed over her. He couldn't destroy the world without her. He needed her. That much she knew.

The demon shouted incomprehensible words. He flipped her over and looked into her dying eyes—his were again endless black. She let hers drift closed, until he wrapped his hands around the incision in her throat. Her eyes popped open, though she no longer had any control over their movement. She watched him close his eyes and slowly inhale through his clenched teeth. Smooth black horns sprouted from his skull. The pigment of his skin darkened, shifted to gray. She felt claws extend from the tips of the fingers wrapped around her throat.

And then she began to sputter blood. Then her muscles seized, contracted, twisted as she went into convulsions. Distantly, she registered that the edges of her wound were melting back together, fusing, fading, and taking the pain with it. At last her body lay still. Her vision cleared. Alastor returned to its previous appearance.

Her mind raced. She was back—breathing. Alive again. He was able to keep her from her death. Her eyes darted over Alastor. She couldn't kill him; she couldn't even take her own life. There was no escape from him. How could this ever play out with her ending up free of him? He would win.

"You are a foolish woman," he scolded her. "Very creativity, though." He paused before he regarded her solemnly and said, "You can't escape this, Kyra. It is our destiny to be together."

"What?" James rose. "That's *my* wife you're talking about." He stood with his chin thrust belligerently forward. Then he cleared his throat, destroying his façade of bravado.

Alastor shot him a glare that made James flinch. Then Alastor threw his head back and released a deep, menacing laugh that shook the room. He stopped and looked at James. "She has belonged to me since before she was born. Your idea that your marriage means anything is absurd. You are just a human and have no idea what you have become tangled in." He looked down at Kyra, still lying on the floor. "She knows. She has had glimpses of our world in her dreams. She knew I was coming, that I would find her." Alastor snapped his gaze back to James. "Now, sit down before I break your neck."

James hesitated, glancing nervously at the others. They had their eyes locked on him. Xavier tugged on his sweater, the shackles rattling on his wrists.

Kyra lifted herself up from the puddle of blood and looked from Alastor to James. She managed a faint, reassuring smile for her husband and he sat back down.

"As for you, my darling," Alastor said, turning back to Kyra, "you may not be afraid of your death, but what about them?" He waved his hand at the captives. "Shall I test the limits of their pain thresholds? Who do you believe could tolerate the most?" When Kyra said nothing, he continued. "She can be first." He pointed to Hailey.

He sauntered over to Kyra's sister. She squirmed away as he reached out for her, but he grinned and grabbed a handful of her hair, pulling her to her feet. Her body stiffened, her fear growing when she looked into his hard eyes. With a click the restraints sprang open, falling from her wrists to clang against the wall behind her. He guided her by her hair to Kyra, who half sat up, leaning back on her arms.

Alastor shoved Hailey to the floor and she slipped through the pool of blood as she tried to catch herself, smearing her arms, chest, and face with Kyra's blood. She fumbled to get off the floor, turned and saw Alastor still standing over her, and chose to stay seated on the floor, mirroring Kyra's position. "She shall be the first to die," Alastor announced.

Derek from the motel entered the room. He carried an antique sword in a leather sheath. His footsteps faltered as he looked around the blood-soaked room. His head swiveled to the corpses and his eyes went wide.

"Ah, perfect timing. Now we can have a good old-fashioned beheading."

Kyra looked at her sister. "I'm sorry, Hailey," she whispered, wishing she could have stopped the demon.

"K-k-kyra, he—he's going to kill me! Can't you even try to reason with him?" Hailey started sobbing softly.

Kyra placed her hand over Hailey's, trying to comfort her, not knowing what else she could do. Even if she gave the demon her soul, he would still kill everyone. "You have to understand. Everything will be okay. You will go to Heaven and be with the angels." Kyra spoke so calmly that it even gave her the chills.

He's a demon, so why would he ever let them go? In the countless dreams she'd had since her early childhood, he'd killed everyone connected to the woman he pursued. Well, not always him; he sent his followers to do it—the damned, the fools who gave their souls to him... How many men were really in this place? There are three less now, she thought grimly, briefly pleased before she felt the wrench of guilt. They may have been bad people, but they were still people. She'd never killed anyone before.

"Please! Wait. Take me in her place." Alexis stood up, pulling against the chains that held her to the wall. "She's just her annoying little sister," she said, assuming a dismissive tone as she indicated Hailey with her chin. "I'm Kyra's best friend. We have been for seventeen years. I am the better choice."

Everyone else looked from Alexis to Alastor, whose eyes remained on Kyra. She held still, not wanting to react to his attempts to unnerve her. He was searching, she was sure, for her weakness; her vulnerability in those among the group. If she protested or even flinched, she would surely sign their death certificate.

Kyra's eyes met Alexis's, then shifted to Axel's concerned face. When she met his gaze, he flashed a hopeful smile. Then it was gone and she wasn't sure if it actually happened or she imagined it.

This wasn't supposed to be the way it turned out. It couldn't be fate for them all to die in this basement dungeon.

"You." Alastor pointed to Iris. "You are Kyra's mother. Perhaps you should join me." He grabbed Hailey's arm and dragged her back to the wall. Nick reached out for his wife and pulled her into his arms as Alastor dropped her.

Alastor knelt down next to Iris. "Give me your soul and I will let you live. You can leave this place."

"My—my soul..." She trailed off, looking confused.

Crap, Kyra cursed in her head, worried that her mother didn't understand what that would mean. "Don't!" she finally blurted. "You can't; he's the creature from my childhood night terrors. I swear it was all real, and this is him, hiding in human form." She turned to face Alastor. "You show them. You show them what I've already seen. Show them what you really are."

Ignoring Kyra's plea, he spoke to Iris. "Give me your hand, my dear."

Trying to catch Iris's attention, Alexis mouthed *No*, but Iris didn't seem to catch it. She glanced at Kyra before cautiously lifting her hand. Alastor gently took it in his own, then started playing with her fingers, deliberately making a creepy spectacle out of it, Kyra was sure. Suddenly he snapped one backward. She screamed in pain.

"Give me your soul and I shall set you free."

Lies!

"How could I, even if I wanted to?" Iris whimpered, choking back her pain.

No. Don't even consider it. He's trying to trick you.

Alastor smiled. "All you have to do is say you'll give me your soul for your freedom from this room, and shake my hand."

More lies.

"Are you actually a demon; not a metaphoric demon, but a real one?"

"Yes. Now how about your freedom?"

"I don't know," she said, her voice wavering, and looked away. "Why do you want it? What would that mean, giving you my soul?"

"Mom don't, you'll go to Hell," Kyra fretted.

"What do you suppose would happen if I asked your other daughter to give me her soul, or maybe your grandson? Perhaps they should go for a swim while you contemplate it." Alastor pushed her to the floor and looked at Kyra. "They can stay under the grate until you decide."

"But they'd drown." Iris looked to the others when Kyra turned away from her gaze.

"Only if you let them," he said casually, and headed toward Xavier.

He can't kill them, she thought, trying to convince herself, *he wouldn't dare. He doesn't care about Mom's soul, he's trying to get mine.*

Alastor grabbed Xavier's arm.

"Get your hands off my son," James said firmly, seizing Alastor's wrist. "I don't know what's going on," he said through clenched teeth, "but you *are not* a demon." Kyra saw Alexis cringe as the words left his mouth. "You're just another scumbag with a bunch of great magic tricks."

"Is that right?" Alastor said coldly. He released his grip on Xavier and pulled his wrist free from James's. Iris looked relieved, but Kyra held her breath, waiting for the backlash.

Alastor's hand snapped out and clenched James's throat, pushing him back against the wall behind him and leaning forward himself until their faces were nose to nose.

James slid up the wall as Alastor straightened up, then lifted him off the floor and high above his head, to the limit of the shackles, now pulling tight on James's wrists. He dangled there, his face red, his eyes wide. Kyra could only stare, her mouth sagging open.

James's gaze left Alastor to find her. "Kyra, please—do something," he wheezed. "What does he want? Please, stop all this madness," he begged her.

"I can't," she whispered, then added, a little louder, "You guys don't understand."

"You're a joke," Axel snapped, his eyes on the demon.

Alastor dropped James to the floor and turned his attention to the new defiant one in the group.

"He *is* an actual demon from Hell," Kyra said quickly, hoping to redirect Alastor's focus. "And if he gets what he wants, the whole world will burn. It would bring on the End of Days. It would mean the extinction of the human race. Isn't that right, Alastor?"

He turned and smiled at her. "Not entirely, but more or less."

She breathed a sigh of relief that he'd forgotten about the others, at least briefly, although his confirming her fears disturbed her.

"You would let your son die? *Our son!*" James exclaimed.

Shut up, James! He's testing me, he has to be testing me. Outwardly, Kyra ignored him, keeping her eyes on Alastor as he pulled Xavier from his father's arms. The shackles fell away from the boy's wrists. *Crap. Poker face. Poker face.*

"He will go to Heaven," she said to James, keeping her voice level. "That's what really matters. I'm sorry." She turned to face Xavier and forced a smile, hoping her fear was not obvious to the demon. "Mommy was just in the water and it's not so bad, honey. It will be over quickly, and I will see you in Heaven very soon, baby. Be brave and strong for me now."

"I will, Mommy. I love you." It ended in a sob.

"I love you too, baby." She kept her eyes from the others, refusing to acknowledge their shock and horror as Xavier was pulled crying to the tank. Tears pooled in Kyra's eyes and, no longer able to hold them back, she let them escape unchecked. She balled her fists, wanting desperately to stop the demon, but she held herself rigid. She couldn't succumb to his demands, or she would destroy the world.

He's bluffing, she told herself. *My son,* another voice countered, *he's going to kill my son. No, he won't—he can't, he has to be bluffing. He's not bluffing!* the other voice countered, high with panic. *He is going to kill my son!* She had to stop him.

"Stop." Iris called out. "I'll do it. You can have my soul if you let Xavier go and don't hurt him."

Kyra gasped, whirling to face her mother. "Mom, no!"

Alastor smiled at Kyra. "Deal." He released Xavier and the boy ran back to his father's arms, crying uncontrollably.

"Shit," Kyra said. *It's all going to go to shit,* she thought, and sighed. "Stop. You can't have her. You don't even want her, you want me. So let's make some kind of deal. Exchange her for me."

"I'm listening."

"They all go home, safe and unharmed." She pointed to the group on the other side of the room. She remembered the redhead who'd been so much like her in her dreams and thought carefully about how to make the deal to keep her loved ones safe. "Neither you nor any of your followers can kill *any* of my friends or family, or take their souls."

"Okay, is that all?"

"No. You can't hurt them, either, and you must leave them alone and not taunt them. Keep them away from all of this." She waved her hand vaguely at the tank, the shackles, Alastor. Her eyes darted over Alexis and Axel, and she hoped they would be able to fix her mess, somehow.

"You accept my offer and join me in exchange for the freedom of those in this room and for the protection of the lives and souls of your family and friends. They shall remain safe from *my* influence and neither I, nor my men, shall be allowed to hurt them, *unless* they try to intervene with you and I. Deal?"

Kyra drew a deep breath. "Deal." She held out her hand. He snapped it up, giving it a solid shake before he pulled her in to him.

She felt the warmth of his breath on her neck as he nuzzled her and inhaled her scent. One hand gently caressed her lower back as he brushed a strand of unruly hair from her face with the other, and she caught Hailey's shiver in the corner of her eye. He stroked her face softly, then grasped her hair and guided her mouth to his. Their lips met and he kissed her.

Her tense body relaxed and she started to kiss him back. Her arms, stiff at her sides, came up to embrace him.

Axel and Alexis exchanged looks of disgust. James grumbled and maneuvered Xavier to look away.

The passion accelerated between them. Finally Alastor pulled back from Kyra and released her.

Mouth agape in shock and confusion, she dropped to the floor, unconscious.

***

Kyra's body convulsed wildly for a few seconds before she went eerily still. Then her chest moved slowly up, down. The dirt and blood on her skin slowly faded away. Her long blonde hair darkened a shade from the roots down to the tips. It too had become clean and free of tangles. It continued to darken, until it was a deep chocolate brown, shiny as satin. Her sun-kissed complexion paled as her lips reddened. Her clothes blurred, so that those watching blinked, not trusting their eyes; when the blur sharpened, her clothing had been transformed into an elegant evening dress, its skirt fanning out on the dirty floor. Her eyes flickered open. She rose, and her hair and dress fell perfectly into place, as pristine as she looked; all evidence of the violence of the past few days had been erased.

"Drug the prisoners before you take them back to where you found them," Alastor instructed Derek.

Alexis and Axel exchanged a worried glance.

"We have many things to discuss. Come darling." He waved for Kyra to follow him.

Kyra looked blankly at the faces of those chained at the end of the room—not without recognition, but without emotion. And then she scowled. Without a word, she turned and followed Alastor out of the dungeon.

Chapter Seven

James Parker sat at his kitchen table across from his son, his newspaper resting on the table in front of him, still folded and unread. Over and over he replayed the moment when Kyra had left him, trying to make sense of it. A cold emptiness had settled behind her eyes after she had kissed Alastor, damping the familiar sparkle he'd always known—or had he imagined it? His hands clasped tighter around the white mug half filled with coffee as his gaze wandered past his son—playing with his cereal—to the kitchen sink, where Kyra would normally be standing as she cleaned up the breakfast mess. Now the sink was full of dirty dishes and the countertops littered with empty pizza boxes and Chinese take-out containers. The fridge was bare and the garbage threatened to overflow onto the floor. He didn't even know what day to take out the garbage. He'd taken so many small things Kyra had done for granted and now she was gone. Everything had changed.

"Dad, can I ask you a question?"

James dragged his gaze to Xavier's worried face. "Well, you just did," he smiled wanly, "but you may ask another."

"When is mom coming home?" All the hope in the world was in his eyes in that brief moment, before the expression on his father's face shattered it.

James sighed. "I don't know what is going on with your mother." Images of Kyra in Alastor's arms flashed through his mind. "I don't think she'll be coming back. There's something wrong with her." He remembered her coldness toward him, and it brought the memory of cold concrete floors and chains with it. He could clearly hear the clank of the shackles dangling from his wrists whenever he fumbled to remove his watch.

The phone conversation he'd had with Iris came to mind: *"Kyra was on antipsychotics and antidepressants when she was young. They kept changing her diagnosis and medications and we never really did figure out what was wrong with her."*

"She must be having some kind of a mental breakdown," James mumbled, more to himself than to his son. "She's in a very dark place; she's sick and needs a doctor." His eyes dropped to the mug between his hands as he mumbled, more to himself then his son, "She was so psychotic when she attacked those people... I've never seen her act crazy like that."

"She's not crazy! And she will come home!" Xavier shouted, abruptly standing up and knocking his chair over. "She loves us."

Unfazed by his son's outburst, James spoke calmly. "She chose to leave us and go with that man."

"She had to go with him! She didn't want to. She did it to save us from him 'cause—because she loves us."

"She will always love us." He wasn't sure if he even believed that anymore. "But... no one can tell your mother what to do. She does what she wants." He cleared his throat. "I don't know, Xavier. Sometimes grown-ups have problems..." He trailed off, deciding that telling an eight-year-old about marital problems would just bring more questions he didn't want to answer. "Sometimes grown-ups change their minds— No, sometimes things happen and—" He hesitated, searching for the right words; he couldn't tell his son that she left them for some kidnapper thug and he didn't quite believe that's what it was. "I still can't explain it. Don't you remember the look in her eyes? I've never seen her like that before; it's like she was a different person."

She was completely insane, babbling about evil surrounding people and being able to do impossible things, and she murdered people—no, that *was* self-defense. Although she had killed those men in horrific ways, more violently than a sane person would have chosen. He thought of her being arrested and hauled off to a mental hospital. "I'm sorry, but Mommy probably won't be coming home."

"No! You're wrong!" Xavier whirled and stormed off to his room, sobbing.

James sighed and considered going after his son, then decided against it, realizing he had nothing positive or comforting to say. He heard his son's bedroom door slam before he returned to his coffee.

James had replayed events in his mind all week, and he still wasn't fully able to understand what happened—*Just a week ago. Is that all?* He still didn't understand what was going on. He had no idea of where he should even start looking to piece together what had happened, and the explanations from Iris and Hailey were far too... out-of-this-world. His phone conversation with Iris shortly after they had all awakened in their own homes had been downright odd.

He had answered the phone, expecting the caller to be the police with more questions, as it was too soon for any news.

"Hello."

"James? Are you and Xavier all right?" Iris. Her voice sounded stressed.

"Yes, Iris, we're okay."

"Is my daughter there with you guys?"

What a stupid question. "No, she never came home. She stayed with that guy, don't you remember?"

"Yes, of course, but I thought—I thought that she might have gotten away and come home, or maybe it was all a nightmare." She sighed. "I mean, I remember him breaking my finger, but it's not broken anymore; it doesn't even hurt."

"Well, she's not here and I don't expect her to be here anytime soon," he said with finality. "I don't know if you were aware of it, but she's been having sort of a midlife crisis for a while now. I don't know how long she has been seeing that guy—"

"*What?* She's not seeing *that guy*," Iris exclaimed. "I don't think he's a guy at all." She paused a moment, then said, "James, I think I can explain all of this."

James sighed. "Please don't tell me you believe all that crap he was spouting. There's no way that was true; it's not even possible it's real."

Iris was silent for a long time, and he imagined her pursing her lips, thinking. "How do you explain the things we saw him do?" she finally said.

"Like what? All he really did was suggest ideas to a bunch of sleep-deprived and starved hostages who were most likely on some hallucinogenic drugs to make his power of suggestion possible."

"What about when Kyra killed him but he didn't die?"

James sniffed his disdain. "Not real. It's just what we thought we saw. We also saw her die by slitting her own throat and somehow he saved her without any medical equipment. It's not possible, Iris. It wasn't real."

"I wouldn't have thought it possible either, if I didn't know about Kyra's childhood secrets," Iris said, her voice solemn.

"What secrets?"

"She never wanted anyone to know, after all the trouble and pain we all went through when she was young. At first she had dreams about angels and would talk about it all the time, then she started making up stories about angels and events that happened in history."

James said nothing. He doubted this story was leading anywhere plausible.

"We just thought she had a wild imagination and it was a normal part of growing up. You know, to cope with the changes when she started school. When she started talking about demons and her dreams turned to night terrors we became concerned and monitored what she watched on TV a little better. Then we spoke to our priest about the contents they were teaching in Sunday school, but he said they didn't talk about demons, so he didn't know where she was getting her ideas from."

"Un-huh." James rolled his eyes.

Iris sighed. "It quickly got worse. She was telling her friends stories about demons and their parents were phoning us all the time. She was getting in trouble at school and church for arguing with teachers about historical facts, then when they challenged her, she would tell them that she just knew or that the angels had shown her. We couldn't get her to stop talking like that, so by the time she was Xavier's age, she was seeing a shrink every day and on seven different types of medication."

James lifted an eyebrow. This was news. "What does that have to do with Kyra running away? You think she has always been mentally unstable?"

"Quite the opposite, actually. I think it was real and she knew more than the rest of us, but we wouldn't listen. I think that man was a demon, or possessed by a demon, and Kyra is possessed now, too."

"Possession?" James said, not hiding his skepticism. "Really, Iris? This is your way of dealing with the reality of Kyra abandoning her family?"

"I think it's at least possible. She was out of her mind when she attacked those guys. That's not normal Kyra behavior."

"That was most likely a result of torture and duress."

James drained his coffee cup and sighed at the memory. The call had not eased his confusion at all. Iris had just added more noise to that already rattling around in his head. It could somehow just stay a bad dream, he thought wistfully, as long as no one talked about it.

His rational mind had been unable to accept anything Iris said as a solid explanation. Regardless of what he had seen.

But if she was possessed, as Iris had suggested, then maybe he could get her back with an exorcism. That other fellow must have been possessed as well, because if demons did exist in the literal sense, then they surely did not walk around on Earth. He shook his head. Even the possibility of possession was too much of a stretch for him to wrap his mind around it. Kyra's mother was just as crazy as the rest of this nonsense. When people asked, "Hey, where's your wife?" he would not be replying, "Oh, she left me because she's possessed; she ran off with the Devil." No. He wouldn't be jumping on the crazy bandwagon too.

In the meantime, he had to figure out how to get his life and his son's life back to normal—as normal as it could be. Neither of them had left the house since the short trip to the police station after arriving back home from the kidnapping. He should have gone to work this week, but he'd extended his absence for another week, while he tried to sort out their lives. He would have to return to work in few days, though, and he was no closer to a plausible explanation than before.

That's it. Enough is enough. He was going to accept that she had run off with a lover in a whirlwind romance and the rest of them had been given some kind of hallucinogenic drugs to explain why they all thought they saw impossible events. *But, the same events? The power of suggestion,* he reasoned; *somehow the men at the hotel must have slipped me something before the fight at the ice machine.*

He walked over to the sink to add the empty mug to the growing collection of dishes. He looked out the window into the backyard. The lawn seemed to have taken over the yard; it was in need of mowing. The buds on the mature trees growing inside the fence line had long ago burst open with the changing seasons. Now their dark green leaves blocked out the view of the neighbors' houses. His eyes touched on the swing set on the west side of the yard, set up by over-eager parents one Saturday afternoon when Xavier was still in diapers. Kyra's vegetable garden on the south side of the yard was thriving, and so were the weeds. She had loved her garden and always took great care of it, out there every day pulling vegetables for dinner.

The flower garden, her pride and joy, stretched along the east fence, which was double the length of the south fence, an abundance of flowers and flowering trees that extended out over most of the lawn now, growing larger as the years went by. Slabs of slate created a walking path through the maze, meandering past the gazebo with vines climbing up its lattice. The most recent—and expensive—addition was a rock waterfall that fed a small stream that moved throughout the flowers before circling back to pumped through the cycle again. She had created a personal oasis where she spent her weekends, working outside.

What was he going to do now, without his Kyra?

***

Alexis dropped the heavy grimoire with a thud onto the table in her motel room, then sat down, opened it, and leafed through the pages in the book's center, searching for the Witch Location spell. It was slightly different from the regular location spells but she hadn't memorized it yet, never seeing the need to learn it before now. She'd been casting it for days, sometimes successfully, sometimes not, while they traveled around the country, chasing Kyra.

Her brother walked through the door and Alexis beamed. "Axel, I'm glad you're here. I was just about to find Kyra."

The buckles on his leather jacket rattled as he kicked the dirt off his boots. "You mean try to find," he said, and handed her a paper cup with steam wafting from the hole in its lid. He took a slurp from his cup. "It didn't work before I left for coffee."

"We will catch up to her, we just have to organize better and plan it properly." She smiled at him as he dropped onto the bed, leaned against the headboard and swung his legs up, crossing them at the ankles then rested his boot heels on the bedspread.

She turned back to the book, flinging her wet hair over her shoulder, still damp from her shower. She found the page she needed and skimmed over it with her finger as she drank her coffee.

"I wish there was an easier way to get to her." Axel snapped his fingers and a small flame shot out from his thumb.

"Like what, summon her like she's a demon?" She pulled Kyra's necklace from her pocket and stroked the mahogany obsidian pendant.

"That wouldn't work, would it?" Axel asked, watching the flame dance into his palm. He flicked at it, sending sparks around the room.

"No, I already tried," she said absently.

He sat up. "You never told me that. When did you try it?"

"After we got back. I tried to steal her away from Alastor, but I didn't really expect it to work on a witch." She kept her eyes locked on the pendant as she cast the spell. Then she stood up to flatten the travel map of California and repositioned it closer to her chair before sitting back down.

Axel tore a page off the motel notepad next to him and crumpled it. "It shouldn't be this hard," he complained. "She never had any interest in learning spells, and demons can't cast." He tossed the ball onto the bed and ripped another page free. "What are they using that would have her popping in and out of our ability to track her?"

"I don't know—a cloaking spell or a protection spell, maybe both." That's what she'd cast on the grimoires to keep them from being found; one could never be too careful.

Axel crumpled up the paper and tossed it at her. "What, like the ones you use to ditch boyfriends after you dump them?"

"Only the stalkers." She winked at him, but he was distracted, telekinetically raising the crumpled ball from the bed.

"Half of them were cops," he teased.

"So?" She started swirling the necklace, holding the clasp with her fingertips. "But seriously, it's not the same. I don't think the spell is on her or us; I think it's on his hideout, if it even is a spell, and she keeps going back there."

He grunted. The ball of paper burst into flames and burned to ash, which drifted to the floor. The smoke detector screamed. Alexis shifted in her chair, careful to keep the pendant swirling, and gave Axel a disparaging look.

"If you spent half as much time studying the grimoires as you do playing with fire," she said, flicking a gust of air toward the smoke alarm to silence it, "you'd learn some new tricks and maybe create some of your own spells to contribute to our family legacy." She smiled to take the sting out of the rebuke.

"Thanks; tips," he said sarcastically.

"Grrrr," she retorted, squinting one eye. He shrugged.

Alexis turned back to the map, then looked up quickly. "Kyra has popped up on the grid again, and it's not too far."

Axel jumped up and headed for the door. Alexis grabbed her room key and followed him into the fresh morning air.

"We have to get her back. I should have known she was in danger," Axel said, ushering his sister to his black Dodge in the motel parking lot.

"I know. I think we both should have known something more was going on," she said, wishing she'd made Kyra tell her what was going on in her head instead of just assuming she already knew. Axel pulled open the passenger door and Alexis continued as she slipped inside. "She'd been acting funny, but I just thought it was normal life issues. I never expected this."

"Me neither," he agreed, closing her door.

The truck rumbled to life and black smoke billowed from the exhaust. The radio kicked on, blaring the local rock station. Alexis blinked her eyes at it and the volume dropped. They pulled out of the parking lot onto the street. The exhaust whistled as he pushed down on the accelerator. He combed his light brown hair from his eyes with his fingers. "Where are we headed? Folsom or San Quentin?"

"She's at Folsom now," Alexis said, turning her head to continue ogling the men in military uniforms. "We'll never get there in time, but she should head to San Quentin state prison shortly after."

"This would be a lot quicker if we could travel like Kyra." He looked at Alexis and wiggled his eyebrows. She knew he was referring to her failed attempts to modify the Astral Projection spell.

"This is so surreal," she said, ignoring him. "I can't believe this is happening to Kyra." Guilt stabbed at her. She regretted not pushing Kyra enough to practice active magic. "Frickin' demon," she whispered.

Axel slowed for the red light. "How's it even possible that she would still be running around with that abomination— unless she's possessed. But even then, it happened too fast and I would expect someone a little more… disturbed, I guess." The truck rolled to a stop at an intersection and he leaned forward, crossed his arms, and rested them on top of the steering wheel, watching the lights.

"Well, she has been off for a while." Alexis took a sip of her coffee and made a face.

Axel reached over and wrapped his hand around her coffee cup. "She's meant for more than the white picket fence and two-point-three children lifestyle." He released his grip as steam seeped from the mouth of her coffee cup.

"Totally, but she wanted to walk that path and have an ordinary life." She sipped her hot coffee. "That was her choice." *A choice she made because she didn't grow up like we did*, she often thought, long after she quit telling her best friend.

"But—" He glanced quickly at her as the light turned green. "If you think about it, it does explain a lot."

"What are you talking about?" She looked at him. "Come on, Axel, how do her lifestyle choices explain anything."

"Not her life choices; the fact that she was always a bit different from us—there really was a demon after her."

"Yes, well, her destiny is to overcome this evil." She faced forward. "We can help her. It must be part of why we're all so close to each other. There are no coincidences. Everything happens for a reason."

The truck roared as he gave it gas. "Damn it, I should have known something was coming," he grumbled. "We have to get her back, Alexis."

She poked her brother playfully to try to lighten his spirits. "We will. It's impossible for us to be separated for any length of time."

Chapter Eight

Axel's gaze drifted over the sign: *DEPARTMENT OF CORRECTIONS, CALIFORNIA STATE PRISON, SAN QUENTIN.*

"Here we go again," he said as he pulled into a parking stall and switched off the engine.

"She should be here soon. It's the last maximum security prison in California that they haven't hit yet," Alexis said as she slipped her feet into her shoes. He thought of the dots they had plotted on the maps as they tracked Kyra, and wondered if they had indeed figured out the pattern or if this would be another miss.

A wave of heat blasted into the truck when Alexis opened her door. The scorching afternoon sun beat down on the asphalt, which shimmered with heat. She climbed out and stretched, pulling in a light breeze that swept through the parking lot with her arms as they raised above her head.

Axel stared out the windshield toward the prison. He grunted and ran his hand through his hair. "What if she doesn't show?" he said to himself.

As soon as the words left his lips, Kyra materialized, standing in front of the hood of his truck. Her eyes fixed on his, and she shook her finger at him. His breath caught in his chest. He fumbled for the door handle, keeping his eyes on her, afraid she would disappear if he looked away.

Alexis spun around as her brother scrambled from his truck. She followed his stare to the dark-haired woman in the parking lot and stumbled around her open door. Before they met in front of the truck, the vision had vanished. The siblings looked at each other and nodded, confirming they had both seen it.

"Crap, they're already here." He surveyed the building. "Now everything's shot to shit. New plan." He headed toward the front gate.

"Wait! So what's the plan here, exactly?" she asked, trotting after him.

"Don't die!" he shouted as he kicked into a run.

Alexis chased after him. "Would you frickin' wait a sec? We have to go in there level-headed."

He slowed to allow her to catch up. He knew she was right, but he didn't want Kyra to slip away. Some part of her might still be in there—she *had* come to see them alone. Maybe. Maybe he'd been too focused on her to notice if the demon was nearby. He wasn't sure.

Alexis caught up to him and they walked quickly toward the main gate. Guards posted on either side of the checkpoint entrance watched them approach. "Halt. What's your business here?" demanded the taller guard. "No visitors allowed until further notice."

"I've got this," Alexis whispered to her brother. Axel grunted and gave an imperceptible nod, slowing his pace to fall behind her.

"Good afternoon, sir," she greeted the guard with a smile. "We're here to have a look around." She tossed her hair. "We have reason to believe that the couple from the news is expected to attack this place at any moment. You are all in danger."

He remained stone-faced. "Return to your vehicle immediately."

She locked eyes with the tall guard and kept walking toward him until she was uncomfortably close to his face. He blinked in surprise, but made no move to stop her or raise his weapon.

"Tim, what are you doing?" the stocky guard demanded, looking from Alexis to the taller guard. Axel shot him a look that made him flinch. He strode up next to his sister, keeping his focus on the stockier man as Alexis worked her magic on the tall one.

"I-I'm sorry, but with all the prison breakouts across the country, no visitors are allowed," Tim said softly. Axel shifted his weight and gritted his teeth, growing impatient.

"Oh, come on." Alexis put her hand on his arm. "Let us in so we can try to stop her and save you."

He tapped his chin and shrugged. "Okay. I'll get you both a visitor's pass." He entered the small concrete booth beside them while the stocky guard looked at Axel and shrugged, then swung open the black iron gate.

"So, could I buy you a drink later tonight?" Tim asked as he handed both clip-on laminated passes to Alexis. "I get off at eight."

"Not today, honey. I have too much to do." She winked at him before heading through the open gate. He stood dumbfounded as she moved past him. Axel grunted and followed.

They looked around for signs of trouble as they took the long walk up to the big brick building. All was quiet. Too quiet. No one was in sight as they entered the building, nor was anyone within range of his ability to sense them.

"Where is everyone?" Alexis said, looking over the empty check-in desk.

"This is odd," Axel agreed. "There's not even dead bodies lying around."

"We know they're here somewhere," Alexis said. "We'll find them."

The security checkpoints were all abandoned as they made their way deeper into the prison, the doors clanging behind them. Axel beeped when they passed through metal detectors. He rolled his eyes when Alexis looked back and shushed him.

"It's my jacket," he whispered, "I can't help it."

It was as if they wandered around in a maze. Axel stopped, his irritation growing as he realized they were taking too long to find her; she was going to slip away again.

"Where are we going?"

"I'd say follow the screams of horror, but… there's no noise coming from anywhere. We'll just have to keep looking until we find everyone."

They wandered the hallways of the deserted prison. Everything was still. There were no signs of struggle—no blood, not even the faint smell of fresh blood; just the consistent smell of unwashed bodies which was more pungent in the smaller enclosed areas. They came to the final door at the end of a long hall. An electrifying energy radiated outward from the other side—there were people on the other side, he could feel it.

As they approached, he heard a deep voice speaking on the other side, the words muffled by the heavy hollow-steel door.

"I guess we found them. So what's the new plan?" Axel whispered, resting his hand on the door.

"It doesn't change. We still need to talk to her and figure out what kind of magic or supernatural being is influencing her."

"Except they know we're here now. Do you think he will just kill us on the spot, as soon as we open this door?" Axel chuckled. "Then we made this whole trip for nothing."

"Oh, don't be stupid. It's not funny. Besides, he can't kill us—it's part of the deal she made." She thought for a moment. "Maybe if he did, Kyra would be released from him… hmm. Why don't you try that for a Plan B?" She nudged him with her elbow. "You can take this one for the team, can't you?"

"Yeah, sure. Great plan." He gripped the handle and pulled the door open, saying, "I guess we'll wing it and hope for the best." He smiled at Alexis as he pushed past her.

They entered a huge oval room, open for three stories from ground level to the high ceiling; they were looking down on the mess hall from the second-floor catwalk. Alexis covered her nose and gagged. The air was heavy with the stench of sweaty men.

Guards lined the walkway, all with guns drawn, some at the railing, looking down on the commotion below. Except all were frozen in place, still as statues. No breath escaped their lips; there was no movement of any kind, not even blinking. Alexis and Axel maneuvered around them to peer over the railing, Alexis poked one of the guards in the chest with her finger. No reaction. She touched his face gently but his eyes never shifted, his body never flinched.

She shrugged. "Well, at least they're not all dead," she whispered.

Axel had his nose inches away from another guard's face. The guard stared through him, focused on something in the distance. He grunted in response to his sister before carefully sliding a statue-guard back from the railing, the man's boots squealing as they skidded across the floor.

"Shhh," Alexis scolded. "Are you trying to get us killed?"

"Oh, please. They already know we're here." He deposited the guard against the wall and stepped up to the railing. Alexis joined him.

Down below, inmates filled the neatly organized rows of tables covering the mess hall floor. Along the walls painted in sepia murals, more inmates stood silently, arms crossed over their chests. Alastor paced purposefully back and forth along a central row of tables, emphasizing his speech with arm gestures now and then. Kyra stood on the floor behind him, her eyes fixed on Axel.

"The choice is yours." Alastor opened his arms out to the captivated prisoners. "Join me, or stay here for the rest of your sentences." He scanned the excited faces. "The decision is simple." His lips curled into devious sneer.

"Oh, crap," Alexis breathed.

"Fuck it," Axel said, then shouted, "Kyra!"

All heads tipped up to the second-floor railing—all but those of the statue guardsmen. They were still stuck in whatever limbo Alastor had created. Kyra slowly exhaled, her nostrils flaring.

Alastor raised his eyebrows. "What, pray tell, do you two think you are doing?"

"We're here to take Kyra home," Axel said. He puffed out his chest and gripped the hand railing firmly. "She belongs with us, not you."

"Axel, I wasn't serious about you taking one for the team," Alexis whispered.

"You are sorely mistaken. She joined me of her own free will," Alastor countered.

"That wasn't free will. You tortured her and threatened her loved ones. She only went with you to protect the people she cares about." He looked at Kyra. "Kyra, please! Please come with us; you're stronger than this. You can fight his evil."

A deep, ominous laugh rumbled from Alastor, echoing throughout the vast mess hall. His eyes locked on Axel. "Now, boy, you are beginning to infuriate me. She shall be mine until the end of time." He swept his arm out, encompassing the inmates around him. "I shall conquer this world, then move on to the next." His eyes bored into Axel, then his mouth twisted in a patronizing smirk. "Leave. Before I unleash my wrath on you."

"Hey, shit demon, why don't you blow me?" he shouted, grabbing his crotch with one hand. *Best to kill the demon, then maybe Kyra will be free from the influence of evil. If not, Alexis will just have to find another way to free her.* If Kyra wasn't being held under the demon's influence, then it would be some kind of possession or maybe a spell cast on her by a dark witch. *Easy enough,* he reasoned.

"Foolish move, boy. Kyra, darling, silence him before his mouth angers me further." He turned to Kyra and she nodded.

Axel toyed with the logic: Demons could be killed just as easily as humans—demon souls attached to human bodies—one less troublemaker on Earth. Apparently this one was more of a threat than the rest of them, so he would be doing everyone a favor—unless this was a human possessed by a demon.

"Good job bro, piss of the demon as much as possible," Alexis hissed from the side of her mouth.

Kyra closed her eyes.

Axel tried to move his hand and flip his middle finger at the demon, but he was stuck in place. His anger flashed, and he tried to shout another derogatory comment, but his lips didn't cooperate, either.

At least he hasn't messed with my head, he thought in frustration as he watched Kyra cross the floor below.

"Well, at least we'll be able to talk to her without the demon in earshot," Alexis observed as Kyra levitated herself to the catwalk. She landed gracefully behind her friends. Alexis turned to face her and smiled. "I love you, hun. I'm sorry I couldn't protect you from all this evil."

Axel strained to watch the girls out of the corner of his eye.

"Kyra please, come home with us." Alexis reached out for Kyra's arm and pulled her far enough forward that Axel could see her face. "Everyone misses you so much. You have a husband who is completely lost without you, and a son who needs his mommy, and I can't lose you to that evil asshole down there." She paused, her eyes pleading along with her words. "Come on Kyra, say something."

Kyra placed her hands on their shoulders and Alexis went still before an unseen force spun her around as if she were standing on a turntable. Now both Axel and Alexis faced the mess hall below, but Kyra didn't drop her hands from their shoulders.

Alastor returned his attention to the gathered convicts. "The time has come to make your decision. If you wish to stay confined, then retreat to your cell now."

Heads turned as the prisoners looked at each other, but no one rose.

"All you have to do—" he grinned at them "—is slaughter the guards."

If Alexis was panicking on the inside, Axel couldn't see it; her face was as frozen as his.

"The two intruders are to be left untouched," Alastor instructed his audience. "They shall bear witness to the great powers of Kyra and myself." His eyes rose to meet Axel's. "She is my dark queen."

There was a flurry of activity below as inmates scrambled to be the first to reach the guards, and the beatings began. The frozen guards were punched and kicked, then stomped when they fell to the floor, where eager hands smashed their skulls against the concrete. A crowd stampeded up the stairs, some spilling onto the second-floor catwalk, others continuing up to the third floor, the steel grating clanging under hundreds of charging feet.

Blood splattered across Alexis's face as the guard next to her was pummeled by fists and anything the prisoners found close at hand. His corpse collapsed against her legs. Blood dripped onto her toes.

Axel could only hear the horror around him and imagined the terror of the helpless victims. He was immobilized and muted, but he could feel Kyra's touch on his shoulder—and if he could feel that, the guards were aware of everything being done to them. The realization sickened him. But then, suddenly, he realized that he could see men continually bumping into him as they pushed past him en route to the next victim, but couldn't he feel it. *What changed?* he wondered, confused. *If I can't feel anything, can the guards?* He hoped that was the case.

And then one inmate pulled a gun from the hand of a guard and opened fire. *That was inevitable.*

The prisoners instinctively ducked, looking surprised, but that lasted only a few seconds before a great cheer went up, and more guns were pulled from the guards' stiffened fingers. The mess hall rang with gunfire, so loud that Axel wished he could cover his ears. And the way the agitated mob was carelessly firing the weapons, Axel worried that a stray bullet might find Alexis—and him. Or was Kyra shielding them—could she?

Finally every guard was down, and after one or two last shots, the mess hall fell silent. Blood was splattered everywhere, and blood dripped from the silent victims to pool around them where they'd dropped. Blood dripped down from the third-floor level, splattering against the railing, onto Axel's shoulders, his head, his shoes. Bodies dropped past his line of sight, dumped over the railings above to plummet down to the ground floor. He heard the sickening thuds as they landed, loud in the sudden quiet.

"Well done, boys." Alastor stood with his arms outstretched. A column of gray smoke whirled around him, engulfing him before expanding to engulf every inmate still alive. The tornado of whirling gray smoke vanished, taking Alastor and the prisoners with it. Only the bodies of the guards and those inmates who had been struck down in the riot remained.

And Kyra. She leaned forward to look into her friends' faces. Then she too vanished.

Chapter Nine

James Parker sat on his sofa, staring at the television. It hadn't been on for hours, but the remote control still rested in his hand. He had hastily turned it off and sent his son upstairs after the news had shown Kyra, once again killing people on the street. This time she was somewhere in Europe. James had begun to wonder if he'd ever really known her at all.

She had kept so many secrets from him: her childhood night terrors, her mental illnesses, the Christmas party, her relationship with this Alastor guy, and whatever it was that had her running around on a killing spree with him. Apparently she *had* been living a double life.

A knock at the door brought James out of his trance, though at first he was unaware of what had interrupted his thoughts, and he sat, bewildered, for a moment until the knock came again.

Doesn't everyone use doorbells these days? he griped. *More annoying reporters, no doubt.*

He rose and headed for the door, preparing to unleash his irritability on them. He pulled the front door open just as the knocker raised his hand to knock a third time. A priest stood on the threshold with his hand raised, a startled expression on his face. Two odd-looking men stood on the porch behind him. James's anger subsided into confusion. *A priest?*

"James—James Parker?" the priest said, drawing James's eyes back to him.

"Yes; can I help you?"

"I sure hope so, Mr. Parker. My name is Father Thomas. May we come in?"

"What for?" James asked bluntly, eyeing the strange men. Their long hair was tied back with thin strips of leather, and strange tattoos ran up their arms. *And robes. Robes! Very... bizarre.*

"We're here to help. There is a way to save us all from the terror that has been going on. Your wife is under a sort of euphoric spell, but we can bring her back from it, with your help."

James hesitated, unsure if they were legit, or as crazy as the rest of the world had become. Could it really be possible to have Kyra come home and be herself again?

"What do you mean, *spell*? You mean she's on drugs?"

Confusion passed over the priest's face before he said, "Yes, in a manner of speaking." He nodded toward the unmarked police car parked across the street. "It's better we speak inside, to avoid prying eyes. May we come in?"

James surveyed their faces for a moment, wondering if they were really there, or if he had fallen asleep on the couch again. They looked harmless enough. He shrugged. "Sure, why not? My life can't get any weirder than it has been lately."

He showed them into the front room, surreptitiously studying them as they entered his home. The two men moved slowly, barely disturbing the skirts of their pale robes. *Like a monk's attire*, he decided, and nodded to himself when his eyes fell on the sandals peeking out from under the robes.

"Have a seat," he said, gesturing toward the sofa.

The priest settled on the sofa; the two men remained standing, taking up a station in the corner of the room.

They look like they stepped out of a time capsule, James thought. *They must be some kind of New Age monks. Of course they're monks! But what on earth are they doing here?*

"Okay, what is going on?" he asked as he sat down stiffly in his favorite armchair.

"Alastor has reasons for everything he does; nothing is random," Father Thomas said. "He has been planning this for a very long time. We need to gather everyone involved—I mean everyone who was at the hostage site, being held captive,"

"Everyone?" James narrowed his eyes at the thought of gathering the group of crazies he'd been avoiding for weeks. *It could be organized as an intervention-type meeting to save Kyra*, he rationalized, *and get her some help—she clearly could use it. Maybe she is a recovering drug addict that went off the rails, and that guy she's with is her drug dealer, and maybe she doesn't know what she's doing, or maybe she's had some sort of relapse in her mental illness.* Anything was possible now, with Kyra's double life bleeding out into James's picture-perfect one.

"Okay, I'll make some calls."

***

As the guests gathered, Father Thomas stood on one side of the front room, where he could see both the sofas and down the hall into the kitchen. He eavesdropped on their conversations, trying to decipher what state of mind they were all in, hoping for an open-minded group that would have an easier time than Mr. Parker was going to have.

James sat in his armchair, staring at the floor. He flinched a little every time he heard Axel's voice as he chatted with Nick about some party they had gone to years ago. They stood in the open space behind James' chair that served as the path from the front door to the kitchen.

Alexis and Iris sat on the sofa, conversing softly. "It's not like her at all," Iris was saying, her expression intense. "She has to be possessed." She glanced at the priest and caught him watching them. He quickly looked away. "That has to be it," he heard Iris whisper; "why else would a priest be here?"

Alexis nodded. "Maybe."

Iris glanced around the room and leaned in closer to Alexis. "I think Kyra has an extrasensory gift or something, which made her more vulnerable to possession."

"Oh yeah? Why do you say that?"

"When she was little she had imaginary friends that she talked to, claiming they were ghosts, but I never believed her. Now I think they might have been, and whatever that was opened her up to possession."

"Could be." Alexis pulled Iris in to hug her. "We'll figure it out soon."

Father Thomas smiled. *It may not be an uphill battle after all.*

Xavier descended the stairs from his room to join the group. He stopped and high-fived Axel before giving Hailey a hug. The boy was beaming as he looked around, seeing all the people who had come to help his mom.

"Xavier," James grunted. "Get over here and sit down."

Xavier lowered his head and quickly obeyed, sitting on the end of the sofa next to his father's chair. "Gee, Dad," he protested mildly, "it's going to be okay—really."

"Just sit down and be quiet, please. We'll hear what they have to say." James turned to Father Thomas.

The priest cleared his throat and tapped on his water-filled wine glass with his pen to get everyone's attention as he walked over to stand in front of the entertainment unit.

"Attention, everyone." The chatter faded away. "I'm Father Thomas. My colleagues here" —he gestured toward the two men in the corner— "don't say much, so I will speak for all of us. We've called this meeting to explain what is happening to Kyra. There is a way that she can come back from all of this, but it won't be easy."

Iris turned her gaze from the two robed men. "Sorry, Father, but you said those men are your colleagues... aren't you from different faiths?" She put her arm around her grandson while she waited for his answer.

"Not exactly. These men are called Majai. They will be of assistance, if needed, but for now they are just going to tag along and observe."

He returned to his topic. "There is an ancient prophecy among many cultures and religions about the end of the human race as we know it. Yes, there are many, many versions and similar stories about the end of days, but this is not one that is found in any religious writings."

He took a sip of his water, scanning the faces. Nick and Axel had sat down on the loveseat across from James. Hailey was half leaning, half sitting on the armrest of James's chair. He had their full attention. Everyone looked captivated ... except the scowling Mr. Parker.

"It talks of a demon coming to Earth when a special child is born. Or, in Revelations, when the first seal is broken, the Antichrist arrives on a white horse. In the prophecy it reads: 'if good and evil unite, war will erupt between the light and the dark.' The second seal is the red horse with war attached to it. That is where we are now." James rolled his eyes. "Alastor and Kyra are presumably building an army with all these convicts they're breaking out of prisons."

Alexis and Axel exchanged a look.

"There are a couple positive points," Father Thomas continued. "First, the one he searches for has to choose to accept him of her own free will, in order for him to have any power over her."

"Oh... my... God... This is all my fault," Iris breathed.

"No, Mrs. Reed. This is no one's fault. This game has been around since the beginning of man."

"Game? How is this a game? He kidnapped us and tortured my wife!" James barked.

"I am terribly sorry, Mr. Parker, but this is a game—or test; whatever you would like to call it—with the rules set by Heaven and the players being humanity and demons. Now, what we know for sure, because it has been witnessed and documented over the centuries, is simple. Every few hundred years or so, a demon rises from Hell and takes human form. The demons can change their physical appearance as they choose. In the 1300s, a witch discovered a demon of a different name in her village, while he was in search of the girl. She thought she had run him off, but later discovered he took on the identities of several townspeople for a few days before leaving."

"A witch." Hailey repeated cautiously, as if she had heard it wrong. "A real witch... like spells and magic, or what do you mean by a *witch*?"

"Yes, a real witch, with real powers. Kyra is half witch." That drew a few gasps from the group. "I'm sure some of you have heard the term 'Nephilim.' They are children born from an angel and a human with some angelic abilities. Kyra is what is called a melhara. She's born from a witch and an angel. She has the great powers of both, but the free will and frailty of humans. Witches are not born good or evil, but have the ability to be both at the same time, just as people are both good and bad."

Alexis gasped and her eyes went wide. "That's impossible. How could she be half angel..." Her eyes swept to Axel, who looked just as stunned.

Chapter Ten

"What? Now my mom is a witch? Is Dad really an angel and not dead?" Hailey looked back and forth from the priest to her mother, trying to discern the truth from their faces.

"Um, not quite. I-I can explain." Her hands fidgeting nervously in her lap, Iris scanned the faces in the group before she looked at Hailey. "You see... Kyra was adopted."

Hailey's jaw dropped and Iris hastened to explain.

"We had trouble conceiving in the early years of our marriage. We thought it might be the only way we would have children. We were going to tell you both when you were older, but then Kyra had so many problems, then your dad died, then you girls moved out, and I never found the right time—"

Hailey closed her eyes and waved her hands for her mother to stop. "What about me? Am I? Oh my—shit. Kyra's not my real sister." She slumped down onto the carpet.

No wonder Kyra was always so good at everything, she thought. She'd spent her life competing with and comparing herself to the daughter of an angel! It wasn't her fault that she could never measure up.

Iris dropped to the floor and threw her arms around her quivering daughter.

"We were blessed and were able to conceive you before we started the process to adopt another child." She smiled and combed Hailey's long hair from her face.

Everyone exchanged silent looks. Nick rose and came to his wife's side. James huffed and settled deeper into his chair as the number of people sitting at his feet grew.

"The prophecy is well-known among the angels and there are legends passed down through the generations in the witch communities. Her birth mother thought she would be better protected this way," Father Thomas said.

"Maybe her mother had no idea," Axel offered, his eyes shifting from Alexis to the priest.

Alexis nodded, leaning forward to rest her forearms on her legs, her fingers interlocked.

"Maybe she didn't know her daughter was a melhara. If she did, wouldn't it have made more sense for her to raise and protect her own daughter?" Axel asked, running his hand through his hair. "To teach her about her powers and to watch out for demons, not abandon her to an orphanage and hope for the best?"

"She knew. She sent an anonymous letter to the Vatican letting us know she'd given birth to the melhara and that she had hidden her daughter. The angel she was involved with would have made sure she knew about the prophecy after she became pregnant. Angels want the child protected from evil as much as we do." He sipped his water and glanced at the silent Majai in the corner of the room.

"Why didn't they protect Kyra from Alastor, then?" Iris asked, moving back onto the sofa.

"Angels have very little involvement in the prophecy, other than creating the child, of course. This battle is for humanity to fight."

"So what's the deal with angels and humans getting it on? How is that even possible?" Nick asked as he guided Hailey to the loveseat, next to Axel.

"There are lower level angels living among us as human beings. They come to Earth and walk among us, guiding people to their destinies... like muses." Father Thomas cleared his throat. "Occasionally, they have relationships, or simply fall in love with a human; children can be produced from these unions, but it's rare. That's where Nephilim and melharas come in. It has been an acceptable practice for them to have close relationships. It's part of the human process."

"Are you sure this demon is the one from the prophecy and not just a regular demon causing trouble?" Axel argued. "There's no way Kyra could have been destined to be evil."

James clenched his fists. Seeing that, Alexis rolled her eyes and sighed. James locked eyes with her and when she shook her head he slowly released his breath, relaxed, and melted back into his chair.

"The large scale of the demon's ambitions after Kyra joined him proves it. It's too big to be initiated by just any demon," Father Thomas answered. "In the prophecy, when the child is born, the demon can sense her existence but he can't locate her until she comes into her full powers when she's eighteen. There is something in the prophecy that has to do with them communicating before they meet, but it's unclear. Other protectors have documented that the child had seen the battles of Heaven and Hell in dreams."

"Other protectors? Protectors of what?" Nick asked, looking up from Hailey.

"Protectors of humanity, Earth, Heaven, the prophecy, God's plan—all of it. We are trying to keep the prophecy from being fulfilled. It is our duty. These types of demons are not here to cause havoc and mayhem while hiding in the shadows, or to collect souls by possession. They come to Earth only to fulfill the prophecy by damning all mankind."

"Well, I guess you missed the boat on that one. You did a great job keeping the demon from getting Kyra," Axel retorted, his voice edged with sarcasm.

"This is getting ridiculous. How can you people be buying into this nonsense?" James blurted, raking a scathing gaze over everyone before turning to Father Thomas. "And just who do you think you are, coming into my home during an already difficult time and spouting this garbage? What do you hope to gain?"

"I assure you, Mr. Parker, this is not nonsense. It's very real and very serious. As we work together to overcome this, I guarantee you will believe it without any doubts."

James glowered at the priest before guilt washed over his face and he yielded, lowering his eyes.

"How has this been dealt with before?" Alexis asked, ignoring James. "Can we kill the demon?" She sat back and pulled her legs up to sit cross-legged, while Iris watched her, nodding.

"This has never happened before—the demon getting his hands on the melhara, that is. Over the centuries the girls were usually found by the protectors and hidden. There used to be a larger group of protectors and a smaller population to sift through." He sighed. "We don't have the manpower like we used to. And people used to be more superstitious and afraid of anything *odd*. Nowadays, there's more skepticism of psychics, and better understanding of mental illnesses and other abnormalities that set people apart. It was simpler when everyone in the community talked about a witch with powers."

"I thought you said they can't use their powers until they're eighteen," James interrupted.

"They still have passive powers like intuition, visions, and other abilities, but it's more like an uncontrolled extrasensory skill that only affects the witch and not the outside world. They come into their active powers when they turn eighteen; then they can use them on other people and the elements of nature. But melharas seem to have access to different types of active power, before they come of age."

"Un-huh…" James mumbled.

Hailey could see by his annoyed expression that he wasn't buying into this. He hadn't seen Kyra the way she had.

Father Thomas continued. "And sometimes the melhara was killed before she could be found by the demon."

"Killed? No wonder Kyra's birth mom sent an anonymous letter," Alexis hissed.

"It wasn't often by the protector, but yes, sometimes they murdered the melhara out of fear that the demon would find her. Some girls were burned at the stake by villagers for being witches, and unfortunately, some took their own lives." He took another sip from his glass. "If the melhara dies then the demon has no purpose here and leaves Earth to wait for the next one to be born."

Axel stood. "Whoa, whoa, wait a minute. If the melhara dies? She can't. She tried to kill herself twice and he brought her back."

"She couldn't die when he was there to stop her. He can't resurrect the dead, but he can bring someone back if their soul is still on Earth."

"Oh…" Axel said, sounding unconvinced. He sat back down.

"If the demon has never got ahold of the girl before, how do you know it can be fixed?" Nick asked, raising his eyebrows.

"It's in the writing, which is the second positive thing about this situation. If the girl is found and does join the demon, the only way to save us all is to get her to switch sides and betray the demon. It says that only *unbreakable* love can set her free from the grasp of the demon."

Still reeling from her mother's confession, Hailey found her voice. "What the eff does that mean? That's not a solution to anything."

"Well, we aren't quite sure exactly what it means. The prophecy was passed down orally through the ages before it was written down, so we're not sure how much is embellishment or interpretation and how much is accurate. It's very vague and twisted around in riddles."

Hailey rolled her eyes and muttered, "Of course."

Father Thomas shifted uncomfortably from one foot to the other.

"Our best approach would be talking to her and hopefully convincing her to betray the demon. It's perhaps foolishly romantic, but the power of love can somehow change her loyalties." He teetered his pen back and forth between his fingers. "Unless…" His hand stopped moving abruptly "…there is some way to trick her into betraying the demon. But we're not sure that would work without negating her free will being involved. Free will is mentioned a few times in the prophecy."

"Okay, so we need to locate her and send someone to try talking to her. That sounds simple enough," Iris offered.

"Yes and no. Simple in theory, but she has the power to kill us all and we can't assume any of the old her is still there. There must be some part of the Kyra you know and love to enable her to come back from this, but we don't know what may still exist," the priest cautioned.

"So, it would be best if just one person went to confront her because she might kill the rest of us?" Iris said cautiously, then added, "I guess James would be her true love."

"We should be relatively safe. She made that deal with the demon to keep us from harm, remember?" Alexis reminded them.

"I don't know if I would put all my faith into that. He is a demon, after all. Who knows how a deal with the Devil really works," Nick said.

"We can't go chasing Kyra all over the globe; we have careers and other responsibilities," said James, his tone irritated.

"I'm sorry; I was under the impression you went back to work for three days and then quit or got fired," Hailey said, calling him out in front of everyone. She wasn't going to let him walk away from helping her sister.

"What?" he blurted, gaping at her. "How do you know that?"

"When you don't answer my calls, I call your office. They told me a few days ago that you are no longer an employee of the company." She assumed the never-ending questions from his colleagues were overwhelming him, especially since he had no answers for any of them. Kyra was on the news daily and her name was being included in the reports now. "Having a wife as a celebrity serial killer probably isn't too good for your image."

James scowled at her, tapping his fingertips on the arms of his chair, but said nothing.

Axel broke the awkward silence. "I'll go with James to help him get close to Kyra. It's too dangerous to send him after her alone."

"No. I don't need your help."

"I think it's a good idea," Iris agreed. "You shouldn't go alone."

"Fine, he can distract the demon while I talk to my wife," James growled, glaring at the carpet.

Chapter Eleven

Sunshine poured down between the buildings and flooded the streets of Manhattan. A little girl in pigtails licked her ice cream as her mother pulled her along the crowded sidewalk. Yellow taxis swarmed the congested streets and city buses roared away from the curb, on the way to the next stop.

A thin cloud of mist, a mere wisp, rose from the sidewalk near a sewer grate. It went unnoticed at first, but as it became denser, the men and women dressed in suits and corporate garb started to navigate around it instead of through it. Still it attracted no attention until it became so thick that it was no longer transparent, but a foggy green. Even then, only a few people actually looked at it as they passed. When it started to slowly swirl, looking like the top of a soft ice cream cone, the pedestrians finally stopped and watched it, curious. The green color darkened. The swirling slowed to a halt, and the column of mist started to fade. As it faded two figures took shape within—a man embracing a woman with her long hair swirled and dancing around them in the fog.

Now the crowd stood in awe. Was this some street performer trick? But then the figures became recognizable. Several witnesses in the crowd gasped and darted off across the street. Others remained still, unable to turn away or flee.

Kyra knew that she and Alastor had become well-known across North America. Their pictures had been on the evening news nightly, illustrating the horrors that they had wrought.

They stepped back from the embrace and stood shoulder to shoulder, scanning the gaping crowd, the outdoor patios beyond that lined the street. There were no empty tables—it was the lunch hour. And every patron was focused on her and Alastor.

She looked to Alastor and he nodded. Taking a step forward, she locked eyes with a woman just a few years younger than herself, wearing a light summer dress. The woman instinctively stepped back, her eyes darting around at the spectators as she clutched the chunky ring on her right hand.

This is the target? she thought, unimpressed. *This nervous girl?*

Smiling sweetly, she moved closer. The young woman tried to step away once again but she was unable to move. She opened her mouth to plead with Kyra, but no sound came out. Kyra brushed her knuckles across the woman's flushed cheek. Her smile instantly went cold and she dropped her hand, unsure of her ability to create an illusion that covered so many minds at once.

She turned to Alastor, who grinned encouragingly at her. Turning back, Kyra grabbed the woman, her fingers digging into the flesh of the woman's upper arms as she squeezed. Blood oozed under her nails. She suddenly released her and the woman dropped to the ground, which opened up beneath her, a perfect black circle that swallowed the woman before it sealed up and vanished.

Screams erupted and the crowd scattered, running in all directions. Hysterical people dashed into the street, and the sound of skidding tires erupted, followed by the *bang!* of impact and the groan of twisting metal, the crash of broken glass. More screaming.

Marveling at the chaos, Alastor smiled to Kyra and whispered, "Excellent work, darling." A glow of pride washed over her at his compliment.

Drivers abandoned vehicles in the street when they couldn't weave around the accidents. Footfalls—the thud of loafers and oxfords, the swift click-click of high heels on the sidewalks echoed off the high walls around them as people moved away as fast as they could.

Kyra tucked her hair behind her ear. "I liked the swirling green smoke entrance," she observed. "It unnerved people." The tinkle of falling cutlery and breaking glass rose behind them as diners overturned tables and chairs, jumped the railings, and ran.

Alastor placed his hand on her lower back. "It will be more effective as they come to know it as the sign of our arrival."

Those moving too slowly were knocked to the ground as the escape turned into a stampede. The little girl in pigtails, her ice cream long gone, had been separated from her mother; she clutched a lamp post, wailing in terror. Cars jammed into reverse as the mob came charging toward them, running down roads and sidewalks alike. More cars crashed at both ends of the street, but one taxi in the middle of the chaos slowly maneuvered around the mess, heading in their direction. The cab crept along the street until Alastor stepped into the driver's view.

The cab stopped for a moment as the driver studied Alastor. As recognition dawned, he stomped on the gas pedal, hoping to escape. It did not budge; the car was frozen in time. Kyra and Alastor approached the cab. Wide eyes glued to them, the cabbie jerked on the door handle once, twice—harder. It didn't move. Frantic now, he jabbed his finger on the buttons for the windows; they didn't move either. He was trapped. Seeing the terror in the man's eyes, Kyra grinned. Alastor opened the rear door and Kyra slid into the back seat. Then he slid in beside her.

"Where would you like to go, darling?"

The cabbie looked into his rearview mirror. If he was trying to hide his fear, he was failing. His breathing was so erratic, he had to be on the verge of a panic attack.

"Central Park, for sure. I've always wanted to see it." She looked at the cabbie in the mirror. "Is it far from here?"

He looked away. "N-n-no—no, ma'am."

"Okay, you can drive us there now." She flicked her wrist and the car lurched forward. Then she held out her hands to the blockade of car collisions in their way; the wreckage parted and skidded aside, clearing a path for the taxi. As the taxi made its way down the street, the cabby avoided looking in the rearview mirror. His clammy hands left moist imprints on the steering wheel, and she could hear his heart racing.

Kyra relaxed back into the seat, wondering why she had hidden from her powers for so many years. Her fears had held back her vast potential, as Alexis—no, as *Alastor* had told her. Now, she was untouchable; feared—and rightly so. Alastor was her savior, her destiny. Kyra took his hand and let her gaze drift toward her window, watching the New Yorkers the taxi passed as it moved toward the park. Everything was clear to her now. Together, they would save the world from itself.

Alastor squeezed her hand gently and she turned to him. "Moving target practice," he said, and nodded toward her window.

Kyra turned back to the window and focused on a couple of women walking down the sidewalk. She flicked her wrist at them. Nothing. As the car moved closer she flicked at them again. The women stumbled and regained their balance as the cab passed by them. Kyra turned around in her seat to view them through the rear window and forcefully flicked both of her wrists at the women. They lurched backward and fell to the ground. She turned forward again and smiled at Alastor.

He gave a half-shrug. "Sloppy." Pulling her hands into her lap, he held his hand over them and said, "Now just your eyes."

She turned back to her window. The cab was passing by the pedestrians too quickly for her to use her eyes alone. She sighed. *Focus, just focus.* She spied a man and a woman up ahead, strolling along with their backs to her. She narrowed her eyes. *I can do this,* she reassured herself. She locked her eyes on the couple and commanded, *Now fly,* and blinked aggressively. The woman fell face-first onto the sidewalk, while the force of her power lifted the man right off his feet and slammed him against the wall of a building; he bounced off the concrete and dropped to lie in a heap on the sidewalk.

Kyra squealed and bounced in her seat. She turned to Alastor, expecting to see his face full of pride but instead saw disappointment. She frowned. "What is it?"

"Half right is not acceptable, darling."

His stern expression annoyed her. She was making excellent progress and had learned so much in these last few weeks, like creating protection bubbles, power sharing, and freezing or selectively traveling a target without accompanying them; soon she would be able to teleport someone without touching them.

"Maybe I meant to only affect one of them," she lied.

"Then the woman should not have fallen." He brushed a loose strand of hair from her face.

She nodded, knowing he was right; she needed more practice or she would put them both in danger when they moved into phase two of his plan, whatever that was. He hadn't told her yet, but he had insisted that she practice initiating specific powers whenever they were between missions.

They pulled up to their destination. Kyra looked at the cabbie in the rearview mirror again. Sweat streamed down his forehead and his right eye twitched. He had a white-knuckled grip on the steering wheel, but despite that attempt to stop it, his hands still shook.

"Th-this is the place," he stammered, careful to keep his eyes forward.

Kyra stepped out of the car and walked around to the driver's door. He glanced at her before facing forward again. When she pulled open his door, he held his breath and squeezed his eyes closed. Kyra leaned in until her face was inches from the trembling puddle of a man and breathed deeply of his sweat and fear. He shivered when she kissed his cheek. She abruptly stepped back, chuckling, and slammed the door shut. Turning her back on cab and cabbie, she walked toward the entrance into the park.

Alastor joined her and she took his hand. They strolled into the park. Kyra smiled when she heard the cab driver peel away from the curb a few seconds later, leaving a whiff of exhaust.

Kyra scanned the place she had only seen in the movies. A dome of bright blue sky scattered with fluffy clouds arched over a lush green landscape. Birds sang in the towering trees. Several joggers passed on the pathways, ignoring them.

Alastor stopped walking and pulled on her hand to stop her. She turned and watched his face morph into the sagging, mottled wrinkles of an old man; his eyes grow watery and fogged by age; his back hunch and his stature shrink. He seemed to shrivel before her eyes.

"Whoa," she said when he was done. "Can I do that?"

"Not without a spell, but you can create an illusion to hide yourself."

She pondered a moment, then took the form of Angelina Jolie.

He frowned. "Try someone a little less conspicuous."

She laughed and her façade shifted into Alexis. He nodded his approval and they continued walking along the path.

A man jogged past, and Kyra saw a pale blue glow surrounding him. A man farther away was walking his dog, which appeared to be surrounded by a white glow that grew brighter as they drew nearer. A few steps before they met on the pathway, Kyra could see that the owner also had a colored aura surrounding him. The dog growled at Alastor and the man tugged on the leash to quiet his pet. The animal moved as far away from Alastor as the leash would allow, and they passed Kyra and Alastor. Kyra turned to watch them as they continued along the path. The color faded away quickly; she wasn't sure if it had even really been there.

"Why did your eyes follow him, Kyra? What do you see?" Alastor asked.

"I-I'm not sure. I think I see colors outlining people, like someone drew them too thick around the edges, then smudged it."

"Excellent. You are finally seeing auras."

She cocked her head at him, confused. "How does it work?"

"Damned souls have gray or graying colors. Mine is black because I am a demon. No human can have a black aura, but it may be so dark a gray that it appears black."

"Oh, I have the power to discern that already; I can sense it when I am close to people. I've never seen colors before."

Alastor nodded. "That was the witch's power. Now you have both. Seeing auras will work on magical beings too, unlike your passive witch powers." He brushed her cheek with his wrinkled hand. His touch made her heart jump, which surprised her; how could she feel excitement, find Alastor as a withered old man appealing? She felt her face flush.

"You will be able to do a lot more than you could ever have imagined, very soon," he finished.

She pondered what she'd seen. "What does blue mean?"

"Blue is the next level after pure white." Alastor sighed gently. "You have a lot of catching up to do, darling. You've been wasting your existence, holding back and hiding. Now it's time to unleash your power and see what you are capable of."

In an instant, they vanished from sight. No smoke, no fading away. Just gone.

Chapter Twelve

The president sat behind his desk in the Oval Office, perusing the papers and file folders lying on the desktop.

"Where's the FBI at with these terrorists?" he asked as he selected a paper and scribbled his signature on the bottom. He looked around at the men and women standing a discreet distance from him, then cocked his head at John Josephs in particular.

Josephs cleared his throat and took a step toward the desk.

"They're still following leads on their whereabouts. The terrorists seem to vanish quickly after infiltrating a prison."

President Beatty grumbled mentally at the lack of progress but revealed nothing in his expression.

"They have determined the pattern of targets, but they seem to be finished with that operation," Josephs continued.

Beatty folded his hands over each other. "They have to be found and stopped, immediately," Beatty said in a level voice, which everyone present knew emphasized the importance of his words. "This country is in an uproar; there are hundreds of thousands of escaped convicts on the loose. We need to stop this now." He swept his eyes over the Secret Service agents standing around the perimeter of the room, their hands clasped together behind them.

"Yes, sir." Josephs nodded crisply, turned, and left the room.

His aide slid another stack of papers across the desk. He skimmed the topmost page:

Effective immediately, all prisons across the United States of America are to be closed down and all inmates pardoned and unconditionally released without need of parole.

"What the hell is this?" Beatty looked up and gaped as the grinning face of the man—one of his trusted advisors—seemed to melt away before his eyes. It left behind the face of the man that had been splashed across the news for weeks now. Beatty jumped up, knocking his chair over behind him. Those gathered in the Oval Office also leapt back—then dropped to the floor as gunshots rang out, echoing loudly throughout the room. The president crouched where his chair had been and covered his ears, watching in shock as the bullets dissolved in midair before they reached the terrorist's flesh.

The burst of gunfire was short lived; Beatty lowered his hands and cautiously peeked over his desktop. The Secret Service agents stood like statues, arms still outstretched, guns trained on the intruder. But they didn't blink; they didn't twitch; they were frozen in place. The advisors and other staff members lowered their hands from their ears, eyes on the president and the man confronting him in the middle of the room. The sprinkler system came on and the alarm started blaring as water rained from the ceiling. As if at an unvoiced signal, the staff members all hurried from the room. The terrorist made no move to stop them.

Beatty's eyes darted around the room, over the frozen faces of his security agents.

"How did you get into the Whitehouse?"

The man leaned over the desk toward him.

"That is the wrong question. The question you should be asking is, why am I here?"

He didn't raise his voice, yet Beatty had no trouble hearing it over the screaming alarm and the hiss of spraying water; it was as if the man was whispering inside his head while he watched the man's lips move. *How can that be?* Beatty wondered; he couldn't read lips, other than basic words that everyone could make out.

Mustering his courage, Beatty rose and braced his palms on his desk so he could lean toward the intruder, mirroring his posture.

"Okay then," he said in his level voice, "why are you here?" His voice, too, came clearly over the raging alarm, which was starting to give Beatty a headache.

"For you to do this." The man tapped a long forefinger on the paper he'd put in front of Beatty, keeping his eyes on the president.

Beatty locked eyes with the man and leaned in. "That's an impossible request," he stated firmly.

"Not a request," the man said, his tone ice. He straightened up.

Beatty also straightened, rolling his shoulders back. "Either way, it's not something that could be done, even if I wanted to," he said, deliberately casual.

The man slammed his fist on the desk. Beatty flinched. "You will do it and it will be done this week," the man shouted, then unexpectedly smiled, throwing Beatty off-balance.

He cursed silently for showing weakness to this man bent on terrorizing the country. *No, it wasn't a weakness,* he corrected himself, *it was an involuntary reaction, like blinking when you get dirt in your eye.* Either way, he would not let it happen again. He leaned toward the man and spoke slowly, to emphasize the reality of his response.

"Those men need rehabilitation and a transitioning program to integrate back into society, or they'll revert to old habits and end up back in prison. It would be a pointless cycle."

"The prisons will remain closed," the terrorist barked. "The men and women will go about their lives in society as they choose."

The president raised his eyebrows at him, shocked by his words. *What is he talking about? Is he completely insane?* There had to be a way to talk some sense into him.

"The economy couldn't withstand such an outpouring of unemployed citizens," he countered.

"That is not your concern. They shall be released, either by you or by me, after the government and its officials are eliminated." The man's hands balled up into fists. "That is the only choice you have to make."

This guy sure has a short fuse, Beatty thought as he glared back. And he didn't like the sound of "eliminated." He softened his voice in hopes of calming the mentally unstable man in front of him.

"Why are you making such a demand?" He motioned for the man to have a seat—a gesture that was ignored—and righted his own wet chair and sat down. "What do you hope to gain from this? What do you really want?" He knew he just had to stall him; soon Security would be bursting through the doors.

"For you to do your part so I can move on," the man answered tersely. He moved around to the side of the desk, leaned over the president, and whispered, "As you are already aware, I have been to all the maximum security facilities in the U.S. and you need only concern yourself with those criminals not yet released. You have until the end of the week to comply, or suffer my wrath."

"I won't be threatened by you," Beatty snapped, annoyed by this man who kept invading his personal space and trying to intimidate him as if they were a couple of high school kids. He met the man's gaze and said, "The United States does not negotiate with terrorists."

"Not a terrorist. Try again," the man sneered, and Beatty thought he'd glimpsed fangs. He couldn't be sure, though, with the water pouring over his face and the incessant ringing from that alarm.

Where is that Secret Service detail? he wondered. And why were the men already in the room stuck in their positions? Beatty experienced self-doubt. What had he actually seen and what were tricks of his imagination? Was it possible for this guy to not be human?

"What, then?" he asked aloud. "Who are you?"

Again offering his sneering smile—*That IS a fang!*—the man took a short step back and sketched a brief, arrogant bow, eyes never leaving Beatty.

"I am he whom you *will* obey," the man said, straightening. "I am the demon Alastor. You cannot stand against me."

Beatty drew himself up. "If you are a demon, as you claim, then God would want us to take a stand against you." He brought his hand up to his forehead to shield his eyes from the sprinkler, somewhat ruining the effect.

A deep laugh rumbled up from the core of Alastor's body.

"God? God does not care about this pathetic place. He abandoned the human race a long time ago."

"The answer is still no." Beatty crossed his arms over his chest.

Alastor's eyes went black and he swiped his hand over the desk, sending the papers plopping to the floor with soggy thuds.

One of the Secret Service men nearest the president dropped to his knees. Blood began trickling from his ears, etching jagged red lines down his jaw and neck to soak into the sodden collar of his shirt. Another man convulsed and violently coughed up blood. Blood gushed from the nose of another. He looked to his leader with fear in his eyes before they turned red and blood began leaking like tears from of them. He crumpled;

the president jumped from his chair and grabbed hold of him as he fell to floor. Beatty stared in horror at the face of a dead man.

One by one, the inert men slumped to the floor as blood flowed out of their bodies. There was not so much as a whimper of pain. When the final man fell over dead, the president stood alone with Alastor in the flooding room. He blinked rapidly and wiped eyes not totally obscured by the torrent from the sprinklers. When he opened them again, a woman stepped out of the blurred surroundings. Beatty gaped at her in recognition: Kyra Parker. Had she been there the whole time?

Beatty's eyes moved back to Alastor when he spoke.

"This is not a negotiation. Release them all." He knelt to bring his face to the president's eye level. Beatty looked away from the dead eyes staring up at him and met Alastor's gaze. "You have one week, or more deaths will be on your conscience."

Parker glided up behind Alastor and put her hand on his shoulder. He stood and stepped back from the president. He grinned and narrowed his black eyes at Beatty as he wrapped his arm around the woman.

"You have a wife and children… then there are always your siblings, their children, your parents, your friends, and everyone you have ever spoken to."

The president clenched his fist under the body lying across his lap.

"Do not test my patience," Alastor hissed.

Alastor and Kyra Parker disappeared in a swirl of green smoke, leaving behind one man and half a dozen corpses.

**

They'd barely materialized in the foyer of Alastor's mansion before he'd dropped his wet jacket on the white marble floor and was yanking at his tie. He threw that down as well. His white shirt, now speckled red, was tossed onto the pile as well.

Kyra slowly unbuttoned her jacket, watching him undress. *This is it,* she thought; *he is my destiny*. He caught her staring and grinned. Holding his gaze, she walked up to him, her high heels clicking on the marble. She stopped with her body inches from his, and moved her shoulders back; her jacket slid down her arms and onto the pile. She knew she belonged to him... and she liked it.

His grin widened. She raised an eyebrow and returned a sly grin before she grabbed his face and locked her mouth over his in a kiss. His fingertips zigzagged down her back to cup her buttocks and lift her up. She wrapped her legs around his waist and her arms around his neck as he carried her to the closed door a few feet away. With a wave of his hand it swung open.

The office beyond was dark but there was still enough light seeping in around the window curtains that she could make out the outline of the desk, and walls lined with books. He brought her to the desk and set her down while he fumbled for the desk lamp behind her, knocking over a cup and spilling pens across the floor. The light clicked on, then the lamp too was knocked over as Alastor swept the desktop clear of paper piles and rolled up maps and everything else. Satisfied, he returned to her, gripped the back of her neck, and kissed her roughly.

She wanted him desperately—she *had* to have him, and she was going to have him now. She gasped when he gripped a handful of her hair and yanked her head back to kiss her neck. Pearl buttons sprayed over the floor as he ripped open her white shirt with his other hand, then slipped it inside her shirt to squeeze and knead her breast.

Staring blindly at the ceiling, she ran her hands over his perfect chest, down his firm abs, to tug at his belt. Pushing the buckle aside, she struggled to unzip his pants before he grabbed her wrist and flung her hand away. Her hands grabbed at his shoulders, trying to pull his body closer. He bit her and she moaned in shocked ecstasy, her nails digging into his flesh. She'd never expected that to be so erotic. He pulled back, grabbed her by the throat, and slammed her down on the desk, knocking the wind out of her. Her back stung as she lay regaining her breath.

He pulled her toward him until her butt slipped off the desk, then wriggled her black skirt up above her hips and shoved her back onto the desk.

Arching her back, she put herself up on her elbows and braced her body with her forearms, her long wavy hair cascading down to pool over the desktop. She brought her chin down, resting it on her chest as she locked eyes with her demon.

His finger toyed with her panties before moving them to the side. He pulled himself out of his pants and slid inside her. Her breath hitched. His hands gripped her waist and his thumbs dug into her pelvis when he pulled her body onto his. She dropped her head back in ecstasy, savoring every thrust.

Afterward, as they lay together on the floor of the office, still breathing hard, Kyra ran her hand over Alastor's biceps, the skin glistening with sweat in the dim light. She smiled. All the years of not being accepted and understood, then years of hiding and pretending she was a normal human, were over. He showed her that she was meant to live out in the open and that she was above the humans, and there was no reason she should strive to be like them; they were weak. She couldn't believe she ever wanted to be one of them.

He rolled his head toward her and looked at her smile, but his expression was hard.

"What was going on with my dreams?" she asked, and Alastor's lips curled into a grin. "Why have I been seeing these things? What is going on with the constant battles and fighting between demons and angels—what is it all about?"

"God started the war when he cast Lucifer out of Heaven for questioning his methods." Alastor paused and took a deep breath, his eyes full of hate. They flickered black before he looked up at the ceiling. "Others shared his doubts and joined with Lucifer. There was war; it raged on for a short while." He paused and rolled his head toward Kyra again. "A short while in the existence of time, that is, before Hell was created for Lucifer to remain separated from God's precious humans and loyal angels."

She ran her fingers through his hair and the blackness seeping into his eyes faded away to golden-brown. "So Lucifer was the first demon?"

"No, demons are different. He is a fallen angel and has since become the king of Hell. God thought separating the leader from the other fallen angels would resolve the conflict. It was less than successful, and they were eventually thrown into the pit by those still loyal to God, but that came thousands of years later, long after Lilith had become Lucifer's queen."

She puckered her eyebrows. "Who's Lilith, an angel?"

Alastor let out a deep, genuine laugh, one Kyra had never heard before. It was the sound of surprised amusement rather than his calculated, menacing laugh when his plans were falling into place. It faded to a chuckle and he regained his composure.

"Lilith became the first demon. She was also the first soul to enter Hell, the first witch in existence and Adam's first wife. Because she was an all-powerful witch, she believed herself superior to the mere mortal, Adam, and abandoned him. She was replaced by the human Eve. It was Lilith who took the form of a serpent and tricked Eve into taking the forbidden fruit. Lucifer was still loyal to God at that time."

"Huh." Kyra digested that for a few minutes. "I think I saw that in my dreams before," she said, then immediately second-guessed herself—as she often did—and wondered if her dream had been a vision of the past or induced by Sunday school stories. She felt foolish for not knowing who Lilith was, and that Alastor had laughed at her ignorance. She lowered her eyes and rolled onto her back, feeling shame from disappointing Alastor.

"After the garden of Eden incident, humans and witches were sent to the earthly plane, where the dinosaurs once roamed. It was now home to huge beasts and the primitive first draft of the human species. This world was one without any magical creatures, until witches were put here."

The timeline on that doesn't make sense, she thought. Afraid of losing more of Alastor's respect, she chose her words carefully.

"If the Devil was still loyal when Lilith was a snake, how did he end up in Hell first?" She didn't turn her head, but looked askance at Alastor.

He smiled. "She was a powerful witch—more powerful even than you, darling. She had cast spells that kept her protected, young, and beautiful. She was immune to any earthly demise and lived for thousands of years. In the meantime, Hell was created and the revolution had begun. She thought she was invincible until a high-ranking angel cut her down. They sent her to be locked up with Lucifer to keep her from ever being reincarnated. She was his only companion for a long time. They experimented on her with both of their powers until she became the first demon."

Kyra nodded. *Witches had joined with the Devil; we were meant to fight against the corrupt creator.* "So what does this have to do with me—why *me*?" she asked, rolling toward him and resting her arm over his chest.

"After a while, to restore balance and give us the opportunity to re-enter Heaven, God created the prophecy."

That must be why I feel so protective of Alastor, she thought. *Witches and demons were meant to fight together against humans and angels. But why me, and not any witch?*

"So what am I, some kind of super-witch?"

"That question requires a complicated explanation." He eyed her and she knew he wasn't going to explain it further. This wasn't the first time he had dodged her questions, she thought bitterly; why was he holding things back from her?

He placed his hand over hers and gave it a squeeze.

But he was honest with her, she rescinded, and he was teaching her more than anyone else could have. In time, when she was ready, she would know more. He was just looking out for her best interests. She trusted him more than anyone, ever.

"You just need to know that you are very unique and have a great deal more power to develop."

She felt as though she had been sleepwalking through the world and he had finally awakened her soul and brought clarity and purpose to her life.

"If we can turn the table from good to evil, then the occupants of Heaven and Hell will trade places. Human beings have free will to choose, however, and both sides can encourage the commitment by any means they choose." He paused, watching her face, and she knew he was looking for her understanding so she smiled and nodded.

"You know as well as I, death in this life doesn't matter; there is another waiting. What truly matters is where that life will be." He took Kyra's hands in his own and pulled her on top of him. "We shall change that and give hundreds of millions of lost souls their freedom."

Confusion washed over her. She thought he wanted to overthrow Heaven, not save the humans. They were insignificant creatures, weren't they? But a vague memory crept in: Alexis saying, "We are no better or worse, just different."

He reached out and stroked her cheek and her confusion cleared. Alexis was wrong, or she had lied—humans were tools, a means to an end. With those souls free from Hell, the damned would outweigh the others and Alastor would win, finally putting the world—no, the *universe* in proper order.

"I've already made my choice, haven't I," she assured him. "It's a funny thing: I've dreamt about you for as long as I can remember, but always in your demon form, until about half a year ago. I've been daydreaming about you—the human you, I mean—for months." She nuzzled his shoulder. "It was so confusing, fantasizing about a man I'd never even seen before. I thought I was just bored with my life and searching for something else, but it all makes sense now. My dreams have stopped. The last one I had was the night before I left Calgary—it must be because I finally found my destiny and I'm at peace."

He nodded reassuringly.

"I used to be afraid of you but I'm not anymore, even when you are not in this very sexy human form," she purred, running her hand over his chest. "I feel like we belong together, like I need to protect you. We're connected somehow. I think I'm in love with you."

"And I love you, my darling."

Chapter Thirteen

"A secret prophecy—of course, why am I not surprised," said President Beatty, looking at the three men in hooded cloaks seated across the table. "So what you're telling me is, you think there is something to his claims?"

"Yes we are, Mr. President," said the Vatican spokesman sitting in the center; the other two nodded. "Demons exist in two forms, the most well-known being those capable of possession, although that occurs less frequently than popular myth would have people believe. Those demons are trapped in Hell and possess their victims from there. They can be sent back to Hell through exorcism, but not killed."

The image of Alastor's black eyes flashed through Beatty's mind, followed by fragmented memories of the deaths of the Secret Servicemen. He leaned forward and clasped his hands together on the table as he forced the memories from his mind.

"You believe this man is possessed, then?"

The spokesman shook his head slightly, his eyes darting around the small room.

"The other types are demons living and breathing here, in the flesh. They create obsession leading to a downward spiral by putting thoughts in the heads of their victims to create chaos. But they live and die like ordinary human beings, and can't do the things that have been reported on the news. They don't have control over your actions; they only breed the ideas in hopes of corrupting their victim and driving him or her mad."

Like the voice in my head that I heard clearly through the fire alarm, Beatty thought. "If this is what you think Alastor is, then why haven't we seen this kind of trouble before?" he asked.

"Those types of demons are very discreet and would never outright claim to be a demon, much less try an attack of this magnitude. Alastor seems to have characteristics of both, which we believe suggests he is the one foretold in the prophecy." The spokesman delivered that last revelation in a whisper, as if he were afraid of someone eavesdropping.

Come to think of it, Beatty realized, *this whole situation has grown more and more paranoid as it's progressed.*

First, the Vatican agreed to meet, but its representatives refused to welcome him to Rome, instead insisting on meeting in the seclusion of an abandoned farmhouse basement hours away from Washington. At first he thought they just didn't want to scare the public and cause more trouble. But then he had to organize discreet transport outside of the official marked cars and hide his identity from onlookers, which seemed over cautious if they didn't believe the claims of Alastor. And now they showed up in regular street clothes—except for the cloaks—and kept scanning the room that they had chosen.

"We are not sure what to expect from the interpretation of the prophecy, but it has to do with war."

The prisons—he's trying to start a war with the prisoners? Why wouldn't he have just released them all, if he had the ability to? Maybe he wants us to refuse his demands and start a war that way? Would convicts make good recruits against the military? It didn't make sense to him, but his team of advisors could work it out.

His top advisor, Petra Humphreys, had accompanied the president. Beatty admired Humphreys for her ability to look at all the angles before making recommendations—sometimes to the fault of indecisiveness. Now he leaned over and whispered to her, "Do you think this is possible?"

"War?" Humphreys whispered back. "Possible. Are we dealing with a demon?" She shrugged. "We have checked security footage; checked commercial flights as well as private planes; we've checked fingerprint and DNA records, and repeatedly questioned everyone in Mrs. Parker's life. That only brought more questions. We still have nothing on Alastor, alias or otherwise. The impossible time frames of their sightings and eyewitness accounts lead us to believe they must both have twins with identical fingerprints—or clones," she joked, and the president gave her a warning look. Humphreys got serious. "This is a possibility we haven't explored fully, although there is a great deal in her psychiatric records about demons. No specific mention of his name, though."

"It needs to be explored fully now," he whispered. "They believe it." He gestured toward the men at the end of the table. "And I need to know if this is what we are up against before the public appearance at the fair this weekend, so we can figure out the best way to inform the country."

"You're still attending?" Humphreys almost squealed, her voice high with stress. "It was recommended the event be cancelled, after the attack at the White House. It's too dangerous—and only a day before the deadline Alastor gave you."

"I have to make a public appearance to show the public that we are not afraid of these two. Besides, it doesn't much matter where we have the conference, as the demon—if that's what he is—has shown us he can get to me, wherever I am."

"But sir…"

He cut Humphreys off with a wave of his hand and turned back to the representatives from the Vatican, his expression serious. "Is there some evidence to back up this theory or prove it within a reasonable doubt?"

***

In a quiet suburban household in southeast Calgary, the workday morning routine had begun. Clad only in a white towel, a freshly showered middle-aged man hovered over the sink in the master bedroom en suite, brushing his teeth. The bathroom light illuminated the patches of shiny scalp beneath his thinning hair, and fell in a long bar across the bedroom carpet to the bed. A stout woman lying there grimaced as the bright light bathed her face, then groaned and tossed the blankets aside. Eyes closed, she fumbled unsuccessfully for her glasses on the nightstand, then abandoned the search and rose. She crossed to the long drapes and whipped them open, flooding the room with warm early morning sunshine. She stood blinking a few times, and smiled.

Kyra grinned as the older woman smiled out to the world, unaware of her presence in the room and the events that were about to take place. Outwardly, Kyra remained calm—but on the inside, she vibrated with excitement. This was her first unchaperoned venture; she could to do as she pleased and not as she was told.

The woman went into the large walk-in closet next to the washroom, where the man had started shaving. As she pulled off her nightgown and dropped it into the laundry basket in the corner by the shelves of shoes, Kyra stepped out of her dark corner. Still unaware of anything else besides what she was going to put on that day, the woman pulled a few items from their hangers. Kyra edged closer as she struggled to pull on dress pants and button them up, then grunted as she did up the clasps on her bra. She stepped out of her closet, shirt in hand.

Kyra stepped directly in front of her. Her face emotionless, she stared into the woman's pudgy face.

***

Startled by the intruder, Colleen jumped and took a step back, squinting as she tried to focus without her glasses. Her fear quickly turned to anger when she recognized the person in her bedroom.

"Kiera! How did you get in, and just what do you think you are doing here?" She quickly held her shirt across her chest, trying to cover herself. "And in my bedroom, no less! You get out of my house right now, before I call the police." Colleen's anger grew when her words stirred no reaction from Kyra. "And you're fired, by the way. I've seen you on the news and you don't scare me," she added confidently.

Colleen's blurred vision suddenly came sharply into focus. She felt the bridge of her nose and found her glasses. But how? She hadn't put them on!

Kyra wore a devilish grin. Her eyes bored into those of her former boss. Colleen watched her green eyes fade away to solid white. Her pupils were gone! Colleen shuddered and stepped back. She could not take her eyes off the intruder. Involuntary chills coursed through her body.

Harold stepped out of the bathroom to investigate. He stopped and looked Kyra up and down. "What the—" He glanced at his wife. "What is this crazy woman doing in our bedroom—wait, is she the girl that's been all over the news?"

"Yes, and she was just leaving." Colleen's face hardened. "Weren't you, Kiera?"

Kyra smiled and moved her finger to her lips, gesturing for her to be quiet. Her other hand swept through the air to point at Harold and motion him over to sit on the bed. His eyes had glazed over and he obeyed quickly and quietly.

Colleen opened her mouth to call to her husband, but no sound escaped her lips. She struggled silently to take a step, to reach out, but her limbs moved as if she were dragging them through wet cement. She could only watch helplessly as Kyra moved toward her husband. She shouted silently as Kyra climbed into Harold's lap.

***

Harold heard a faint melody luring him over to the bed. The room faded away, along with everything in it. He no longer saw his wife or any furnishings in the room, just endless empty space. The music in his head grew louder as a goddess stepped into view. At this moment, the only things that existed were this beauty and himself.

***

Kyra caressed his face as he wrapped his arms around her waist. He pulled her body against his own, tilting his head as he kissed her soft lips. They toppled over onto the bed. Her soft curls brushed his face as she straddled him and he held her body pressed against his.

"I want you," he whispered desperately.

She turned to face her boss as she spoke. "What about your wife?" She grinned, her eyes locked on Colleen.

"Who, Colleen?" He rolled his eyes. "I would leave her in a heartbeat for you. I haven't loved her for years."

Kyra held her fingertips in front of her mouth and made a dramatic 'O' with her lips, watching Colleen. She pulled out of his grasp and sat up.

"Would you die for me?" she asked him.

"Of course. I would do anything for you."

She turned back to him. "Good. I want you to kill your wife." She swung her feet to the floor and slid off his lap.

"Yes." He reached for Kyra but she slapped his hand away and stepped back from the bed.

"You can't touch me until you get rid of Colleen. Understood?"

"Understood."

Kyra looked back to the shocked face of the woman she hated and smiled coyly. "Have fun." Then she vanished.

***

Back in the secluded hideaway, Kyra strode down one of the cold concrete hallways of the basement dungeons, the click-click of her high heels echoing ahead of her. She stopped in front of one of the small holding cells. The smell of mildew, unwashed skin, urine, and blood hung in the stale air. The soft buzz of the fluorescent lights and the muffled sobs coming from the dark cell were the only sounds in the basement when her feet stopped moving. She peered into the eight-by-ten cell, where the only light was that cast by the glow in the hallway.

A mattress lay on the floor, a couple of ratty quilts and blankets spread over it. In the other corner stood a porcelain toilet, once white but now mottled by years of filth. The sobbing came from a young woman sitting on the mattress, her legs crossed and her face buried in her hands. Her summer dress was torn and grungy, her hair stringy and dirty.

She looked up and wiped away her tears when Kyra's footsteps stopped at her door. She barely resembled the woman she'd been on the streets of New York, the day she came face to face with Kyra for the first time.

"What do you want from me? Why did you put me here?"

Kyra smiled then turned away and wordlessly headed back toward the stairs.

She emerged from the basement into the great marble foyer. The mouth-watering smell of roasting meat filled the air. Alastor's office door was half closed, voices murmuring softly on the other side. His tone was light and carefree, unlike his usual bold, harsh voice, and a woman giggled. Kyra's guard went up. *There are no women here.*

She pushed the door open and walked into his office. A beautiful woman in her mid-twenties, with long, straight, bright white hair, had one hip hitched up on the desk, one spike-heeled black boot on the floor, her other leg draped casually off the desk. Alastor leaned in to her, inches from her face, with his hand gripping her thigh.

They both looked over when the heavy door swung open. Alastor stepped back from the vixen and released her leg. She smiled politely at Kyra without flinching.

"And what are you up to now?" Kyra asked with a little more snarkiness to her tone than she had intended.

"Kyra, darling, this is Celista. She is one of the most loyal and reliable soldiers in the underworld. I was finally able to release her from Hell this morning."

Kyra eyed her suspiciously. "Welcome," she said dryly.

Celista nodded with a smile. Her coppery complexion enhanced the silvery sheen of her white hair and her electric blue eyes. This woman had sultry enchantress written all over her, Kyra thought bitterly.

"What type of demon are you?" she asked.

"I'm a siren. Just one rank below our beloved Alastor," she said, leaning over to rub Alastor's arm.

"I see. So you lure *stupid* men to do your bidding?"

"Not just men, honey," Celista snarled, rising from the desk.

"I did that earlier today." Kyra put her hands on her hips. "I don't see how that makes you some great asset to us. Do you have any useful powers?"

"Enough," Alastor barked. "We have to prepare for this evening."

Chapter Fourteen

The smell of sizzling hot dogs and hamburgers filled the air as Alastor and Kyra approached the crowd. Young children laughed and ran to the next ride as their parents chased after them between rows of booths containing a variety of carnival games and food. Teenage boys played the shooting games while the girls watched, whispering and giggling. Parents gathered in circles, chatting with each other while youngsters pulled on their parents' hands, impatient to move on to the next activity. There was a time when she would have enjoyed mingling in a group like this, blending in as an ordinary family with her husband and son, making new ordinary friends and enjoying the atmosphere. Now, the thought of her old life made her sick. Things were different; her eyes were open and she couldn't believe she ever wanted to be part of that distorted illusion.

Kyra reached out, took Alastor's hand, and wriggled her fingers between his.

"Wow, they sure seem to be putting on a big show," she said as they walked unnoticed through the crowd.

"They are feeding the delusion that nothing has changed." He pulled his thumb out from underneath hers, repositioning it over her thumb, and pressed down, squeezing her hand. "Soon enough they won't be able to pretend any longer."

Kyra's eyes drifted over the crowd. Police and security personnel roamed the crowd. There seemed to be an overabundance of security present, she thought as they moved past another pair of officers.

They made their way to the outdoor stage, decorated in red, white, and blue bunting, with an American flag draped over the front of the podium and several microphones sprouting from its top. It stood on a raised dais before a backdrop decorated with more American flags. Two large red and white pillars held up a huge white canopy that shielded the stage from the hot sun. The pillars looked like giant candy canes. A green metal fence ran along the front of the stage, preventing spectators from getting too close. A large security detail filled the gap between the stage and the green barricade, each guard standing only three or four feet from the next, all of them focused on the crowd. More security officers lined the three exposed sides of the stage itself, standing inches apart, their backs to the podium, hands resting on their holstered guns.

The crowd had started to gather around the stage, though the man of the hour was not yet on the grounds. The MC was killing time, droning on and on: "The president has been in meetings with his council and outside experts all week to determine the best course of action to deal with these terrorists. For the safety of all American citizens, the public is advised to avoid contact with them." The man had one eye on an aide at the back of the stage who was waiting for the limo to pull up as he tried to sound upbeat in assuring the crowd that any new violence would be suppressed.

Kyra glanced at her watch. "We have ten minutes to kill." She frowned, crossing her arms over her chest.

"Not yet," he said, watching the stage.

"Huh? What—that's not what I meant, but we could, if you like." She looked at Alastor, then stepped in front of him, grabbing his hands and tugging on his arms until he looked at her. "There are a few dark souls in the crowd you could bleed out, and I could take care of the security before the president even comes on stage." She tapped her chin as her eyes wandered to the sky. "Or we could just burn it all down and kill everyone." She squeaked with pleasure, bouncing on the balls of her feet at the thought of it.

"Ah, Kyra, you truly are my dark queen." Alastor smiled at her. "So many beautiful ideas from my beautiful melhara. Have patience, darling." He pointed to the limo pulling up beside the stage.

The doors on both sides of the limo opened, and Secret Service agents stepped out and looked around before signaling the president to leave the car. Kyra's eyes lit up as she watched the president step up the stairs to the stage.

"Do you think they'll give in to the demands to stop all the slaughter?"

"Nuh-uh. No way; it wouldn't never happen," said the crusty old woman next to her. "They wouldn't negotiate with the likes of them." Her eyes fixed on the stage as the president walked up to the podium.

Kyra turned to the old woman. "Really, eh? You don't think it would be in the best interest of the nation to stop them from murdering more people?"

"Absolutely not. They'll catch this Bonnie and Clyde couple and lock them up." She flashed a smile of reassurance at Kyra.

Kyra stiffened. "And if they can't? Just let the world burn? Kyra and Alastor have a little more going on than Bonnie and Clyde did."

Alastor nudged Kyra when the president started to speak.

"I know these last few weeks have been difficult and unsettling for many of us. We are dealing with something we have never seen before. At first we thought it was some kind of new technologically-advanced body armor or weapon, but the surveillance tapes have been thoroughly investigated and that possibility has been eliminated." President Beatty scanned the crowd before continuing. "Then we investigated alternate possibilities. After much deliberation, we have a new, admittedly wild, theory." He cleared his throat. "Some of our advisors believe, as I do, that there is a high probability that the man calling himself Alastor is not from this Earth."

He set down his speech cards and gripped the sides of the podium. "This may be hard for some to wrap their minds around, but most of us do believe that he is a demon. A real demon, in the flesh, that rose up from Hell—the biblical kind of Hell. All that we know for sure is that Alastor and his accomplice Kyra Parker are extremely dangerous, and all contact with them should be avoided. We have dedicated a hotline number solely for tips about them, so if you see them, call the number."

Alastor smiled at Kyra. She leaned in and whispered, "I guess they've been busy trying to figure out how to stop us, rather than working on releasing the rest of the prisoners."

He jerked his head toward the stage, motioning for her to listen, and wrapped his arm around her waist to pull her against his side. She felt a rush of excitement course through her body and her worries washed away.

President Beatty lowered his voice and spoke more slowly. "We have decided that we have to fight these terrorists, demon or no demon. They will be caught and locked up in one of the prisons they want us to close down so badly. We will use any means necessary to stop them."

"I have heard enough," Alastor hissed. "We shall educate them on their limitations."

"Do you want them silenced, as well?" Kyra asked, unsure.

"Screaming is beneficial for morale."

The wave of audible terror rushed through the crowd before the first drop of blood spilled. They quickly realized they were in trouble when their limbs no longer moved. Bodies in the crowd went limp and fell to the earth, their internal organs liquefying and spewing from their orifices. Those nearest the wailing victims looked on in helpless horror, unable to reach out and comfort them in their final moments of life.

One of the security men's feet burst into flames. The others rushed to put out the flames and were halted in mid-stride. Then cries erupted from the crowd as blood sputtered out of select spectators.

"Looks like we're all going to die today. No one can escape them now," said one of the men in the president's personal detail.

"Don't say that shit," the man next to him scolded. "We're going to win this one and kill them both."

Kyra put out the fire with a wave of her hand. The flames had done some damage to the man's pants but not the man himself, save to his pride. She leapt effortlessly into the air and floated over the crowd, the barricade, and security, the sapphire-blue evening gown she wore flowing out from her hips like a parachute as she descended to land delicately on the stage.

Her eyes burned into the two men who had spoken as she moved toward them, her dress trailing behind her, dusting over the stage. She stopped two feet from them, the jeweled sequins on her dress catching the sunlight and casting bright speckles over their faces. She smiled an overly bright, friendly smile. The men smiled back nervously, squinting, then glanced at each other.

Alastor appeared beside her. "So, you think you can defeat us." He raised an eyebrow. "And he thinks you are all dead." He pointed to the other man, keeping his eyes focused on the confident one. "Speak, boy."

"Yes, that's what we said," he confirmed, his voice wavering.

"How do you intend to defeat me? I have the power to destroy you."

The man met Alastor's gaze with a glare. "I suppose you probably do."

"He shall live," Alastor said, pointing to the other man, "because he understands human limitations."

He raised both arms. As he did, fires ignited under the feet of the security and police officers in the vicinity of the stage. Flames shot into the air, followed by screams of pain as the fires danced upward to engulf the immobilized officers. Their clothes melted into their flesh; their skin blackened and crisped. Black smoke billowed skyward, filling the air with the smell of burning hair and flesh. The cries went on for what seemed an eternity. Spectators in the crowd were unable to turn away from the horror before them; some kept horrified eyes locked on the stage, while others squeezed their eyes tightly closed.

Kyra gagged on the smell and quickly brought her hand to her mouth, then retched again. Her eyes popped open. She faded from the view of everyone except Alastor, then rushed to the edge of the stage and vomited into the grass off the side of the platform.

Alastor vanished slowly in ripples of heat before he went to her. "You all right, darling? What happened?" He took her elbow and moved her away across the stage, invisible to everyone but each other.

"Yes, I'm fine. The smell of burning flesh got to me." She brushed off her dress before combing her fingers through her hair. She absently scanned the crowd, still frozen in place, silently watching the only living security man on the stage with the president. She smirked. There was nothing they could do but await her next whim, or witness what was next.

The second wave of Secret Service agents flooded onto the stage, only to falter and gape in the horror at the blackened corpses. Fragile shells of the people they'd once been, they were beginning to crumble under the pressure of the light breeze, the charred bits wisping gently across the stage to settle in morbid drifts of ash against any vertical obstacle. The stench hung in the air, trapped under the massive white awning over the stage.

The only surviving security man sank to his knees, his face buried in his hands. Two of the new security officers rushed over to him after hastily scanning the area. The other four surrounded the president, facing outward, their guns drawn.

Alastor and Kyra looked at one another and nodded.

A swirl of green smoke drifted up between the president and the stage backdrop. Gasps from the crowd alerted the security officers, who whirled left and right, eyes darting everywhere, until they saw the green smoke and quickly gathered between it and the president, blocking access to Beatty.

Alastor stepped out of the smoke to the blaze of gunfire. Bullets zinged around and against him but none pierced his body. The echoes from the gunshots ricocheted deafeningly through the air. Finally they stopped firing.

Alastor grinned. "Have you finished?" He scanned the shocked faces, then stepped forward.

Howling in wordless rage, one of the men charged toward him, teeth barred and fists clenched. With a flick of Alastor's wrist, the Secret Service agent's head jerked around to an unnatural angle with an audible snap. His body took another step before it dropped to the ground. The sight of the prostrate body with the head facing skyward, the facial expression frozen in a grotesque state of shock, unnerved the others. There were gasps; involuntary steps back; the sound of retching from two of them.

Alastor closed in on the president, parting the security men in the way with casual sweeps of his hands.

"You have no intention of meeting my demands. Now you shall pay with your life." He moved slowly, inexorably closer, and narrowed his eyes. "I am not of this Earth; there are no means to defeat me."

"What you're asking is irrational," Beatty stammered. "It's not a possibility to release every inmate, in every prison."

A shot rang out, echoing through the air. Alastor faced the crowd in search of the source. The bullet hung, suspended before his face. He scowled at it before he plucked it from the sky and rolled it over in his hand.

Kyra had already identified the source. Directly across from the stage, a sniper lay on the roof of a large burger booth, concealed behind its tall façade. A small hole had been cut in the plywood sign, just large enough for him to aim and shoot through and strategically disguised by a painted pickle. The shooter must have lain there since before events began to unfold, waiting for his chance.

Kyra materialized inches away from the sniper, hovering in midair at the level of the roof. Her scowling eyes drilled into him. He gulped and swallowed hard. She reached out, grabbed the man by his shirt, and yanked him from his hiding place. The sniper was airborne for a short while before he slammed into the ground headfirst. She slowly floated down to the ground and stalked toward her target as he picked himself up. They locked eyes. She felt a twinge of sympathy for this man— he was, after all, just trying to protect his leader, as she protected hers. *Run, run for your life,* she wanted to yell at him, but the words were frozen in her mind.

She tapped her forefinger against her lips as she watched the fear in his eyes turn to aggression. He pulled a knife from a strap on his leg and slashed at her. Kyra nodded at it, and an invisible force ripped the knife from his hand and sent it through the air to land in Kyra's grip. She looked the knife over, then looked back to the sniper. She saw his aura—a vibrant yellow, meaning he was in opposition to Alastor and unlikely to see the way—but he was a good man, she knew, and she needed to help him.

Her vision blurred suddenly, and she felt faint. Her thoughts became cloudy, as if a fog had settled over her mind. She clenched her teeth and shook her head. The fog cleared.

The sniper has to die, she thought; *he is evil and trying to stop Alastor from saving the world.*

She grinned at the man, then leapt forward and sliced open his throat. His mouth dropped open in surprise. The blood drained from his face, flowing in a bright red cascade from the slit she'd opened in his neck. He dropped to his knees, then toppled over.

The crowd screamed as one and fled in a frenzy of terror, though some stood riveted in place, paralyzed by shock. Kyra disappeared from the audience to reappear on stage next to Alastor.

"Why did you free them?" Alastor barked.

"I didn't, someone else did." She scanned the crowd and caught a familiar face. Alexis. "It was them." She pointed to the group of familiar faces.

Alexis, Axel, and James pushed their way toward the stage. She looked past them to the entrance to the fair, where Hailey and Nick, along with Kyra's mother Iris and Xavier, hung back. Between them and her former friends, the priest and his two Majai companions stood on the edge of the scattering crowd, a small island of calm in the rushing sea of people.

Alastor glared at the Majai men. His eyes went black and the stragglers in the crowd slowed to a stop. He turned back to Kyra. "Finish the objective, quickly."

She wrinkled her brow and cocked her head. Alastor touched her shoulder and she understood what he wanted her to do. She nodded and lifted her arms. Her eyes closed and she threw her head back. The remaining security detail dropped silently, falling dead to the hard floor of the stage.

President Beatty grabbed at his chest and dropped to his knees. Red-faced, mouth working like a goldfish's as he gasped for breath, he doubled over, his forehead pressing to the stage floor. His body relaxed as his life drifted away, and his body toppled sideways and lay still.

Kyra dropped her arms and opened her eyes in time to see Alexis stop in the center of the trampled grassy field, her eyes locked on the stage as her brother and James ascended the stairs together. Kyra watched the men she knew—she once knew—move toward her. Alastor moved to her side. James caught Alastor's hard stare and hesitated. He looked away and cleared his throat. Kyra saw his hands trembling. When Axel passed James, closing the distance to Kyra, James jolted upright and quickly push past Axel, moving Axel aside with his arm as he hurried to his wife. He stopped a few feet shy of her, carefully eyeing Alastor.

"Kyra..." James looked over the bloody, charred graveyard they stood in. "I-I—" He shuddered. "We need you to come home. We love you."

She cocked her head, baffled by his request. She had no home with him; he was a time-filler—a waste of time; a distant memory of a life lived wrong; her rock-bottom, before she turned her life around; a mistake she'd made while she was on the wrong path—the path of evil.

"This is not you." He glanced at the demon beside her. "How could you ever let yourself be involved in all this senseless murder?" His voice sounded more and more distant as his image shrank away from her, like reversing the zoom on a camera lens. "Kyra!" His temper flared. "Enough is enough." He reached out and grabbed her wrist.

She felt the jolt in her arm and he shot back into focus. He pulled her toward him and stepped farther away from Alastor.

His eyes—his serious eyes—danced back and forth from hers to Alastor as he leaned in and went for a kiss. She pulled back on impulse, but found her resistance weakening as he struggled to reach her with his mouth. He loved her and she knew it; she had loved him, or at least thought she might have—but Alastor was her one and only love now.

Mere inches away from her lips, James froze. She pulled away from her husband and he began to cough and sputter blood. He groaned and pawed at his stomach and chest, his eyes pleading with Kyra.

Kyra, devoid of emotion, watched James being torn apart. He was an insignificant mortal that had tried to touch her and she belonged to Alastor.

James brought his hand to his nose as blood gushed out with every cough. His eyes blurred red as blood seeped from their corners. He dropped to his knees.

A Celtic sword materialized in the hands of the angry demon beside her. He sliced the blade through the air.

Chapter Fifteen

The head of James Parker rolled when it hit the stage floor, spraying blood. His body took a moment to catch up; then it dropped to its knees and toppled over beside Axel's feet. *So much for the protection of the deal*, he thought bitterly.

Chaos.

Utter chaos erupted as those still nearby scattered, stampeding over each other. Kyra's horrified family ran for the car, Nick carrying Xavier as Hailey and Iris stumbled after him, being pushed and shoved by others running past them, crying and screaming as they all fled for their lives. All but one…

Alexis.

The crowd divided and flowed around her. She stood still with her eyes fixed on the stage, mouth gaping open and her arms outstretched, unmoved by the hordes scrambling past.

The remnants of the audience dissipated quickly, leaving behind only a few stragglers.

Kyra and Alastor turned their attention to Axel. Kyra's expression emotionless, Alastor's full of fury. Axel's eyes fixed on Alastor as he took a step back from Kyra and the growing pool of blood at his feet. The two men were locked in a battle to stare each other down.

"Kyra, what are you doing? How could you let this demon kill James? He was your husband and your son's father." His eyes shifted to meet hers. "I know you're still in there somewhere. Fight him and come back to us."

She gave no indication that she'd heard his words. She stared blankly, her eyes glazed; she didn't even seem to notice that he'd spoken. Axel wasn't even sure that she could see him.

Alastor's face hardened. "Do you want to be the next body on this stage?"

"I'm leaving," he said, then looked to Kyra once more, his heart full of sadness. "There's nothing here for me anymore."

He backed away slowly before he turned and headed down the stairs. Other than bits of garbage and flattened grass, there was little evidence that a large crowd had been gathered here only a moment ago. A few casualties sat on the edges of the field, nursing broken bones and cracked skulls. Where hundreds of people once stood, only his sister remained, watching and ready to fight.

Before Axel reached Alexis they witnessed Kyra and the demon disappear from the stage with neither swirling smoke nor pyrotechnics to herald their exit.

***

As the sun set over the hills, leaving a magical pink glow in the distance, Kyra rested her hands on the railing of the old wooden deck and mulled over the events of the president's last appearance. Resistance was to be expected as they traveled the globe, making demands on the political leaders. They were in no real danger, as she could usually sense the threat before it happened. In circumstances like those today, when she didn't see the sniper attack coming, her protective powers would instinctively take over and shield them both.

Together, they were unstoppable.

Alastor stepped out from the mansion onto the deck, walked up behind Kyra, and slid his arms around her waist. She leaned in to him and breathed in the faint scent of his cologne as his chin slipped over her bare shoulder and nuzzled her neck.

"Tell me about this Axel character," he whispered into her ear.

Kyra sighed. "He's in love with me." She released the railing and rested her hands over his. "He's Alexis's brother, so I've known him as long as I've known her. When we met there was that raw animal magnetism, and I found him extremely irresistible. The first time I saw his testosterone-fueled fighting, I wanted to rip all of his clothes off right there."

"What stopped you?"

"His flavor of the month girlfriend was sitting with us. And I didn't want to be with a witch—"

"Fantastic," Alastor cut her off and pulled away. "That makes his sister a witch, as well, and adds two more under the protection of the deal," he grumbled.

She turned to face him, confused by his outburst. *Didn't he know they were witches? And what does he mean, two more witches?*

He cupped her face in his hands and pulled her to him. "I need to know about your history with him," he said, his eyes blazing with something Kyra couldn't decipher.

"There's not much to know. We were just friends for the longest time."

"Were you ever *with* him?"

"No, not really." A memory of Axel stroking her naked skin as they lay in his bed flashed through her mind. "Well, not back then, but kind of in the last six months. It's hard to explain."

"Try. He has interfered with my plans twice, now."

She pulled her face from his grasp. "Okay, at the last work Christmas party we had, James ended up working late and didn't show. Alexis never really commits enough to a guy to even consider bringing one to a work party, so she brought her brother. Axel had just moved back to town. I hadn't seen him in so long…" She trailed off as her eyes drifted to the deck boards. "I don't know exactly why it happened, but the normal innocent flirtations we'd always played with intensified. They got progressively more provocative as the night went on until we eventually kissed."

"Interesting; is that all?" he asked, taking her hands.

She shook her head. "We took off and went back to his place. I didn't even tell Alexis, but she probably knew it was coming. She called me on Axel's phone the next day to tell me James had called her and she lied for me. I was supposed to go home that night but decided to take a break from my responsibilities and shut off my phone to disappear from everything in the world, except Axel."

"Did you love him?"

Kyra sighed and brushed her hair back. "I was lost and confused about the men in my life and couldn't focus on either of them. I couldn't really be with them both, not without betraying them both. Axel was tortured by it and things got worse before you stepped into the picture and changed everything."

"So you did love him before you came to me." Alastor stroked his chin, speaking more to himself than to her.

"I always did on some level, I guess, but I don't think I realized it until Christmas. I was with him the day before I was brought here."

Alastor smiled. "See, Kyra? More evidence that you were not such an angel before I found you."

She shrugged. "I did feel guilty about it, but I don't remember why. Now I don't feel bad at all. It's like I can look at the situation with emotional clarity. I couldn't leave James and Xavier, but I couldn't leave Axel, either. I needed them both; how could I have chosen?" She sighed, tucking her hair behind her ear. "I was back to having nightly dreams about you and wasn't sure if it just added more confusion to those two relationships. At first I thought that I dreamt of a man that didn't exist because I wanted something they couldn't offer;

because neither Axel nor James was the right choice. Now I think, on some subconscious level, I knew I wasn't going to be with either of them for much longer, so there was no point in making a decision. The choice was already you." She smiled at him.

Alastor brushed her cheek with his knuckles. Her pulse quickened as he pressed his lips on hers for a slow, deep kiss. He pulled away, leaving her disappointed and wanting more. "And your useless human husband just allowed you to do as you pleased?"

"James never knew about the affair, or that I was a witch. He was always too preoccupied to notice anything that wasn't work-related." She laughed. "In fact, I bet you when he was sitting on that cold concrete floor in the basement, surrounded by all that fear and chaos, he was thinking about work. And probably how dirty the floor was."

"What are you rambling on about?"

She rolled her eyes. "I didn't let all this happen to be a terrible person. I loved them both, but for different reasons. They'd have been the perfect man if they were combined into one man."

"What about the witch? Did he love you before you married the human? Did he want you to be his wife?"

"He never said and I never asked." Kyra dropped her gaze for a moment. "Then the years just filled up with the things that we never said to each other."

"Is that why you seldom used your powers—because of the useless mortal you married?"

She looked up at him. "Mostly I didn't use my powers because I didn't want them."

"That truly made my search for you more troublesome."

"Well, we're together now."

He smiled. "Indeed."

Chapter Sixteen

The group reassembled at their chic downtown hotel suite, where hysteria created a cacophony of voices. Iris and Nick were trying to talk over each other. Hailey was shouting at Axel. Alexis and the priest were trying to console Xavier, who had gone silent, and sat in one of the oddly shaped modern chairs, staring into space. The two Majai men stood off to one side, silently observing everyone.

"What the hell happened?" Nick exclaimed to no one in particular, scratching his head.

"I can't believe that she just stood there and didn't say anything," Axel said to Alexis, who only waved her hand at him before crouching down next to Xavier.

"This is all your fault, Axel," Hailey said, nudging him on her way to Nick and Iris. "You distracted her and got James killed!"

Axel grunted.

"What's wrong with her?" Nick asked Iris. He dropped his voice to a whisper. "It's like she was a zombie."

Iris shifted uncomfortably. "Don't talk about Kyra that way. She needs our help."

"So, what now?" Nick asked her, his tone more sympathetic.

"I can't believe this is happening," Hailey interrupted as she walked between her mother and her husband. She whirled to face them. "How are we going to save her?"

"Xavier, honey," Alexis said, her voice soothing, "I know you are probably confused right now, but that bad man…"

She flipped her hair over her shoulder, searching for the appropriate words to comfort a child. One day she would have her own children to carry on the family line—if she ever met someone worthy; someone had to, and she was more likely to settle down than her brother. Xavier was different; he had an understanding of the world that went well beyond his years, thanks to her—so what could she say now to comfort him, without lying?

"I'm so sorry, sweetie."

"No, it's okay," Xavier said, his voice flat. He turned his head toward Alexis. "My dad's not dead and my mom's not evil, either."

"I'm sorry, child," Father Thomas interjected, resting a hand on Xavier's shoulder. "That man killed him. But he's safe in Heaven now."

Alexis put her hand on his. "You're just in shock, but everything will be okay, I promise."

"We need a new plan!" Axel shouted above the noise. The chatter stopped and they all turned to look at him, waiting. He ran his hand through his hair. "I'm sorry, but James was not the one to bring back Kyra. He was in denial. He didn't understand her, or what is going on. Someone else has to be her unbreakable love and I know—"

Everyone started talking over each other again.

"Maybe it's me," Hailey offered. "Sisters have an unbreakable bond. Maybe it's not a guy."

"What about Alexis?" Nick suggested. "They've been attached like Siamese twins since they met." Hailey shot him a hurt look. "It's not a dig at you, sweetie; we just have to consider all the possibilities so we don't make another fatal mistake."

Alexis stood. "Yes, and I think it's time for the truth and secrets to come out—"

The shrill ringing of the hotel room's phone interrupted her. The chatter stopped and they all stared at the sleek silver phone hanging on the wall as it rang again. Then a third time.

It's not possible, Alexis thought. She pushed past Iris and Nick and snatched up the receiver.

"Hello?" She gasped. "James! James! Is it really you? We thought you were dead! We saw the demon kill you."

Xavier's eyes had been glued to the phone from the moment it started to ring. The room was dead silent as everyone stared at Alexis, straining to hear the other end of the conversation.

"See you soon," Alexis finished, and hung up the phone with a smile.

"Was that really James?" Hailey asked, her eyes wide.

Axel's mouth sagged open. "But how is he alive?" His eyebrows rose. "I saw him get decapitated!"

Alexis rubbed her hands together before smacking them together in a loud clap. "Well, he doesn't know how it happened, but he just woke up a couple minutes ago, in the street. He'll be here right away."

"I may have a theory," Father Thomas interjected.

As the priest moved to the center of the room, Hailey and Alexis plopped down on the floor in front of Xavier's chair, and the others slowly found seats. He waited until everyone had settled in.

"When Kyra made the deal with the demon, you told me that she said he could not kill any of you, that everyone who was in that dungeon is protected from his evil. That was part of the deal she made."

"Wait a minute... how could he even hurt James, then?" Iris interjected.

"So why did Kyra attack just James and not Axel too?" Nick asked, eyebrows pinched in confusion.

"Kyra didn't kill James, Alastor did. He obviously sees James as more of a threat than Axel, or he would be dead too," Hailey offered.

"No one is actually dead," Axel corrected her.

"You know what I mean," Hailey retorted. "Alastor removed James, not you."

"Because he tried to kiss Kyra, not necessarily because he's the one to turn her."

"All right you guys, that's enough. Hot tempers don't solve anything," Alexis scolded, her eyes darting between Hailey and her brother. "Father, do you have any thoughts on the demon's wrath toward James and not my brother?"

"He interfered, and in the deal she made with the demon, he can't hurt you unless you interfere with his plans, but apparently he can't permanently kill you, as is evident from this event. I don't know why he *only* attacked James, but Axel might be right, and it was because James tried to kiss Kyra. The demon did, however, physically cut down James rather than using any powers, for some reason. Demons kill people with their powers, for the most part."

"What the hell does that mean?"

"The prophecy isn't overly clear on this," Father Thomas warned. "And it's hard to tell if Kyra is in control, but regarding James, the demon felt threatened enough to dispatch him."

Iris nodded. "The demon did it because Kyra wouldn't. James could still be the one," Iris said glancing at the others.

Father Thomas opened his mouth to speak, then closed it and shrugged slightly.

Hailey stood and put her hands on her hips. "Or me," she stated firmly.

"What about Iris? She's Kyra's mother. Or at least the only mother she's ever known. That's possible, isn't it?" Nick looked to the priest. "Or Alexis."

"Anything is possible, I suppose," he muttered.

"Enough." Alexis rose and started to pace the room. "It's time you all knew the truth." She stopped and looked to her brother. He nodded. "It's Axel."

"What?" Hailey exclaimed. She glowered at Axel. "I knew there was some ulterior motive for you going with James, you scumbag."

Eyes on Axel, Iris slowly sat down next to Xavier, reaching out for the floor behind her.

"Hailey, stop," Alexis urged. "You can't help who you're in love with."

"Yeah, but you can control your actions." She glared at Axel. "How could you? She's married, and they have a child."

"It's not like that, Hailey," Axel protested, then dropped his voice and glanced meaningfully at Kyra's son. "And we don't need to have this conversation in front of Xavier."

***

Iris watched as James entered the suite to be ambushed by hugs and happy faces. His son crawled onto his lap when at last he found a seat.

"That didn't go over very well. So, what's the plan now?" James asked, looking to the priest.

"I think we're all in agreement, mostly, that the demon took you out, not Kyra. So there is a strong possibility that you could bring her back. The fact is, we have no way of knowing except by trial and error, which in this case can get people killed."

Axel grunted. "This is stupid. She didn't even try to stop him!" He stopped and looked at Xavier. "Xavier, why don't you go to the other room while we talk," he said mildly. He looked around at the others and murmured, "He doesn't need to hear everything."

Xavier looked around at their faces. They were all looking at him, nodding their agreement, except for his father. James was glaring at Axel, his jaw tight and his fists clenched. "Go," he growled through his teeth, though he kept his glare on Axel. Xavier took one look at his dad's face and hurried into the other room, closing the door behind him.

Iris stared at James, confused by his anger. Did he already know?

Axel met James's glare. "Kyra has been unhappy for a long time and was considering leaving you, James. I'm sorry to have to be the one to tell you, but I don't think that's very *unbreakable*," he said dryly.

"Women like Kyra don't fall in love and run away with the wandering grease monkey bad boy," James sneered. "What kind of life do you think you could have provided for her? You would have been a fleeting phase in her life. She'll never leave her family."

"Never leave, eh?" Axel retorted lightly. "I'm sorry; where is she now?"

"She left you too, jackass!" James snapped, making both Iris and Hailey gasp in surprise. She had never heard him speak like that—Axel yes, but he'd always had a strong personality; James had better manners, like her husband had when he was still alive. But, she supposed, if he was ever going to act out, this would be a justifiable reason, even if it was dreadful timing.

"She wouldn't have come to me if you were taking care of her," Axel said. "She's always been a very special woman—but you seem to have forgotten that."

"I have never forgotten how great she is! Life isn't all rainbows and lollipops. We have demanding careers and other adult responsibilities that you wouldn't be able to comprehend," James said, sneering again. "You move around all the time and go through jobs like you do women."

Axel lifted his eyebrows. "It was obvious to me that she needed a little less responsibility and a little more fun," he said. "Kyra and I have a connection that you could never understand. She loved you at one point, but face it, James—you're boring. You couldn't have held onto Kyra forever."

Alexis sighed and tossed her hair over her shoulder, then walked over to the sofa and plopped down next to Iris.

"If I'm so boring and you're so exciting, then why did she never date you? I mean, you did know her first, but you've always been 'just friends.' She dated *me* and married *me*. She didn't want you, she wanted me."

Axel charged over to James. "You're not the one that is her great love!" he growled into James's face. "I am. She loves *me*—I know it—and I have loved her since the day we met."

"Then why were you never with her? Your love couldn't have been that great," James said coldly.

Hailey's eyes dropped away from James, then drifted from the floor to her husband, who stood slack-jawed, his head swinging back and forth between the arguing men.

"Kyra and I do have an unbreakable bond. We are meant to be together, I know it. I can feel it. I don't know why it's become so difficult in this past year, but it was always there, just under the surface," James said. "Look, I know about the Christmas party." He crossed his arms over his chest.

Hailey and Iris exchanged looks of confusion, then Iris remembered hosting the Reeds' family dinner. Axel never made it and Alexis had told her he was ill with the flu. Was this what they were talking about? Was he not really ill?

"It may have happened because she was bored and wanted some excitement," James continued, "but it wasn't because she loved you. She would have ended it when she grew tired of you."

"She loved every minute with me. She couldn't get enough. Was she always a screamer, or was it just with me?" Axel smirked.

James lunged at him, fists swinging furiously. Axel threw up his arms to shield himself and both men tumbled to the floor, where they rolled around on the carpet, throwing punches at one another.

The others looked on, paralyzed by shock at both James's outburst and Axel's confession. Alexis simply sighed and rolled her eyes.

"Stop it! Stop this right now!" Iris pleaded as two boys she loved like her own children thrashed around, trying to pulverize each other.

"You two are unbelievable. You're acting like children," Alexis added.

Xavier came barreling out of the bedroom, screaming, "Stop, don't fight!"

Hailey grabbed Xavier before he could reach them. The two men broke apart and shuffled away from each other.

"It's okay, Dad," Xavier said, not trying to pull free. "I know Axel loves Mom."

Hailey glared at Axel while Iris shifted uncomfortably on the leather sofa.

"I know it's kinda weird to you, but Mom and Alexis and Axel are best friends forever. They have another best friend too." He paused and fidgeted uncertainly, twisting his fingers. "Someone is missing."

"What, honey?" Alexis said, trying not to sound too urgent, though her eyebrows drew together. "Who's missing?"

Xavier looked down, frowning. "I-I'm not sure. The fourth friend is lost."

Axel and Alexis exchanged puzzled looks.

"Ah, the naive innocence of youth," James grumbled. "Best friends forever," he said sarcastically.

"No, Dad. For real."

Chapter Seventeen

Jensen Harris and Vance Carter stepped into the sunshine and paused to fill their lungs with the crisp, clean air. It had never before smelled so good to them; it was the air of freedom. Vance stood on a patch of freshly cut grass, his eyes closed, inhaling the invigorating scent and absorbing the warm sunshine bathing his face.

Jensen glanced behind them, back to the prison, where all the convicted felons were filing out from the behind the fences, flooding the parking lot in a river of orange overalls that flowed around the cars like water breaking around rocks. Their faces ecstatic, they headed for the highway. Armed guards stood high on the walls, watching as everyone left the concrete walls behind and headed off into the world.

Jensen grunted. "We need to have a plan."

Vance looked at him. "I don't have one. This was all very sudden."

"Well, neither one of us have any family alive, and if we're really gonna try to turn over a new leaf, we can't look up our old friends. So where are we gonna go?"

Vance shrugged. "We've gotta get real, honest jobs so we can pay for a place, I guess."

"That won't be hard," Jensen said sarcastically. "Where we gonna sleep in the meantime?"

Vance scratched his head.

Jensen watched a dust trail snake along the gravel road, kicked up by an old pickup truck approaching the prison. The roar of its engine grew louder as it got closer, and rocks flew up behind the tires as the truck whipped into the parking lot. The truck's paint was chipped and faded, and years of rust had eaten at the body. A loudspeaker had been mounted on the roof. The truck screeched to a stop in an open area of the parking lot, and the loudspeaker crackled to life.

"Hey you guys," a man's voice said through the speaker, "any of you looking for a job and a place to stay? We have a few openings at Alastor's manor."

Vance beamed at Jensen. "Well, that must be fate."

"Or bad luck," groaned Jensen.

"Don't be such a bitch," Vance growled. "Let's go check it out."

Jensen rolled his eyes. "That's kinda counterproductive, dontcha think? He's the root of all evil... or something like that."

"Well, I'm not saying let's work for the guy, I'm just saying he must expect a lot of people to be homeless and jobless when they get out of the pen, so he might have a plan to help us guys get back on our feet." Vance stroked his chin. "After all, he fought to have all the prisons across the country shut down, so he must have a plan."

They walked over to the truck, where a small crowd had already gathered. Two guys, one bearded and the other just plain nasty-looking, had already gotten out of the truck and were chatting with the former inmates. Men were quickly moving on after talking with them, some muttering expletives and accompanying those with rude gestures.

"Hey! You two." The bearded man pointed to Jensen and Vance. "You got any special skills?"

"Well, I'm good with computers, and break and enter-type stuff like lockpicking and safecracking," Vance offered.

"Yep, so much for turning over a new leaf," Jensen muttered beside him.

"And this guy," Vance jerked his thumb at Jensen, "can complain like it's nobody's business. What's it pay?"

"It pays food and shelter. You'll be financially compensated once you leave, or if you move up the food chain."

"It pays nothing?" Jensen shook his head and looked at his friend. "No way; there's no point if we can't make any money."

"You heard him. We don't need money. They feed us, and we'll have a place to stay until we figure out what we're gonna do." Vance turned back to the men by the truck and smiled.

"Part of the deal is, you can't have any contact with the outside world, and you can't leave the grounds until we trust you. Then you'll be given more assignments and privileges. Does that work for you?" the nasty-looking guy asked.

Vance nodded. "Works for me. I've got no one to talk to anyway."

"Okay, get in the truck." The bearded driver glanced around the faces. "Anyone else got any skills?"

Jensen swore under his breath.

As the crowd started to disperse, the other man added, "Cooking, cleaning, reading, writing, computers, assault, talented at talking people into what you want them to do?"

Vance looked back at Jensen with wide eyes, silently pleading with his buddy to get in the truck and come with him.

"Okay, fine, I'll go," Jensen said reluctantly, grimacing at Vance.

"Okay, get in."

As Jensen climbed into the back of the truck, Vance said brightly, "Looks like we're getting a place to stay and free meals."

"It's not free. Everything comes with a price," Jensen grumbled. "I think this is a very bad idea and I'm gonna say I told you so, eventually."

A couple more guys climbed into the truck and sat down on the floor of the box.

The nasty-looking guy clambered over the rusty side with a handful zip ties and black hoods. He tossed a hood at each of the new recruits.

"Put these on and pull the drawstrings tight. If they come off on the trip, you'll be getting a bullet in the head."

With his hood in place, the heat from the summer sun burned onto Vance's head and his brow had already beaded with sweat. Only tiny specs of light filtered through the suffocating material. He struggled with his breathing as his wrists were bound behind his back with zip tie handcuffs. That was nothing new to him. He'd had these makeshift handcuffs on his wrists before. The police used something similar when they'd run out if actual handcuffs during a mass arrest.

The voices from the other inmates faded into the distance as they walked toward the highway and their freedom. The truck bounced around on its worn out shocks as the nasty guy crawled out of the box and into the cab. The truck door slammed and the truck roared away from the prison. A cooling breeze flowed through Vance's hood, allowing him to breathe easily again as they headed from the prison into a new and unknown chapter of their lives called freedom.

***

"It is done." Alastor strolled triumphantly into the sitting room. "All the prisons across the US have been emptied. Soon the other counties will follow their lead."

"That's great!" Kyra beamed. "So what's our next move?"

Celista rolled her eyes. "Obviously, it's to shut down the legal system. No cops, no security, no lawyers or judges… no punishment for any crime."

"That makes sense…" Kyra said, drawing out her words, unsure. Celista always seemed to know more than she did; she wondered if Alastor shared his plans with her while he kept them from Kyra—or did she simply know Alastor better? Her eyes lingered on Celista, then shifted to her demon. "Is this how we are going to tip the scales on Heaven?"

"Leave the plotting to me and just do what you are told." He marched past the crocodile-skin chesterfield and sat down in the armchair across from them. The girls were on opposite ends of the sofa; there was room for three more people between them.

"Yes sir," Celista responded immediately.

Kyra grinned at her obedient reaction. "Alastor, don't get so defensive and agitated. We are just excited and want to keep things moving in our favor." She leaned casually on the armrest and tucked her feet up on the couch. "After all, it took a while for the prisoners to be released."

Alastor leaned forward, his eyes widening. "Five and a half weeks since you turned is not *a while*. I have been waiting and planning this since the beginning of time, and if it takes us a hundred years to take over, so be it."

"I'll be dead by then and you won't have access to my powers anymore." Kyra rapped her fingers lightly on the armrest.

"No, darling." He sat back in his chair. "I will keep you alive and young until we are finished our work."

"I should've guessed." She smirked, remembering her attempted suicides.

"Now listen," he said, sitting up straight and looking back and forth at the two women. "We shall dismantle the justice system, but not until the other counties follow the lead of the Americans and close down their prison systems." He lowered his voice. "In the meantime, Kyra and I shall embark on a journey through the planes to bring back some horrors for the world to experience."

"What? Are you kidding me?" Celista threw her hands up, arms outstretched. "You're taking her through the planes." She carved her fingers through her hair, pulling her face tight, then whipped her hands out, releasing her locks to fall over her shoulders. "She'll get killed for sure, and this will all go to shit."

"Celista, you shall remain here," Alastor said in a tone that left no room for argument. Her shoulders slumped, but her eyes burned into Alastor. "Ensure my plans remain on target, and feed the prisoner. We shall return as soon as we are able."

"And how long will that be?" Kyra asked, hoping to prompt him to bring her into his confidence.

"A few days, maybe a week, depending on how smoothly our journey proceeds."

Celista crossed her arms. "I'm the babysitter? Unbelievable," she huffed.

"Dismissed," Alastor snapped, looking at Celista.

She stormed out of the room, her hair swishing behind her.

"Well, I quite enjoyed that." Kyra smiled and patted the chesterfield next to her. "So where are we going? How does this plane thing work again?"

He drew a deep breath. "There was a time when all the planes were together as one in Atlantis—"

"Like Atlantis that sank into the sea?" Kyra interrupted.

"Yes, that is the way humans have heard of it." He leaned back in the chair, resting his muscular arms over the armrests and stretching his legs out in front of him.

The memory of Axel telling her to fight him flashed through her mind. She winced and shook the memory away.

"But," Alastor continued, "Atlantis is still thriving and it was never here on this Earth. When all the planes coexisted in one place…"

His words faded as a series of images flickered through her mind: her smiling friends gathered on her wedding day; the birth of her son, Xavier; Alexis covered in paint from their joint attempt at the masterpiece resting on the easel; meeting Alexis in college; her first kiss with Axel.

She felt a hand squeeze her leg and flinched. Her head shot to her left and she saw Alastor smiling there. She held her breath and looked back to Alastor's chair. It was empty. As he rubbed her leg she released her breath and relaxed, slowly forgetting the visions.

"The different planes are more suited now to the creatures living within them," he said, his fingers trailing up from the base of her neck. "They are set up so you have to go through one to get to the next. Earth and this Solar System are the least magical of them all, and relatively safe. On the opposite side from us is the plane holding the most powerful creatures you can imagine. That's where we are going."

"To get what?"

"A dragon egg."

***

"I am not going in there," Kyra said, eyeing the mirror inside the archway. "Isn't this the gate to Hell? I thought the other mirror was the doorway to the planes." She glanced behind her, down the long corridor to the identical archway at the other end.

"The gate to Hell only opens if you read the inscription." He pointed to the scribbles carved into the stone of the archway. "This door takes us through the planes in reverse order. It will be faster and safer for you." He reached out for her hand and smiled reassuringly.

Her eyes wandered from his hand to the mirror and back to his hand before she took it. He pulled her into his arms and stepped toward the mirror. The mirror felt cold to the touch as he pressed her hand against it.

"Ready?" he asked, watching her face. She nodded, holding her breath. Her hand slipped through the glass. He held onto her waist as he stepped inside his reflection.

They vanished.

Chapter Eighteen

The hooded passengers bounced around in the box as the pickup slowed to a stop. The tailgate dropped down with a bang and a jolt. The springs under the truck box sagged as someone climbed in, and moments later someone cut Jensen's hands free.

"We're here. Take off your hoods and get out of my truck," the bearded guy commanded. "This is your new home. Alastor is worse than all the hype, so do what you're told or you'll end up buried in this field." He swept his arm out toward a green expanse of rolling hills around a massive, modern-day castle.

"And... I told you so," Jensen whispered, looking over the area.

He was right—it was more of a field than a lawn, and severely neglected for decades; the weeds choked out the grass. Closer to the house the overgrowth had been mowed down, revealing patchy growth patterns. The massive mansion itself was a beautiful example of brick and stone architecture.

Vance shrugged. "We're here now, so let's make the best of it," he said, dropping to the ground and moving toward the grand mahogany double doors with the others.

As they entered the large marble foyer, Jensen and Vance exchanged glances. It was a far better setup than either of them had imagined. The sound of high heels clicking over the marble floor drew their attention. They turned.

Vance's mouth dropped open at the vision of beauty approaching them; a short, skinny little thing that Jensen imagined he could easily toss around in the bedroom. Her flawless dark glistening skin with the perfect amount of cleavage—larger than an apple and smaller than a watermelon—was enhanced by stunning bright white hair; and her bold, hypnotic eyes seemed to be glowing at him from across the vast marble room.

She smiled as she reached them. "Hey boys, I'm Celista. Now, which two of you are going to be dealing with the computers and media monitoring, and all the rest?"

Jensen elbowed Vance when he didn't respond. His mouth still hung open. Vance shook himself. "Me—um, I am. Sorry, I'm Vance... and I'm your man," he said, extending his hand.

She grinned, stepping closer to him. "You most certainly are."

His mouth dropped open again and his hand dropped with it. Jensen rolled his eyes.

Another of the convicts moved up next to Vance. He too was rendered speechless by their hostess as he feebly raised his hand.

"I'll take these two. Travis, show the others the kitchen and then take them to get settled into their rooms." She smiled sweetly.

"Kitchen?" Jensen searched the face of the scruffy guy—Travis.

"Yep. You'll be a-cookin' and a-cleanin' like a little bitch."

Vance and the other con followed Celista over the marble floor, past the cascade of mahogany stairs, and into one of the wide corridors heading in opposite directions just before the kitchen entrance.

Jensen stood in the archway of the kitchen, watching his friend wander away with the creature of beauty, mesmerized by her narrow hips and tight, swaying bum.

"Figures, he gets the hot chick and I get stuck with a woman's job and the hillbilly who's never heard of soap," he mumbled.

"What's that?" Travis demanded. Jensen shook his head and stepped into the kitchen.

An hour later, Jensen had settled into his room and was still waiting for Vance to show up. Travis had let them pick their rooms, but informed them they would be bunking with someone else, so naturally Jensen had told his new kitchen coworker that his buddy Vance would be his roommate.

The room was bigger than his first apartment. It made perfect sense to put two guys in one room. Two queen-sized beds sat on opposite sides of the room, complete with clean white linens, and bedside tables with reading lamps; two huge dressers were against the wall across from the foot of the beds. A couple of chairs and a full-sized couch with a wrought iron coffee table in the center of the room faced a fifty-six-inch TV mounted on the charcoal-dark brickwork above an oversized gas fireplace. The walls were smoke-gray. The room smelled of pine air fresheners, which he thought was odd, but it was definitely the best man cave Jensen had ever been in, in all of his thirty-seven years.

Vance burst into the room, beaming, as always.

"I see you got us a great pad." He spun around as he strode around the room. "Wow, this place is awesome—everything about it. Dontcha think so?" He never waited for a reply. "This house—no, this *castle*—the job, our room, and..." he paused for effect. "...that smoking-hot chick."

"Oh, great. Did you hit on her already? Now we're going to get kicked out of here because you're stupid." He frowned, wondering if they could ever get kicked out, or just end up dead and buried in the field, as Travis had said.

"No, no," Vance said, shaking his head. "She just showed us how everything works and what we're s'posed to be lookin' for, all day, every day." He wandered over past the TV, running his hand along the base, then stopped and turned to Jensen. "But I did stare at her ass whenever she was lookin' at the computer screens."

"Whatever you do, don't try to hook up with her." Jensen stepped toward Vance. "She may be smoking hot, but she'll probably shoot you in the face if you try anything. I imagine she deals with a lot of stupid, horny men."

"Yeah, whatever." Vance shrugged and headed toward one of the beds. "She's kinda different looking, and she gives off this weird vibe when she gets close to me, so I just made a joke about this operation being run by demons and she got all serious." His hand slowly moved to his neck before he scratched at the stubble. "She told me that it is, and that she is. But I'm not totally sure if that was a joke or not."

"Well then, definitely keep your distance from her." Jensen's serious expression only lasted a few seconds before he burst out laughing, finally letting go of his worries.

"Don't be a dick. I'm serious. I think she might be an actual demon," Vance said, sitting on the bed.

"Well, if that's the case, we should *not* be staying here and working for them. But that shit can't really be real… can it?" he said as his eyes drifted to the ceiling. *Demons don't exist; these guys are just really evil people with a lot of power, like the mob or a biker gang. But… none of those organizations had enough power to close down the prisons.*

"I don't know." Vance looked away. "I guess we'll have to wait and see if they do anything… anything demony."

"Demony? Really? Like what?"

"I don't know. Shoot fire from their eyes."

Both men chuckled.

"Well, I'll see if anything out of the ordinary happens when I'm cooking your dinner for the next two hours," Jensen said, moving to the door.

Sauntering along the hallway on his way to the kitchen, Jensen passed several doors, some closed and others open, with the room's occupants sitting on sofas, drinking beer and shouting at their TVs. A few of the bedrooms were vacant, or had suitcases packed and waiting to be retrieved.

At the far end of the hall, Celista stepped out of a room and marched toward him, both, apparently, en route to the kitchen. But just short of the kitchen she glared at him, then whipped around the corner, a ring of keys she held in one hand jangling together, and strode toward one of the mahogany doors near the main entrance. Jensen slowed to watch her. She grew increasingly agitated as she tried key after key on the large ring; finally the bolt clunked open and she disappeared through the doorway.

He shrugged and went to join the others in the kitchen.

With five guys helping in the kitchen, the meal was easy to prepare. An entire pig was roasting on the barbeque just outside, on the patio. The smell that drifted in through an open window made Jensen salivate. Someone else had taken care of the potatoes, prison-style—a vegetable peeler sat atop a pile of potato skins, lying in long curls on a piece of newspaper in front of a chair, and the quartered potatoes were already in a large pot of water. All he had to do was chop and boil some carrots. *Maybe this kitchen duty thing isn't going to be so bad after all.*

When everything was prepared, the kitchen crew dropped it off in the dining room, where some men had already gathered, and returned to the kitchen. The kitchen had to be cleaned before the cooks were allowed to eat, Jensen had been told. Washing dishes while people kept filing past the kitchen on the way to their dinner was torture for a hungry man looking forward to finally having a home-cooked meal. As more and more voices filtered in from the dining room, Jensen rushed to finish his chores. There was still plenty of food left on the table when he finally sat down and dished up a plateful.

He was almost finished scarfing down slabs of pork dipped in mashed potatoes swimming in gravy when Celista stomped into the room with a ferocious look on her face. She grabbed Jensen by his forearm and jerked him to face her.

"You, take these keys," she thrust the keys into his dangling hand, "and go feed the bitch in the basement."

"Wha—who? What basement?"

She huffed. "The door on the left side of the entry leads to the basement. Just follow the crybaby's sobs and give her a plate of food." She let go of his arm. "Don't forget some water, and *whatever* you do, don't unlock her cell. Make sure you lock the basement door back up again when you're done."

"Yes, ma'am," he said as she turned away in a wave of white hair. She left the dining room without looking back.

Jensen rose from the table just as Vance wandered in. "Hey man, is dinner over already?"

"It's been almost an hour. Everyone is going to start packing up, but I guess they always put any leftovers in the fridge for whoever wants to eat it later," Jensen told him.

"Oh, I better grab a plate now." Vance shoved a chunk of pork into his mouth. "What are you doing now? Do you wanna eat with me?"

"I just finished. The hot chick told me to... get this." He leaned over the table and whispered, "Feed the girl that's locked up in the basement."

"What?" Vance mumbled through his mouthful. "They have some kind of prisoner? Is she hot?" he asked, absently spooning food onto his plate, eyes on Jensen's face.

"You're an ass." He plopped a massive scoop of potatoes onto a clean plate and followed with carrots. "Why the fuck do they have someone locked up here, is the better question."

"That's what I meant. I wonder who she is and why she's here."

Jensen shrugged. "Who knows. But I'm going to find out." He looked down at the plate. He stabbed his fork into the pile of pork and added a slab to the plate, then picked it up. "Later."

Stopping by the kitchen, he grabbed a couple of water bottles from the fridge, then headed down to the basement.

The staircase descended deep underground, much farther down than the depth of a regular basement. The air was damp and musty. He stepped off the last stair into a corridor lit by a dull orange glow that didn't reach the shadows along the high ceiling. The demon chick was wrong about one thing—he couldn't follow the sobbing, as it was totally silent, except for the sound of his footsteps echoing off the cold concrete walls. He passed several open doors that revealed large, open rooms, all with the odd chair or table as the only furniture. When he peered inside some he saw floor drains and dried blood spatter. A couple of the rooms had shackles mounted to the walls, and one contained an enormous tank filled with water.

He eventually entered the holding cell area. Here the barred doors were all closed, even though they were currently empty of occupants—until he reached the fifth cell in the cell block. A woman with short blonde hair lay asleep on a mattress on the floor, curled into a fetal position and wrapped in old, torn blankets.

Jensen examined the wall of bars in front of him, then looked at the heaping plate of food in his hand. That wasn't going to slide under the bars. Celista had told him not to open the door, but the prisoner was just a girl, and she was sleeping. Even if she woke up and attacked him, he was sure he could handle her.

He reached through the bars and set the water bottles down on the grimy floor before thumbing through the key ring, looking for the ones that likely unlocked the cell doors. There was a cluster of similar keys with different numbers engraved on them. *Probably these.* He slid the first one into the door and jiggled it. *Nope.*

As he tried the second key the girl sat up and pushed herself back against the wall.

"Hi," he said, looking up at her. "Sorry. I didn't mean to wake you. I-I just brought you some dinner."

She stared at him. "Why are you coming in here?"

He held up her dinner. "The plate won't fit under the bars. I guess I got a little carried away. I'm not going to hurt you, I promise."

She cocked her head. "I've never seen you before. What happened to the other guy?"

Jensen shrugged. "I don't know. I was just told to bring you some food and water." He tried the next key. "Why are you down here?"

"I don't know. They won't tell me." She sighed, twirling a ring around on her finger.

"How long have you been in here?"

"I don't know; a couple, three weeks maybe." She stood and started toward him. "It's hard to tell time without daylight."

The lock clunked heavily. "Okay, I'm coming in, so just stay back a second." He swung the door open and stepped inside. "Hope you're hungry. I kind of overloaded your plate." He held out the plate in both hands, his eyes locked on hers.

She was dirty from head to toe, but her bright blue eyes still sparkled. She was about five foot eight, slender—nothing about her seemed threatening or dangerous. She was amazingly beautiful, considering she was in desperate need of a shower.

When she reached for the plate her fingers brushed his, and a spark of static electricity jolted them both.

"Thank you. No one has ever brought me this much food." She went back to the mattress and sat down with the plate on her lap. "They don't even feed me every day."

"What? Are you serious?" He retrieved the bottles of water from the floor. "I'm Jensen. Who are you?"

"Jezabelle," she mumbled through a mouthful of food, covering her mouth with her hand.

He sat down beside her and set the bottles at her feet. She dug into her food like he was about to steal it from her. Pausing with the metal fork in one hand, she guzzled some water, her eyes drifting over to the open cell door. She set the bottle down and stared at the pathway to freedom.

"Are you okay?" Jensen asked.

She turned her head toward him. Her face was inches from his. She tightened her grip on her fork. "Please help me," she whispered, her eyes desperate.

He wanted to help her. He wanted to touch her sad face and make her happy again. "How?"

She relaxed her grip on the fork. "I need to get out of here or I'm going to die."

"There's guys everywhere all the time, and we're in the middle of nowhere. Even if I could get you out of the house without being seen, I don't even know where we are. I couldn't tell you how to get away from here."

"I need to try. It's better than dying in this cell." She tilted her head down and looked up at him with big doe eyes full of sadness.

Jensen shook his head. "They'd know it was me and they would kill me."

"Then come with me."

Her hand brushed his arm and for a moment he enjoyed the thought of running away with her, then he remembered Vance. "I can't. I have a friend here. They might kill him, too."

Her hand tightened on her fork. "I'm leaving, with or without your help." She lunged at him.

He reached out for her wrist as they tumbled across the mattress, her forgotten plate scattering food. She got on top of him, using all of her body weight to hold him down while she lifted the fork above her head with both hands to stab him. It was hopeless; did she really think she could overpower him? He held her wrist in one hand and pulled the fork free of her grip with the other, tossing it aside. He rolled her over on her back and pinned her down with his body, careful not to crush her, and secured her wrists above her head. She squirmed briefly before she surrendered, breathing hard. He felt her chest touch his each time she inhaled. As she calmed, he loosened his grip.

She smiled and his clenched teeth relaxed into a grin. He leaned in and kissed her. Releasing her wrists, he moved his hands underneath her. She ran her fingers through his hair before pulling him deeper into her mouth. Her legs wrapped around him and she melted beneath him.

Jensen drew back. "I'll get you out of here, I promise. Just give me some time to figure out how," he whispered.

Chapter Nineteen

The flat surface of the boulder had been polished to a smooth glimmer that reflected the image of the fields surrounding it. The reflection rippled from the center as long, slender fingers pushed out through the rock. A bubble of energy exploded outward, flattening the grass and leaving an indent in the ground surrounding the boulder.

Kyra emerged from the boulder and collapsed onto the ground; Alastor trailed behind her, holding her hand.

"Damn it, Alastor, this is getting ridiculous." She jerked her hand away from his.

"We are nearly finished," he said, standing over her.

"I'm exhausted. I can't go through another plane. I need to rest." She glared up at him. "You never told me the doors would be scattered around the globe."

"The goal remains to locate the eggs and return here, then you can rest."

"Are you deaf?" she exclaimed, gaping up at him. "I said I can't do it. We did three plane jumps to get here so it will be three home, unless there is some shortcut you know about." She eyed him suspiciously. She was growing tired of him keeping things from her until the last minute. She liked to know what was going on in advance, so she could prepare herself for it.

"No shortcuts. But it will be less of a struggle to return." He brushed off his shoulders, eyes wandering over the fields.

"We fought the natural current of the doorways, going through Atlantis first; it was like swimming upstream. It would have been less arduous going through the ghost plane, but there are four stops that way. I wanted to save time."

"Are you shitting me?" She pulled her hair back and swirled it around in a bun, wishing she had a hair tie, before she dropped the pile of hair behind her shoulders. "We should have gone the longer way. I don't want to deal with any more stupid, annoying creatures."

"Every plane has its own annoying creature." He held out his hand to help her off the ground.

"Great. Let's go the other way home," she said, ignoring his attempt to get her moving.

"That would be pointless, darling." He dropped his hand and focused on her face, looking vaguely concerned—or maybe he was just trying to mask his impatience and annoyance at her probing him. "It would still be fighting the current, and we would have to deal with bloodsucking creatures that would be particularly interested in your human flesh."

"Bloodsuckers? Like what, vampires?"

Alastor grunted. "Yes, and werewolves, among other things." He extended his hand toward her again and flapped his fingers, urging her to rise.

"Vampires!" She slapped his hand away and saw his jaw tighten. "Why didn't we just grab a handful of them and unleash them on humanity? They'd cause great devastation and chaos." She knew she was irritating him but she didn't care. He needed her and she wasn't going to follow orders blindly, like Celista, anymore. She had the right to know what his plans were and how he intended to carry them out.

"Yes, but they have limitations," he said through clenched teeth. "Dragons are virtually indestructible; humans cannot kill or tame them. They have to be black dragons, for poetic symmetry. They are the third seal."

"What? Isn't the third seal supposed to be famine?"

"Yes. They will cause famine by burning the crops and eating the livestock. Humans will have a difficult time harvesting whatever is left, with dragons flying around hunting for their dinner."

"Fine." She crossed her arms. "I'll wait here and you go get a dragon or an egg or whatever, then we can go."

"Kyra darling, you are behaving like a spoiled child. We need only stroll a short distance and we shall find what we came for. Our powers are strongest together."

She sighed as she picked herself up and took in the new landscape. They stood in a bowl-shaped depression, the grass in their immediate area flattened from their arrival and a dirt trail leading away through the tall grass. She turned slowly in a full circle. A breeze shifted the long green grass in waves. A herd of wild horses grazed the endless sea of green. An unremarkable forest stood in the distance, with a few trees dotting the plain farther away.

"These worlds are all the same."

"What did you expect?" Alastor said. "They were all the same place, once. The differences are created by the creatures living in that plane. Earth is destroyed, but it's to be expected, with creatures of such limited... abilities."

"So, where do you suppose a dragon lives? In the mountains?" she asked, looking at the ragged purple line of a mountain range on the horizon beyond the forest. "Can you use your powers to get a couple of those horses to take us up there?" She nodded toward the animals grazing in the distance. "I don't want to take us; I want to conserve my strength."

He let out a laugh. "Those aren't horses, and we would not be able to control them."

"What are they?" She squinted toward the animals. "They look like horses to me."

"Pegasi or unicorns; we are too far away to tell. And dragons do not reside in caves. They live in nests."

"A nest? What, like in a tree?"

He snorted. "On the ground. They are the most dangerous wild creatures in existence simply because they are a carnivorous species that lives without fear or predators."

"So how do you plan to control them on Earth?"

"I have no intention of controlling them. When they hatch they will head out in search of fresh meat even as the people turn on each other, and the world will burn."

***

Hooves pounded along the riverbank as the demon sprinted over the rocky terrain, moving faster than a cheetah past the grove of trees. Alastor's wings flapped open and he took off into the sky, a trail of liquid fire following his path. Screeches echoed through the hills, uttered between bursts of flame that shot from the mouth of the massive white dragon pursuing the demon up the river.

Whatever he did, it certainly angered the dragon, Kyra thought, watching.

The two creatures darted around a distant bend in the river and disappeared behind the hills. Kyra melted away from the tree that she had infused herself into, and ran in the direction from which the dragon had come.

She slowed her pace as she came upon a structure made of logs—no, she amended, trees, whole, huge trees—and mud. It reminded her of a cross between a beaver dam and a bird's nest, though it was larger than her old house. The top of the nest was five feet high; she couldn't see over the side to see if there were any eggs inside.

She leapt upward and glided over the wall to land softly inside the bowl-shaped nest. There—seven eggs against the near wall. They were smaller than she expected, only three feet high and two feet wide; tiny compared to their enraged mother. They sparkled in the sunlight: two blue, three black, one red, and one purple. Alastor wanted four—they would have to find another nest. Maybe the purple was dark enough for him to accept, she thought—but she knew he wouldn't.

She glanced around the sky, listening to the silence before she turned back to the eggs. She lifted her hands and the three black ones rose from their resting place; the others shifted into the empty space. The glittering black eggs drifted over the wall and Kyra levitated after them, gliding quickly over the hills on the way back to the gateway home.

Chapter Twenty

They walked the long path to the holding cells, the eggs floating along in front of Alastor as Kyra followed behind.

"Why can you use my powers down here and I can't?" she asked.

"I never put up anything that blocks the powers of a demon."

"Oh, what blocks powers?" She stopped, crossing her arms.

He turned and looked her in the eye, his face serious. "Not your concern."

Kyra sighed and followed after him to the empty cells.

Alastor unlocked the first cell door. They went in and he gently set the eggs on the mattress on the floor.

"It's oddly quiet down here, don't you think?" She motioned toward the cells farther down the hall.

"Indeed."

"She might have died from malnutrition or dehydration," she said, stepping out of the cell. "I'm going to check it out." She stepped out into the hall. Alastor locked the cell before following her.

"Well, is she dead?" he called out to her, knowing that she couldn't be.

Kyra whipped around the corner, back into Alastor's view. "Worse. She's gone," she said, approaching him.

"*Whaaaat?*" he roared.

Kyra stiffened and bit her lip. "What does this mean?" she asked, avoiding his eyes. "What's going to happen now?"

"She is a threat."

Her body relaxed and she moved toward him. "Oh, please; how can she be a threat? We are the most powerful things on this planet."

"Perhaps she may not be a threat alone, but there could be serious repercussions. I have come too far for this to crumble now."

Kyra scowled. "That fucking bitch Celista was supposed to be taking care of Jezabelle. She probably killed her and dumped the body. She was pissed about being left behind."

"She would never dare to defy me," Alastor said, his eyes darkening into black orbs of anger. *And, Celista is not able to kill her anymore than I.*

Kyra's eyebrows drew together as she pursed her lips. "What do you mean, she..." Alastor glared at her. "I mean, where did Jezabelle go then, if she's not dead?"

"A head is going to roll for this," he said, ignoring Kyra. "Get the men to scour the grounds immediately. I have a hellspawn to find."

Alastor traveled Kyra to one of the servant bedrooms before he appeared in a flash of light in the hallway in front of the sitting room, blocking Celista's path. Without fear or hesitation, she morphed into the manipulative siren and flipped her fingers through her hair, her chest thrust forward, a provocative smile on her lips.

The house was quiet, everyone sleeping. Then he heard Kyra yelling and saw lights flicking on in the bedrooms. Kyra emerged from one and strode across the hall into the next bedroom and repeated the process.

Celista glided down the dimly lit hallway toward him and he braced his arms on either wall, blocking her path. His eyes narrowed as she approached.

"Celista, explain."

"Somehow she escaped." She shrugged, looking away. "There was only one guy that I sent down there. I already questioned him and he's telling the truth about not letting her out." Her eyes found his face. "I've questioned everyone. No one is missing and the keys are where they should be. I don't have an answer."

"Someone has to pay for this, and I left you in charge."

"I'll find her and I'll find who's responsible for this, with your help." She fluttered her eyelashes.

"It should have already been resolved," he said through clenched teeth. "When is the last time you saw her?"

"The day you left." She slid up beside him. "And then last night I went down and found her missing." She placed her hands on his outstretched biceps.

"She went missing at some interval in the last twenty-four to ninety-six hours?" He let out a deep howl of rage and shook her hands off him. "I should pulverize you."

"You know, I would like that." She pressed up against him and slid her hand into his pants. "I have a much better idea to clear your head."

"Old siren tricks to escape my wrath, I see."

"It always worked before; you know you love it." She looked up at him and grinned.

He grabbed the back of her head, twisting her neck to an unnatural angle. His mouth came down on her neck, his fangs lengthening, and he bit her. Blood trickled from the punctures into the corners of his lips before he moved off her. She dug her claws into his flesh, tearing his shirt. Blood dripped from both of them as he released her.

They stood there, panting, their blood dripping onto the floor, and stared into each other's eyes. She leapt into his arms and he welcomed her. Her legs wrapped around his waist as they devoured each other, their claws and teeth breaking skin and drawing more blood.

Celista's head jerked backward. Alastor pulled back, surprised and confused. Her head jerked back again, the force pulling her whole body with it. Alastor released her and she fell to the floor with a loud thud. Celista looked up to see a pissed-off Kyra standing over her, glaring.

"Who the hell do you think you are?" Kyra demanded. Celista groaned, rolling her eyes, and picked herself up, brushing herself off. "How dare you use your powers on Alastor?"

"I don't need to use my powers with Alastor; he wants it on his own." Celista smiled smugly. "He's always preferred *me* over any other, for millennia."

"You're fucking dead." Kyra raised her arms. The earth trembled beneath their feet. The hallway vibrated and hummed as jagged cracks cut through the drywall. Books and lamps crashed to the floor in the rooms around them. Celista rolled her eyes, laughing at Kyra's anger.

"Kyra, stop." Alastor edged closer to her. "We need her. She has a huge role in my—our plans."

"Get someone else." Kyra jabbed a finger at Celista. "I want this bitch dead."

"You can't kill me, you stupid witch." Celista flipped her hair. "I am a demon."

"Is that a challenge?" Kyra dropped her arms, her nostrils flaring.

"Enough!" Alastor slammed his fists down on an invisible surface.

"If I do kill her you can just resurrect her from Hell again—or maybe bring back someone more useful," Kyra said, her hate-filled eyes locked on Celista.

He shook his head. "It takes a great deal of power to pull someone up from Hell." He stepped between the two women, facing Kyra. "As the world grows in darkness I gain more power, but it weakens me to bring others here; the trip through the planes has taken a toll on me, as well." He caressed Kyra's cheek, tilting her face to look up at him. "I have already set the plan in motion for who shall be next, and I cannot afford any setbacks from ridiculous female jealousy."

Kyra let out a cry of frustration and pulled away from his hands. "Fine. I won't kill her on one condition."

"Name it."

"Alastor, don't be crazy." Celista rolled her eyes. "She can't kill me, I'm more powerful than her. And since when do you negotiate—"

"Hold your tongue," he barked, shooting her a warning look before he faced Kyra. "What is your demand?"

"I want her out of this house—permanently. And I don't want you to have any sexual contact with her, ever again. She's your past. I am your future."

"Done."

"What!" Celista gaped at him. "You can't banish me. I have been by your side for thousands of years."

"Those days are over. And be grateful you are on Earth and not in Hell," Alastor said, watching her face, hoping that she understood. "Now go."

She turned and stormed off, her hair swishing behind her. She paused before turning the corner to look back at Alastor and Kyra. Kyra flashed a tight smile and flipped up her middle finger. Celista glared back at her before stomping off into the foyer.

Chapter Twenty-One

Jezabelle stumbled through the forest in the predawn darkness, hampered by the heavy, mud-soaked hem of her dress, which kept wrapping around her knees, and bare feet that were cut and bruised. The morning mist hung heavy in the air and settled as dew on the long grass, which also clung to her legs like a thousand grasping green tentacles. Moonlight filtered through the canopy, casting pools of wan light and shadow over her path; the overhead branches blocked sight of the moon itself.

She had been on the run for hours. The sun would be up soon and she knew she had to put as much distance between her and that house as she could. She had chosen to head in the direction opposite the driveway, dashing instead across a field behind the house to the treeline. No roads in this direction. Creeks and rocky gullies, yes, but no sign of civilization yet. Maybe she should have chanced the road.

She shook her head. *No point making it too easy for them. That would be the first place they look.* She needed to find a car and leave this nightmare in the dust before anyone noticed her cell was empty.

The demon—and Kyra—had imprisoned her for a reason; she had to find out why. She knew where she was going to start looking for answers. She just had to get her hands on a car.

***

After a week of escalating street violence, the vice president declared martial law. Grocery stores were being ransacked in broad daylight. Store security couldn't control the sheer volume of thefts. Some of the stores tried to cut their losses and close, but that just gave thieves free rein and kept the honest people out of the way.

After the supermarket invasions, the supply and hardware stores became madhouses, as people swept items from the shelves, trying to stock up on supplies to get them through these uncertain times. Who knew when things would return to normal—or if they ever would? And facing an impending apocalypse, did it really matter whether they paid for the goods they took?

Public parks had turned into campgrounds for the new homeless—both former convicts and people driven from their homes by record-high home invasions and break-ins; squatters took up residence in the abandoned homes. The 911 operators couldn't keep up with the calls. All firefighters, police and health care professions were on twenty-four hour duty with first responders patrolling vigilantly to solve or prevent problems. The National Guard had been mobilized and a call for volunteers to aid with the chaos in any way they could had been sent out via media channels; that had been a great success in the beginning, but as the violence worsened, volunteers dwindled.

The public had been told to stay off the streets if they could. Despite the mid-August heat, kids no longer played in the parks and playgrounds. Their parents watched the constant breaking news bulletins on TV. Deadbolts were added to doors and main floor windows were boarded up. Husbands patrolled their homes and yards with shotguns. Very few people still ventured out to go to work. The risk of not coming home after a day at the office was too great.

As the late afternoon sun moved across the sky, Alexis and Axel walked down the center of the street, surveying the damage. Broken glass glittered on the pavement and sidewalks. The odd car was on fire and abandoned shopping carts lay flipped on their sides in the middle of streets barren of traffic, save for military vehicles.

In a few hours the vice president's speech would begin in a live televised broadcast. They expected that Kyra and Alastor would be in attendance—it was an important address and would be hugely publicized, so how could they resist? Alexis and Axel had volunteered to scout the area and find a way to acquire press passes to get everyone inside the building.

They arrived at the White House pressroom and were redirected to another area where the Secret Service were preparing a larger room for the press conference for tonight. An outdoor event had been deemed insecure so they were under the false assumption that staging an indoor, press pass-only event would be more secure and controllable.

Axel veered off toward the young reporter from Channel Five who was carrying a handful of press passes. Alexis waited, looking around. There were guys walking up on the catwalk above her head. Men were combing through the building while others were setting up rows of chairs in front of the stage opposite the entrance. Cables and cords clustered up near the stage were being checked over, with security men watching every move in the room.

Axel returned with four passes in hand, grinning.

"I'm impressed. That was fast work," Alexis said.

"She only had four but that will get the job done. The others will have to stay behind. See anything important?" Axel asked, glancing around.

"Nothing that stands out. Why do they keep repeating the same process for security? It's like an open invite for the demon. Haven't they figured out he likes to make a spectacle?" she said dryly.

"People are stupid. They're all sheep." He chuckled.

She shot him a withering look. "Are you sure you're not on the wrong side? Let's get out of here; we have one more stop to make."

"Nathan?"

Alexis nodded.

***

A woman relaxed at a small round café table on the empty patio, sipping espresso in the mid-afternoon sun. Dark, oversize round sunglasses hid her eyes. Tendrils of her vibrant red hair framed her face and spiraled loosely down her back. She leaned back in her chair and crossed her slender legs, watching occasional pedestrians scurrying by.

Colleen clumsily slipped into the chair across from the redhead, dropping her oversized purse onto the ground beside the table.

"This better be something worthwhile. I rushed all this way," she said, her eyes darting around the empty streets.

Without so much as a glance toward Colleen, the redhead pushed a press pass across the table with her fingers, still holding the espresso cup with the other.

Colleen frowned down at it. "What am I supposed to do with this? I don't give two hoots about the statements or Q and A session tonight."

Red turned to face her, tipping her head down to peer over the top of her shades, revealing her electric blue eyes.

"Are you dense? Kyra will make an appearance." She shrugged. "But it's up to you, what you do with that."

Colleen glowered. "My husband is dead because of her. She deserves the same."

Red pulled a crumpled brown paper bag from her Gucci purse and set it gently on the table. Colleen reached for it and peeked inside. She looked up at Red.

"How am I going to get this in the building?"

"Keep everything together in the bag and it won't be detectable. Remember, you have to get close to her for it to work."

Colleen nodded and closed up the bag. She stuffed it in her purse before grabbing the press pass. Her chair whined in protest as it scraped back along the cement. She stood, nodded, and waddled away. The redhead rolled her eyes and groaned before returning to her coffee.

***

The priest, Alexis, James, and Axel walked through the main doors with their passes around their necks. Most of the reporters had already filled the seats close to the stage, eager eyes on the raised platform, awaiting the vice president. The security detail stood around the perimeter of the room, stance poised-casual, eyes constantly scanning the crowd.

Axel surveyed the ceiling; there were snipers on the catwalk, also continuously scanning the crowd.

"They didn't even try to hide the snipers this time."

His gaze drifted to the fiery redhead leaning against the wall. She smiled at him and winked. He returned the smile and chuckled to himself.

Alexis caught his distraction and elbowed him, hitting the buckle on his jacket.

"We aren't here to pick up chicks." She glowered, rubbing her elbow. "Pay attention or we could all end up dead."

"As long as I'm not the one that ends up shot, I'll be happy." Axel smiled at his sister.

"This better work. Our variation of the plan, I mean. We're risking a lot, doing this on a live broadcast for the world to see," she whispered to Axel.

"It will. And if it doesn't the world will end soon enough anyway, so it won't much matter."

They made their way down the carpeted aisle to the front of the crowd; with no seats open, they joined those leaning against the wall near the stage.

"I should go blend into the crowd somewhere, I guess," Alexis said after slipping Axel a tiny, flat piece of plastic. "Good luck, you guys." She kissed her brother on the cheek and whispered into his ear, "Make sure it's hidden."

"Thanks, tips," he said sarcastically.

"Grrr." She playfully squinted an eye at him.

"Where are you going?" James asked.

"I'm going to head over to the other side and find a seat so she doesn't see us all together," Alexis responded casually.

A security man approached them. "I'm going to have to ask you all to find a seat."

Alexis put her hand on his arm. "Sure, sweetheart. Just give us a minute alone."

The man smiled and walked away.

"Okay, remember to stick to the plan and improvise when necessary. Hopefully this will work," Father Thomas said.

"At least we know the demon can't kill us," offered Axel.

"Yes, well, not permanently, anyway," James grumbled. "It still was unpleasant dying temporarily."

"Well, let's try not to get killed today," Axel countered.

"Father, if you would please come with me, I'll help you find a seat near the aisle." Alexis smiled and headed around the front row of chairs.

He nodded and turned to Axel and James. "Good luck, and have faith."

Alexis cleared a seat two seats in from the center aisle as the priest caught up to her. After a brief exchange he smiled, placed his hands on her shoulders, then moved to his seat. Then she went to the far side of the room and made her way down the aisle. She leaned over a seated man and whispered in his ear; he stood and sought an open seat near the back of the room. Alexis smiled at the people next to her as she sidled into the seat.

The chatter died away as an aide took the stage and announced the vice president.

The door at the rear of the pressroom burst open. Alastor stood in the doorway. Dressed in a sharp black suit and tie, he looked like he was about to attend a wedding... *Or a funeral,* Axel thought. The camera crews pivoted around to him as the photographers started snapping away.

"I never received my invitation, but I assume I was expected." He started down the carpeted aisle.

"Halt!" an FBI agent shouted as he drew his sidearm.

Alastor flicked his wrist and the agent slammed back against the wall. Another flick of the wrist and the snipers fell from the catwalk. People scrambled to move out of the way, knocking over chairs and stepping on each other. Screams erupted when the bodies struck the audience. Chairs flew and more people were knocked over.

On the stage, the Secret Service hustled the vice president toward the stage exit.

Snap. Snap. Snap.

Crack.

Boom.

The boom was amplified in the enclosed area, ricocheting from wall to wall. A blinding flash of lightning followed, and Kyra stood in the faint ring of smoke it left behind. Clad in a low-cut crimson red cocktail dress that hugged her every curve, with bright red lips to match, for a moment it was as if she were a flame rising from the ring of smoke. Big, thick waves of her luscious dark hair framed her chest.

The security men opened fire. The rapid-fire gunshots rang around the room. She stood motionless, her eyes narrowed and her hands on her hips.

As the bullets dissolved into thin air, the vice president yelled for the men to stop shooting. They ceased fire after the third shout, but barely lowered their weapons. Kyra tilted her head down, her eyes locked on her targets. Screams, quickly cut off, escaped the security men as they simultaneously evaporated, leaving the vice president standing alone.

Father Thomas rose and stepped into the aisle facing Alastor. Clearing his throat, he held up a crucifix and started whispering prayers.

Axel elbowed James. He lifted himself slightly from his seat and, crouching low, they made their way to the aisle near the wall. He glanced back to the priest after they stood up next to the wall. Alastor was still casually approaching Father Thomas. The demon and everyone in the room were focused on the priest. All the cameras in the room had turned toward them. Everyone, including Kyra, watched and waited.

Axel and James moved quickly and silently toward the stage.

Alastor strode up to the priest before cutting a grin. "You think a little prayer and a crucifix can stop me? Ignorant, foolish old man."

The crucifix started to glow red. The priest's hand began to tremble, then shake. The crucifix burst into flames and he dropped it.

"You don't belong here, demon!" Father Thomas shouted. "Go back to where you came from."

Alastor threw his head back and laughed. "Did you honestly believe that would accomplish anything? This world is in transition. Soon it will all be mine."

"I may not be able to stop you, but good always conquers evil," the priest threw back.

"That delusion was constructed by humanity for their peace of mind. You and I know the truth." Alastor glanced over the fascinated spectators' faces, then raised his voice. "Have you any desire to know the truth about the good and evil in this world?" The crowd remained silent. "Good does not triumph over evil; they are in a perfect balance all the time."

"He lies like the demon he is," Father Thomas growled, turning and looking over the room. "He means to frighten us and lead us to believe there is no hope to defeat him." He turned back to the demon. "God will help us rid the Earth of you."

"Foolish old man... God will not be coming to save you. There is no hope."

"There is always hope, and it rests with the angel you stole." He pointed to Kyra on the stage.

Chapter Twenty-Two

The heads in the crowd turned toward the stage. Axel and James were by Kyra's side, each holding one of her hands and trying to talk to her. Her eyes darted back and forth, looking distracted and overwhelmed.

"Kyra!" Alastor called.

Kyra shook her hands free of theirs and pushed James and Axel back with quick flicks of her wrists. James crept closer to her and kept talking. Axel moved away from them and searched the crowd for his sister.

Alastor's eyes narrowed, darkness swirling inside them. Father Thomas pulled his rosary from his pocket and stepped back. The demon's eyes were solid black by the time the priest knelt and started praying.

Alexis kept casting as she watched the angry demon walk up behind the priest and reach for the back of his neck.

James continued, "You've lost so much already, darling: your job—" She snickered. "Your home—"

She cut him off. "I live in a castle."

Axel swung around and met Kyra's eyes. "So you do still have the ability to speak."

She grinned. "Jealous that it was to him?" She pointed to James with her thumb.

"Nope." He faced James. "Keep doing what you're doing; I think you're making progress."

Kyra's eyes narrowed as Axel turned his back on her again.

"Kyra, what about the people that love you, your friends and family... Xavier and I need you. We can't lose you."

She flinched before looking at James, her expression soft. She stepped closer to him and touched his face with the back of her hand.

"What is this!" Alastor bellowed.

Alastor's outburst centered Kyra's focus back on him and the priest.

"Witch trickery to give hope to the humans?" Alastor said. His outstretched hands quivered with effort, but they could not reach the priest. Prayers poured from his lips. "It is all for not, I am Alastor, the demon from Hell."

Kyra whipped her arm out and James flew from the stage. She walked up behind Axel and grabbed his bicep, flinging him around to face her.

"What are you up to on this stage, my dear Axel? You've had your back turned to me for too long now. You haven't lost interest in me now, have you?" She frowned.

"You always have my interest, babe." He winked.

Kyra pushed past him to search the audience. Axel started coughing loudly and clearing his throat. Kyra turned back to him and raised an eyebrow.

"Really? Wow."

She turned back to the seats. "That is witch magic and we are missing just one witch... Come out, come out, wherever you are... *Alexis.*"

Kyra found her and raised her arm, holding her palm toward Alexis. Alexis's chair began to slide over the floor toward the stage. Axel grabbed Kyra's waist and lifted her off her feet. Alexis stopped casting, stood, and flung her arms open toward the stage. Kyra flew from his arms and crashed into the back wall of the stage.

Alastor made a sound not far from a growl. Axel rushed toward the fallen Kyra. Alexis sought out the priest, but she was too late. Alastor lunged toward the priest, grabbing his head with both hands. Blood seeped out of Father Thomas's ears as the demon squeezed his skull, crushing it between his hands.

Snap. Snap. Crunch. Groaning, then a pop like a burst watermelon as Father Thomas's skull gave way to the pressure. His lifeless body toppled to the floor, eyes bulging from their sockets.

Screams erupted from those closest as they scrambled away from the demon. His eyes still black, he stalked toward the stage.

James crawled back up onto the stage. Kyra pushed Axel's hands away and leapt to the front of the platform to stare down at her former friend.

"Bad, Alexis. That was very foolish of you."

"Kyra, wait." Axel touched her arm. "Do you know what you are now? Do you know what he is doing to you?"

"Yes. I'm the most powerful witch on Earth." She jerked her arm away.

"Kyra, you're the melhara. You are part witch and part angel. *Angel*, Kyra, not demon. He has turned you to evil. Remember your dreams. Angels fight demons, they don't join them."

She didn't hide her surprise very well before she looked to Alastor for confirmation. He shook his head. "Lies, darling."

She threw Axel to the floor with her glare. He slid up the center aisle, bunching the carpet before him. Kyra whipped around toward Alexis.

Alexis raised her hands. The air in the room whirled, faster and faster, tighter and tighter. Papers and video equipment spun inside the tornado as it grew. Alexis's colors streaked into the tornado like the strokes of a mad painter as she faded into the wind. The wind carried her to the stage before she became visible again.

Kyra's hair whirled around her face. She put her palm out and the air around her grew still. She flipped her head and her hair whipped away from her face. Her eyes went white. She moved her arms up toward the ceiling and the building rumbled violently.

Pieces of the ceiling broke free and crashed down around them. Chunks of concrete and rebar exploded on the floor. Smaller pieces crumbled on the stage as they landed, and a few larger ones burst through the wooden floor of the stage. Splinters flew into the air.

Reporters moved farther away from the stage, backing toward the far wall as they continued filming and taking pictures.

Alexis continued her approach. Kyra stepped toward her with one hand outstretched and the other pointed to the hole in the ceiling. Her eyes again went white as she squeezed her hand.

Alexis's movement slowed, her steps were stolen from her; her raised foot hovered a moment before slowly drifting to the floor. The whirlwind ceased. Everything in the air dropped to the floor. Alexis struggled to break free from Kyra's control; she dropped to her knees as Kyra came down on her.

"Nice try." Kyra grabbed Alexis by her shoulders. "Bad, bad, bad. You shouldn't misuse your powers," she scolded, shaking her. "Especially on someone who is stronger than you."

"Kyra, please. Please come back to us. Let's send this demon back to Hell together." Alexis stared into her white-glazed eyes, searching for something—anything—that she could recognize as her friend.

Kyra held her tight and flung her head back. Alexis thrashed around in her grip. Axel rushed the stage and leaped onto the four foot high platform, rolling out of his landing. Kyra dropped Alexis to glare at him. The seizure stopped, and

Alexis rolled away from her. Kyra's eyes returned to their normal emerald green and she stared at Axel, who stopped and returned the hard stare.

A bolt of lightning crashed through the hole in the ceiling, electrifying the air. Flames erupted to coil around Kyra.

"Enough! You're interfering with our task." She smacked her hands together. Axel and Alexis vanished from the room.

The flames settled and snuffed out.

***

"You!" Kyra said, pointing to the vice president. "I've run out of patience for the day."

Alastor stepped up, glaring at Kyra with his black eyes. He bared his teeth, revealing long fangs, and his fingertips began to elongate into claws. Kyra backed down and moved to the side of the stage. James followed Kyra to the front corner of the stage and the vice president focused on the demon as he morphed back into human form.

"No second chances," Alastor barked. "You are to immediately disband the military, police force, FBI, CIA, Homeland Security, and anything else of that nature."

"No. It's impossible," the man protested.

"You will do it or join your predecessor… and your family will have the same fate as his did." Alastor turned slightly to face the cameras. "Anyone caught on duty will be killed on sight. I have no tolerance left for disobedience."

When James tried to speak to Kyra, she held up her hand. His lips moved but no sound came out. She watched Alastor intensely. The silent words from James's mouth slowly became audible. Baffled, she looked over to him and glimpsed a figure approaching behind her.

She whirled around and came face to face with Colleen's angry mug. "Ha. You're still alive. That's surprising."

"My husband is dead because of you." Colleen's eyes bored into Kyra.

"Me? No. If you killed him to save your own skin, that was your choice, not mine."

Colleen held a paper bag in one hand. She raised a knife in the other. Kyra rolled her eyes and flicked her wrist toward her. Nothing happened. She looked at her hands, confused. She waved her arm out, vigorously shooing at Colleen but she was still not affected by Kyra's powers. Colleen lunged at her. Kyra jumped back. The blade skimmed her left arm.

James stepped forward and grabbed Colleen by the arms. She wriggled in his grip. Kyra's shock faded to anger; her eyes narrowed. She used both hands to wrest the knife from Colleen's fingers. Before James could react, Kyra swept the blade through the air, slicing it across Colleen's throat. Blood sprayed, splashing on Kyra's dress. James released her, horrified. Colleen dropped lifeless to the floor and he stepped back, his eyes on the growing pool of red.

"Kyra, what have you done? Oh my God, what have *I* done?" He looked up at Kyra. "I just helped you murder someone."

She snatched up the brown bag and looked inside. Two crystals, one silver and one white with dark flashes, nestled inside. She handed the bag to Alastor as he walked up beside her.

"What are those for?" she asked as he peered into the bag.

"They block your powers," he whispered. "How could she have known this? Was she a witch?"

Kyra sniffed. "Definitely not a witch."

Alastor placed his hands over the bag and rubbed them together. The bag vanished along with its contents.

"What is this parasite still doing here?" He pointed to James, who was still looking at the lifeless body crumpled at his feet.

She shrugged, then strolled up to James. She put her hands on his face. He looked up into her eyes and she leaned in and softly kissed him. His hands floated to her hips as his eyes closed and he returned her kiss.

She pulled away abruptly. Her eyes narrowed and went white.

James tried unsuccessfully to pull from her grip. She released his face and stepped back. His head whipped around in a circle with a snap, and his body slumped to the floor.

***

"Dad!" Xavier screamed.

Hailey rushed over to her nephew. "What's wrong, hun? Are you worried?"

"My dad's dead," he choked out.

"I'm sure he's fine. He's with Axel and Alexis and the priest. They should be back soon. Hopefully, with your mom, too." She smiled and combed her fingers through his mop of hair.

"No, Aunty Hailey, he's not coming back." Xavier rubbed the tears from his eyes.

"Shhh. It will be all right," Hailey promised, hoping it wasn't a lie. She pulled him close and hugged him.

"Hailey." Nick's head popped in the doorway from the adjoining room. "You need to get in here. We just saw the end."

"It's over?" She faced Xavier. "See, honey? They will be back soon."

"Um, not the speech, but the attempt to get Kyra," Nick said. "We're not sure if anyone might be coming back here."

***

Alastor reached out for Kyra's hand; she took his and he led her to the center of the stage. He pulled her close and kissed her, then shot a quick scowl toward the vice president before surveying the room, mentally tallying the body count. He smiled.

Green, slowly swirling smoke engulfed the stage. Still holding Kyra in his arms, their eyes locked on the center stage camera, they vanished.

"Bitch," muttered the redheaded vixen under her breath. She shook her hair and the red flowed out, leaving brilliant white. Her facial features molded back into the face of a siren.

Celista.

Chapter Twenty-Three

Alexis Bennett wandered down the street, her mind lost in thought. She'd revealed herself as a witch to the world and lost her powers, all within the span of a couple of minutes. And despite this sacrifice, her friend was still lost.

She flicked her wrist at the empty pop can sitting on the curb. It stayed sitting there, defiantly mocking her. She kicked it into the street as she passed. Twirling her finger at the sky added to her frustration when not so much as a gust of wind circled her. She slumped down onto a bench and looked up to the orange sky as the sun set behind the skyscrapers.

The hum of an engine drew her attention as a car pulled up on the street in front of her, its engine idling.

"Give me your purse!"

Her eyes dropped to the revolver pointed at her, then drifted to the man behind it. "I don't have a purse," she said, holding up her hands.

"Your wallet, then."

"Sorry—no wallet, no cash, no cell phone."

He lowered the revolver. "What do you have, then?"

She rose carefully, keeping her hands up and eyeing the gun as she edged closer to his car.

"I don't have anything that would interest you, but you could really help me out by giving me a ride to my motel," she coaxed, touching his arm.

His eyebrows furrowed. "You're fucking nuts." He jerked his arm away and sped off.

Alexis let out a heavy sigh. Even though it wasn't possible, somehow her passive powers had vanished. She sauntered back to the bench and dropped down, feeling defeated and hopeless.

The priest had given his life to aid their cause and she had failed him. He was their best link to the prophecy and now he was gone. Alexis had grown up hearing stories about melharas, but they were just children's stories meant to teach witches about abuse of powers and fighting the lure of dark magic. She'd never expected melharas to exist. Everyone would soon know what she was, if they didn't already. Including all of her human contacts that she had manipulated over the years, like her FBI friend, Nate. She could only hope that Axel had done his job and Nathan would still be willing to help her, without the extra prodding. She didn't know if she would be able to get what she needed from him without her powers. She'd used her power of persuasion so often that it had become a natural reflex, like squinting your eyes when blinded by the sun.

***

The curtains were partly drawn over the windows, the setting sun casting an intense orange glow through their rust-colored material. Hailey and Xavier cuddled on the tiny sofa bed that faced the two double mattresses. The two Majai men stood in the far corner with their backs to the mint green wallpaper, their hands clasped together. Nick and Iris sat on the bed, Nick with his back resting against the wall, Iris on the corner, one leg on either side. Everyone was focused intently on the motel room's closed door.

The door opened. Still holding the doorknob, Axel scanned their gloomy faces.

"Am I the first one back?"

Iris sprang up. "James didn't make it," she sobbed as she hugged him.

"What do you mean, he didn't make it?" He pulled back to look down at her face.

Iris met his gaze. "Kyra killed him after you and Alexis vanished."

"Well, I don't imagine Father Thomas will be able to come back; he wasn't part of the deal. But James was. He hasn't called?"

"Xavier knows his dad is gone," Hailey said quietly. "He knew as it unfolded on TV."

"What the hell were you guys doing, letting him watch it?" Axel snapped.

"We didn't. He was in the other room. He just knew," Hailey stated defensively.

"Xavier's been kind of weird lately. We think he might have some kind of powers like Kyra," Nick offered.

"That's not possible; he's too young." Axel combed his hand through his hair, watching Xavier.

"What do you mean, he's too young? How would you know? Oh right, your sister is a witch too, isn't she," Hailey said, her voice sharp.

"Yes, she is, but witches don't get powers like that until they're older."

"Kyra did. Well, sort of. I've never seen her as she is now, but she had dreams and visions all the time." Iris gently kicked at the carpet. "We sent her to a shrink because of it." She looked up. "Xavier is sounding like Kyra used to when she was that age."

Axel moved to the sofa bed and sat down next to Xavier. "The only thing he would be able to do as a witch, at this age, is have the odd vision about future events—not the present." He gave the boy a quick squeeze, then left his arm draped around his shoulder. "Hey, little buddy, you know how you could tell that your dad wasn't dead after the demon had killed him before… is that the same way you can tell that he won't be coming back now?"

Xavier sniffled. "Yes," he said, nodding.

"How does it work? Did you see him in your head, like a dream but you're awake? Is it a feeling, or you just know?" Axel coaxed gently.

"I can tell that he's not in his body anymore."

The door opened again, and all eyes jerked toward it as Alexis walked in and tossed her key on the dresser. She flung the door closed. Iris sprang to her feet again and hurried to Alexis with outstretched arms. Alexis turned to the cluster of people in the room, then dodged back toward the door as Iris rushed toward her; her eyes went wide as the older woman wrapped her arms around her.

Axel nodded to his sister, then turned his attention back to Xavier. "What, like he's a ghost?"

Xavier shook his head. "No, it's different. He's not staying here; he's going to Heaven. If he stayed, then he would be a ghost."

"James got killed again?" Alexis asked, pulling away from Iris.

"But for real this time," Xavier whimpered.

Alexis glanced over the faces in the room before she focused on her brother. "Am I missing something?" she asked cautiously.

As Axel opened his mouth to speak, Hailey blurted, "Kyra killed him and Xavier knew he was dead as it happened. He can somehow tell that James is in Heaven."

"He's not in Heaven, but he will be on his way soon," Xavier corrected her. "He went to talk to Mom."

"I think maybe Xavier is suffering post-traumatic stress or something," Nick said. "This is a little *too* bizarre."

Alexis tilted her head to the side. "What do you mean, he's on his way to Heaven?" she asked Xavier.

Xavier sighed as if he were explaining something everyone should know. "It takes time to get there. You don't just die and you're there. He's got to walk there—but he's gonna hang out in the ghost plane until he gets used to being dead."

"Walk there? Where is it; can we walk there too?" Iris whispered.

"Not until we die," Xavier said matter-of-factly.

An uncomfortable silence settled over the room, everyone searching the others' faces for some kind of confirmation. They were all still processing what Xavier had said. How could he be so insightful and accurate? Or was he just a regular eight-year-old with an active imagination? They were hopelessly unaware—they all were, even Axel and Alexis, though to a much lesser degree—of Xavier's potential. Axel grunted, breaking the silence and making Hailey flinch, though she kept herself from looking over Xavier's head at him.

"Okay, so if James is gone," Alexis said slowly, "why now and not before?"

"Because Kyra did it," Iris sobbed.

"Huh? So what? He should still come back, like before."

Axel scratched the stubble on his chin. "Alastor killed him before. The deal she made bound him or his men; she said nothing about herself."

Alexis looked to the Majai men silently standing in the corner of the room for confirmation of Axel's theory. They nodded, expressionless.

"Xavier, can you sense where your mom is?" Alexis asked him.

"Yeah, duh. Can't you?"

"Hey!" Axel scolded.

"Sorry, Aunty Alexis," Xavier apologized quickly. "Yeah, I can."

"It's fine." She shot her brother a look. "My powers don't work like that. I had to cast a spell to locate her, but she keeps popping on and off my radar abilities. Where is she?"

"Well, I don't know exactly, but she's far away now."

"How far? Same country, other side of the planet, or not on this earth far?"

Xavier frowned in thought. "Um... I think she's still in the US, but like *far*, not like as far as my house."

"She's kind of hidden, right?"

"Yeah, *but* more like... kinda fuzzy."

Alexis looked up. "I think they're in the hideout, where we were taken prisoner. She's concealed while she's inside the place. I can't locate it. She just shows up once in a while, then vanishes again." She sighed. "I tried to use my powers to escape when we were held there but he must have put up crystals or had a witch cast spells to block witch magic, because Kyra never used hers, either."

"It blocked good magic, not witch magic," Xavier added.

"What? How do you know that?"

"'Cause—" He hesitated, looking at the others. "Mom couldn't use any of her powers, not just the witch ones."

"Wait a minute." Alexis placed her hands over his. "Xavier, do you have more new powers already?" She glanced around at the confused faces of those listening. "Well, it makes sense that Xavier would inherit Kyra's gifts," she explained. "He is part angel and witch too, after all... and Father Thomas did say they have different powers that develop at an early age."

Alexis had been babysitting Xavier one day, years ago, when he'd told her that he dreamt of angels and demons, and that he knew they were different from other people, but didn't understand why. Shortly afterward, she had shown him her family grimoires and the lessons on magic had begun; it became their secret—one they both hid from Kyra—and they both looked forward to the days when Alexis would babysit Xavier.

She had explained that Kyra didn't practice magic, but she did, and quickly became the person Xavier could confide in and learn from about his heritage. They would read the grimoires together and she had cast spells and shown him her elemental powers. He was eager to learn and excited to grow into his powers, but he didn't have any active powers—that she knew of.

Alexis's gaze darted around the room before focusing on Xavier. "Did you tell her you had *special* abilities already? She never said anything to me about it."

He shook his head. "Heck, to the no. Anytime I did anything funny, she would act all weird and I didn't wanna freak Mom out, so I pretended I was normal. "

"Oh my…" Iris breathed. "That's what she did with us, after all the trouble when she was young."

"It's okay, Mom. Don't feel bad," Hailey reassured her. "I know some stuff; she was okay. Well, I didn't know that she was a witch or anything, but she told me things after you and Dad thought she was fine."

Iris's face pinched. "What kinds of things?"

"I remember Kyra telling me scary stories when we were little, but when we grew up and started dating, she would tell me which boys were jerks and I always thought she was just being judgmental, but she was *always* right. And… she talked to dead people, but it wasn't scary when we were older, just *strange*. She kind of grew out of that before we left for college."

"Why didn't you tell us, sweetheart?"

"Why didn't you tell us she was adopted!" Hailey retorted. "Sorry… still accepting *that* family secret." She sighed. "You'd have taken her back to the doctors. I don't know why she didn't tell me she was a witch, or a melhara or whatever."

"Because she didn't know until college, after we met." Alexis surprised everyone with her statement. "I knew what she was when we met but had no idea she didn't know. I was open with her about my abilities and being a witch, and we went from there. I never knew she was a melhara until Father Thomas told us."

"What about you, Alexis? What's your story?" Hailey urged.

"Yeah, what was going on with you and Kyra on that stage? There was a lot of strange stuff happening," Iris said.

"You should have told us, especially when all this stuff started happening with Kyra," Hailey added.

"Oh yeah, I almost forgot!" Nick interrupted. "There was some woman on the stage that confronted Kyra, and she couldn't use her powers—she almost got killed. James actually had to pull the woman off Kyra. Then she killed her and Kyra got her powers back."

Axel ran his fingers through his hair. "Were you guys able to record the news broadcast? I would like to see it."

"Yeah."

They filed into the adjoining suite and sat where they could view the TV. Xavier started toward the doorway, but his grandmother grabbed his arm and shook her head. He sighed and rolled his eyes before dramatically falling back onto the bed. Alexis and Axel sat on the floor directly in front of the TV. Nick flipped open his computer and searched the recorded files.

"So Alexis, have you always been a witch?" Hailey pressed. Axel wasn't surprised that Hailey wouldn't be sidetracked by a change of subject.

Alexis sighed. "Yes, I've been a witch forever. Like most witches, I came into my full powers on my eighteenth birthday. You don't just pick up a book and become a witch. You are born one because of your parents. Over the generations witches and humans got together, and their offspring gradually became less powerful—like diluting the gene pool; no offense." She glanced at Iris. "Psychics and prophets tend to be bled down through the generations, but they have a fraction of the abilities their ancestors would have had. Seeing the future is a risky business—you can't control what you see and you can't change what you've seen. The ones that publicize and make money from it are breaking the rules—they aren't supposed to reveal abilities to the public. At least they don't claim to be witches."

"You did today. Well, you revealed abilities."

"Yes, to try to save my friend, and I may get into trouble for that later. Kyra has the most powers an angel-bred child can have. Xavier is now one-quarter angel and one-quarter witch and half human. Make sense?"

"Yeah, I guess." Hailey was the only one that responded. Nick nodded, only half listening.

"Don't forget to tell them the part about where every witch gets their powers from." Xavier chimed in from the other room.

Alexis laughed. "What Xavier is talking about is the origin of witch magic. It comes from nature. The foundation of an individual's powers is one of the four elements." She waved her hand. "There's a lot more to it and it's really complicated to understand."

"Here's the recording. I zipped past everything to this woman that Kyra couldn't use her powers on," Nick said, looking up. The recording appeared on the TV screen.

Axel squinted, then shook his head. "I have no clue."

Alexis gasped. "That's our boss from the bank. She's a bitch, but there's no way she's supernatural in any way, shape, or form. How odd."

They spent an hour watching the whole recording twice, finally deciding there was nothing on it that would be helpful. Axel flipped off the TV and stood and stretched, pushing his arms above his head. His shirt lifted above his belt with the movement, and he caught Hailey eyeing him intently before she turned her eyes away.

"Nothing to help us improve our plan of attack?" Nick asked hopefully, oblivious to the silent exchange.

"No, but we may have something else—" Alexis started.

Hailey cut her off. "Every time you guys have approached them, they've had their guard up, looking for a fight. And that damn demon is always close by."

The four of them sauntered back into the other room, where Iris and Xavier were now playing card games.

"We have a Plan B. Axel slipped a tracking device onto Kyra's clothes. We can track her to the hideout and approach her when they least expect it," Alexis said.

Alexis swiveled around from Nick and Hailey to face him. "Did you get it on her somewhere she won't notice it? Hopefully for a few days, if we're lucky."

"Few days? Hope that's a joke. She'll probably find it when she showers or changes. I stuck it under her belt on her dress when I grabbed her around the waist, but you hurled her against the wall so quickly afterward, I don't know if it was on securely yet or not."

"How did you get a tracking device?" Hailey questioned.

"I have a friend in the FBI. I'll go call him and see if it worked."

"Of course you do," she said sarcastically.

Alexis left the crowded suite and dialed her cell phone as she slipped into the adjoining room.

"If it works we can find the hideout location with technology instead of magic," Axel explained. "They shouldn't be expecting that. This could really open a lot of doors for us." The doubt on their faces told Alexis, watching from just beyond the doorway, that they weren't as excited about the possibilities as he was.

"So does that mean you are her true love, or unbreakable love, or whatever we need?" Hailey asked cautiously.

"It's a strong possibility. She twice allowed James to..." he trailed off, watching Xavier. "Kyra never did anything to me, and Alastor never tried. She was annoyed when I was ignoring her, but that could have been because she knew that I knew Alexis was up to something."

Alexis wandered back into the room and they fell silent, waiting for her to relay some good news.

"He's not sure if he wants to help," she told them. "I just told him in the sweetest way I could, without the ability to use my powers to influence him, that he owes me one, and he would be helping us save the world from the demon and this nightmare. Then, after he continued to protest, I had to add that I'll be coming after him if he doesn't help."

"You think that will work?"

She lifted her hands in a helpless shrug. "I don't know. I've never used threats before to get what I wanted. I never had to."

Axel checked his watch. "Either way, we have to get going, or Nick's corporate jet is leaving without us."

Chapter Twenty-Four

Incoherent shouting echoed in her head, the words bouncing around in layers over each other like echoes in a cave. Kyra cupped her ears as the voices grew louder, unable to ignore the noise any longer. Over the past several hours, the whispering had dialed up to shouts and invaded her thoughts more frequently, making it all more and more difficult to brush off.

"Kyra!" Alastor called as he stepped into the sitting room.

She looked up, dropping her hands, hoping he hadn't noticed her weakness.

"I have a task for you," he said, sitting down in the armchair across from her.

She cocked her head and focused on his words, forcing the voices to diminish. But as she stared at him, the image of James in his favorite armchair appeared between them; he sat comfortably, legs sprawled in front of him. Alastor's words drifted away when James's image solidified, blocking the demon from her view. He looked at her with pain in his eyes. A thin red line appeared on his neck, then grew wider; blood began to run from the slit. Blood gushed between his lips as his mouth opened. His head tipped back and toppled off his body.

Kyra jumped in her seat, fingers digging into the leather upholstery.

"Kyra! Are you listening?" Alastor barked.

She shook her head and James vanished. Then she quickly corrected herself and nodded, meeting Alastor's eyes.

***

The thunderous music vibrated through the floor. People crowded the bar, shouting their drink orders. Behind them, in a sunken area surrounded by small tables in front of the stage, strobe lights flashed over the dancers packed on the dance floor, the rapid bursts of light making their movements look choppy.

Kyra made her way across the club, looking larger than life in the flashes of light. She was one of only a few Caucasian women in the Hong Kong nightclub, and a good six inches taller than anyone else with her high heels on. She strode up to the roped-off VIP area. A burly bald guy stepped into her path and put his hand out to stop her. Without interrupting her stride, she raised an eyebrow at him and shooed him away. He put down his hand and stepped aside, pulling the red velvet rope with him.

Kyra walked up to the man in the middle of a group of petite young women wearing far too little clothing. He grinned at her as she pushed past them and entered his space.

"You're the saharki?" She looked him up and down, disgusted. "I have a package for you."

"And you must be the fabulous melhara. Have a drink with me."

"No."

"Come on, just one."

"No. Alastor has a job for you and I was sent to deliver the egg. That is it."

"All business and no pleasure, then? What a waste of a perfectly good existence."

"Stop wasting my time, you pathetic little cretin."

He snorted. "You think you are better than me? We are cut from the same cloth, you and me."

"No, we are not."

"Opposite sides of the coin, maybe, but still the same creation, belonging half in this world and half in another."

***

Hailey stopped in shock when she walked through the front door of the Parker residence; Axel, Alexis, and Nick bunched up close behind her, momentarily confused. Iris and Xavier were still coming up the walk, the silent Majai men trailing behind.

Movie cases and couch cushions had been strewn around the living room. In the kitchen beyond, half-open cupboard doors were visible, and boxes and cans of food were scattered all over the countertops.

Axel looked over her shoulder. "What the…"

"Who would be rummaging through here and what on earth would they be looking for?" Hailey wondered as they all moved slowly inside.

"Reporters wouldn't do this. Maybe government guys?" Alexis suggested.

There was a crash upstairs; they all looked up to the ceiling.

"They're still here," Iris whispered. "Axel and Nick should go check it out." She nudged Axel with her elbow.

Hailey grabbed Xavier's hand and headed back toward the front door.

"Calm down. Just wait here," Nick said, looking to his wife before following Axel. "We're not likely in any danger from the police."

"What if it's a burglar or a crazy person?" Hailey called in a stage whisper.

The two men crept up to the first landing, Axel glad that the carpeted stairs muffled their footfalls. They paused and looked behind them to the second-floor railing. Nothing. They slowly moved up the next flight of stairs with their backs pressed against the wall, listening to things being banged around upstairs. After a moment, Axel identified the sound: dresser drawers being pulled out, then slammed shut after a pause while the contents were rifled through.

Axel poked his head around the corner at the top of the stairs, peering down the hall. The noise was coming from the master bedroom. The door was open but all he could see was the shadow of movement. The rest of the rooms were quiet. He turned back to Nick and shrugged. They stepped into the hallway and moved silently toward the bedroom. Suddenly Axel put his hand out to stop Nick. He motioned for him to listen.

The rustling in the bedroom had gone quiet.

Axel closed his eyes and held his breath, searching for the aura of the intruder but couldn't sense anything.

Silence.

He took a deep breath and opened his eyes. Calm washed over him. He stepped into the bedroom doorway.

Something slammed him off his feet and he hit the wall behind him hard, sliding to the floor despite his attempts to catch himself. He finished on one knee, his other foot underneath him. Bracing himself with his fingertips, he looked up at his assailant: a sprightly young woman in her late twenties with short, wild blonde hair. He hadn't sensed her, and he should have, if she was that close to him—unless she wasn't a human.

Nick whipped around the corner, arms outstretched, ready to attack.

"No! Wait!" Axel shouted, but he was too late. Nick too was hurled backward. Axel dove out of the way. Nick crashed down where Axel had been a moment ago.

Axel stood up and brushed himself off. "Another witch, eh. What are you doing here, trying to save the world from the demon apocalypse?" He grunted. "Who the hell are you?"

She stood feet apart and her hands on her hips, glaring at him. With a jerk of her head she flipped her bangs out of her face.

"I could ask you the same question," she retorted.

"I'm Axel and this is Nick." He pointed to Nick, who was trying to pick himself up; every time he shook his head to clear it, he slid back down to the floor, still dazed. "Kyra's a friend of mine and he's her brother-in-law. We actually know her, but you sure don't, or we would have met before."

"My name is Jezabelle and I'm *trying* to get to know her. She kidnapped me almost a month ago and I don't know why."

"Let me guess: a crappy windowless basement that blocks out magic?"

"Y-yes, how did you know?"

"I've been a guest there myself. Not really my favorite vacation destination. Had you met her before she took you?"

A stair creaked. Jezabelle and Axel swiveled their heads to the staircase.

Alexis sighed. "I can't even creep up stairs now."

"And this is my sister, Alexis. Kyra stole her powers last night. After they had a showdown during a very public TV broadcast." He snickered.

Alexis shot him an angry look. "Hello. We should go downstairs and talk this out with everyone—the suspense is killing them."

Jezabelle followed Alexis down the staircase while Axel helped Nick to his feet. They hurried after the women.

***

The confusion was palpable as Axel and Nick joined those waiting in the living room, their eyes on the young woman with the blonde pixie-cut, as Alexis called it, who accompanied them.

"Everyone, this is Jezabelle," Alexis said, waving a hand toward her. "She's a witch and was just about to explain what she's doing here," she shot her a disapproving look and plopped down on the sofa, "rifling through Kyra and James's stuff."

"Please, just call me Jez." She scanned the faces in the group.

Xavier smiled brightly and rushed up to her. "Hi, I'm Xavier." He held out his hand. "Nice to meet you."

Her eyebrow lifted and she smirked. "It's a pleasure. You must be her son," Jezabelle said, shaking his hand. "You have your mom's eyes." Her eyes softened as she smiled.

Nick took Hailey's hand and guided her, with Xavier in tow, to the love seat.

"Kyra kidnapped me from the streets of New York, in broad daylight, and sent me to a tiny cell in a windowless dungeon out in the middle of nowhere. I'm trying to figure out why."

Axel strode up to her as she spoke, eyeing her suspiciously.

"Had you met her before that?"

"No," she said, shaking her head. She looked over the group. "She barely even spoke to me, but she would swing by my cell every few days."

"Can you take us back there?" Alexis asked, leaning forward in her seat. "We need to find the hideout."

"It's all jumbled now, like an old memory or a dream that slips away. I remember running through acres of forest and fields, and some odds and ends here and there, then I was here." She shrugged. "I can't focus on where I was; my mind is a blur. I don't know how long it took me to get here or how I got across the border." Her hands came up and she shrugged again.

"Damn." Alexis pulled her hair back and twirled it around in her hands. "It's still okay; Nathan should help us."

Jezabelle's face scrunched up and she cocked her head to the side.

"I'm trying to help," she said in a pained voice.

Axel touched her shoulder. "What about the demon, Alastor?" He moved to sit next to his sister and Iris. "Did you see or talk to him?"

"I only saw him that day in New York. He was with her but didn't say anything, just stood back and watched."

"He's always with her when we've seen them," Axel mused. "I think James might have been getting to her before everything went to hell."

Jezabelle looked around the room. "Where is James? He's helping you guys, isn't he?"

"Kyra, or some version of Kyra, killed him," Nick whispered to her behind his hand, hoping to spare Xavier, but everyone heard him clearly.

"Oh..." Her gaze drifted to Xavier. "Sorry about your dad, little man."

"He's okay. He's gonna take off soon," he said. Jez nodded as her lips formed a sly smile.

"What? You can see ghosts—I mean, your dad... you can see your dad right now?" Hailey jerked her head to Xavier.

"Yeah, but I have to try hard to see him. Mostly I can just tell he's here and then he talks and I can hear him. He's going to go to Heaven soon but he wants me to tell you guys some stuff before he leaves."

Axel knelt down in front of Xavier. He caught Hailey squirming slightly in the corner of his eye, but when he looked at her she froze; her eyes briefly locked on his before she looked at the floor. Axel turned back to Xavier. "Is he here right now?"

"Yeah."

"What does he want to tell us?"

"He wants me to wait until Jez finishes her story."

Jez shrugged her shoulders. "There's nothing more to tell. I was in a cell with no contact with anyone else, other than a white-haired demon girl and some guy that brought me food every other day, but they never spoke to me. Then this cute guy brought me dinner and helped me escape. I really hope it worked out for him and he didn't get killed. He wouldn't come with me." She looked sad. "Then I came here to try to figure everything out." She motioned to Xavier to have his say.

"Okay, so... Jez is the fourth friend." Xavier smiled, bouncing excitedly in his seat. "She has the power of water. I knew that when I saw her." His face went serious. "Dad didn't tell me that part. He wanted me to tell you guys that the four of you can banish Alastor back to Hell."

"The four of us? You mean me, Jez, Axel, and Kyra? Or who, you? How's that supposed to work when you and I have no powers and Kyra is under the demon's influence?" Alexis said.

"Axel is a witch? But he's a guy; I thought witches were all women," Hailey interrupted.

"Come on, Hailey, keep up. Xavier is part witch, my sister is a witch, so, naturally, I would be too."

Hailey shot him a glare. "You're an asshole," she said bitterly.

"Hailey! Watch your mouth. I raised you better than that." Iris's eyes moved to Axel. "And as for you—you don't have to be an antagonizing butt-head jerk to her; it doesn't help anything."

"Yes, ma'am." He winked at her.

Iris raised her eyebrows. "Ma'am is a little over the top for you, my boy."

Axel snickered and turned back to Xavier. "Okay, X-man, what does your dad want us to know?"

"He wanted me to tell you that the four of you complete the circle with your powers, and have to fight the demon together. So if Mom doesn't come home, the demon will never leave."

"That's not the only way to get rid of the demon," Nick reminded them.

"That's helpful," Axel said sarcastically.

"I get that they can't kill me or Axel, but why didn't Kyra and Alastor just kill Jezabelle, if we need her to get rid of him?" Alexis quickly smiled at Jezabelle. "No offense, Jez."

Jezabelle shrugged.

When Xavier shrugged, their heads turned to the silent men in the corner, standing with their hands clasped together and their heads lowered.

"Do you guys have anything to say, ever?" Axel prodded.

They didn't move.

"Do you even understand English?" Hailey added, sneaking a glance at Axel.

They nodded in unison.

"So help us out a little. Tell us something," Nick pleaded, folding his hands in his lap.

"They can't," Xavier piped up, then recoiled back against the sofa.

"What the hell are they here for, then?" Axel shot them both a withering look that didn't seem to bother them.

"They were sent here, but not for us." Xavier clutched at his arm.

"Sent by who?" Hailey asked.

"God," he said, his eyes darting over their faces. Axel realized Xavier was always guarded whenever he spoke about something supernatural. He wondered if it was from the stories Alexis had told him about his mom and his grandparents when Kyra was growing up. Maybe she had made him afraid that he would be thought of in a negative way.

"Well, that's just great." Axel shook his head.

"Did your dad tell you that too?" Iris asked softly.

"No. I know because I'm part angel."

Axel stood. "Well, is there anything else we should know about?"

Xavier thought about it before he responded. "Not right now."

"What? Now you have to tell us."

"I can't. I will when I'm supposed to."

"Okay, deal." Axel looked around at all their hopeful expressions. "Now, what's the plan?"

Alexis smacked her hands together and jumped up from her seat. "We have to pay a visit to Nathan and persuade him to help us now. We don't have time to wait around for him. Xavier, can you... *travel* like your mom yet?"

Chapter Twenty-Five

Kyra rounded the corner into the foyer just as Celista closed the door to the mansion.

"How dare you come back here." Kyra glowered at her as she stomped toward Alastor's office.

"I'm on orders, toots." Celista flung her hair behind her shoulders and also started toward the door to Alastor's office. "How's my lover been keeping?"

"He's your *ex*-lover. Past tense." Kyra increased her pace, her arms swinging as she moved as quickly as she could without breaking into a run.

"Oh?" Celista cocked her head. "Does that mean that your ex-lover is up for grabs?"

They both reached for the door handle at the same time.

"What are you talking about?" Kyra slapped Celista's hand away.

"That sexy witch that's always in jeans and a biker jacket." Celista smirked. "Brown hair, brown eyes, chiseled arms. He's kind of deviously delicious-looking. I bet he'd be a lot of fun."

"You stay away from him," Kyra said, her face hard.

"Why, what does he matter to you now?"

Kyra let out an exasperated snort before she opened the door and stepped inside. Celista scurried past her, dodging a swing from Kyra. Alastor looked up from his papers and pushed back from his desk.

"What's this *skank* doing here?" Kyra demanded, her hands on her hips.

Celista glared back at her. "You're sure self-righteous for someone who's only recently been added to the roster in this war."

"Without me there would be no war," she retorted.

"Bitch, please. It has been raging long before you and will be raging long after you're gone. You're still mortal, after all."

"Enough, you two," Alastor interrupted. "Celista is here on my orders to report back after she dropped off the other eggs. Did you find your guys all right, darling?"

"Yes." She crossed her arms over her chest.

"Any problems?"

Kyra stole a glance at Celista. "No."

"Then give us a minute."

"Fine, I'll grab some food—but then we need to talk... privately." Kyra focused intensely on Alastor.

Alastor nodded and waved his hand to dismiss her.

"Your mortal body must be famished after an exhausting journey like that," Celista said, her tone mocking.

Alastor cleared his throat and Celista slumped her shoulders, pouting.

Annoyed, Kyra left Alastor's office and headed for the kitchen.

That siren is not supposed to be here—ever, she fumed. *He babies the whiney little brat too much, and she's a constant nuisance.* She should have handled all the dragon eggs—Kyra didn't understand why he would trust Celista to deal with them. *She hasn't proven overly reliable—she would have cozied up to that saharki in China and not done her job.*

She scarfed down her food, then went to rest in the solitude of her bedroom. *And calm down,* she added, still seething as she lay down on the bedspread and closed her eyes. Calm didn't come, though—nor did rest, really—and twenty minutes later,

Alastor still hadn't come looking for her. Kyra marched out of her room and returned to his office. She burst through the closed door without knocking.

Alastor stood over Celista, who was bent over his desk with her skirt up around her waist. Alastor stood behind her, his hand gripping the back of her neck, holding her down as he thrust into her.

"What the—"

Alastor held up his free hand, and Kyra's words caught in her throat; her legs froze in mid-stride. Celista twisted her head to catch the look on Kyra's frozen face. With a sneer, the siren turned her attention back to Alastor and thoroughly amped up her show of enjoyment.

When Alastor finished, Celista pulled her skirt back down and casually strolled past Kyra to the door. Their eyes locked. Celista half smirked at Kyra's murderous stare as she struggled to break free of the lock on her voice.

"You can wipe that smile off you face, you're still banished from the manor," Kyra said.

Celista's smirk spread into a grin, her teeth gleaming between her lips. Their challenging stare-off never broke until Celista had passed by Kyra. Neither of them turned their head to glance at the other. Kyra couldn't, even if she wanted to—until Celista had left the room and closed the door behind her, and Alastor waved his hand, freeing her from her petrified state.

"Took you long enough," she snapped as she started walking toward him.

"Don't get snarly with me," he barked, and she stopped advancing. "Remember who you are talking to."

"What the hell was that all about?" She felt the pain of betrayal deep inside her chest. "I thought we talked about her and you agreed."

His face unresponsive, his eyes blank, Alastor said, "Listen, Kyra. I am a prince of Hell and do not answer to anyone, especially some little witch." He casually straightened his desk.

Her breath faltered in shock, then her pain turned to anger. "You need me for this plan of yours to work. If I go, your world crumbles and goes to shit."

"My silly little whore, you gave yourself to me. I own you and can do as I please with you, including allow you to exercise your free will or not, like the other souls I own."

"Then why don't you, if you're so powerful?" she asked in the most sarcastic tone she could manage, knowing that he drew most of his power from her and she drew very little from him. She mostly drew on his unnatural physical strength and the power of hellfire—which was basically just elemental fire on steroids.

"It would be inefficient to waste my time micro-managing everyone." He narrowed his eyes at her. "Do you recall the times when your mind was in a fog and you heard a whisper in your ear before you reacted? That was me, pushing you."

She closed her eyes, trying to remember. Images of the security guards, police, Secret Service agents, and the president flashed over the backs of her eyelids before she saw James, standing in front of her as a stranger, speaking incoherent garble... then being decapitated by Alastor... then as he stood next to Colleen's corpse, looking horrified, and finally—she saw herself kill him. Was that all her, or some sort of power he held over her? She wasn't sure.

"You bastard," she whispered, and opened her eyes. "Is that why I feel bound to you? I thought we were in this together. All this time, I thought I was making my own decisions. I thought we were partners."

"A demon prince has no *partners*, just soldiers and servants." He pulled his chair out. "And you have been an acceptable soldier so far, but I find I still have to prod you to get things done."

"Well, I'm *finding* that you are leaving me out of the loop a little too often," she said as he sat down. "I can't just follow orders blindly, I need to know what is going on before I happen to stumble upon it."

"You have no reason to be jealous of Celista," he said. "We have a long history and she is a good warrior." Alastor motioned for Kyra to sit in one of the chairs facing his desk. "Celista has her own ambitions of being the queen by my side. It matters not what either of you desire. *I* shall decide, and if I choose to have you both on my arm as queen or one as my concubine, then so be it."

"It's not just her," she said, fists on her hips. "One of the saharki guys said that we are cut from the same cloth, or the same coin, or something like that. Is that what I am, half witch and half demon, like them?"

Alastor laughed. "Not quite, darling."

"Good. They are such vile, disgusting creatures. So then, what am I, besides half witch?"

"Half angel."

"What!" she shrieked. "We shouldn't be working together!" She started to pace the room.

"One of the meddling witches already told you, but I blocked it from your memory. There is no longer a need to hide this information from you."

"You tricked me into crusading with you. How did this happen?" she muttered to herself.

"No tricks. You joined me of your own free will, to save your family. It was meant to be. It is written that I would need divine intervention. I can only escape Hell when a melhara is born."

"That seems like a different life now." She rubbed the back of her neck and added silently, *or someone else's life*. She remembered making the deal, but the memory was so distant, it seemed as though it were the childhood dream of a being that had been alive for thousands of years. "Wait—if Heaven is at the end of the planes, then where's Hell? They have the same door." She pursed her lips and lifted her eyebrows, watching Alastor.

"Hell is in the center. The planes are in a circle, there is no *end*. One has to go through them in sequence, except for Hell. Anything going there, from any plane, goes straight there—do not pass go, do not collect two hundred dollars."

She tucked her chin and looked at him as if peering over the frames on a pair of glasses. "Is that a Monopoly reference?"

He smiled and motioned for her to sit in the chair across from his desk. She shook her head. He continued. "No one ever escapes Hell except for a son of Lucifer, when the melhara is born."

"You got Celista out," she said flatly, "and a bunch of other insidious cretins."

"The gates are crumbling as the balance of power turns." He folded his arms and rested them on his desk. "The stronger demons are able to escape, with assistance from other powerful demons."

She started pacing again, slowly shaking her head. "Great. Just great."

She was part angel and had helped a demon. Now the gates to Hell were crumbling and demons that belonged in Hell were running loose—in the flesh, on Earth, because of her. The dreams of angels and demons that haunted her childhood came rushing back to her and she felt sick. Her memory focused on the dream of the vivacious young redheaded melhara with electric blue eyes that she had told her son about on the last night of her old life. The redhead had put up a far greater fight against Alastor than she had. Kyra pushed the heels of her palms into her eyes, her fingers combing into her scalp, as she tried to remember the details of that old dream. The redhead had been different and obviously under his influence after joining Alastor, but she'd eventually escaped the demon—at the cost of her life, and not by her choice.

Alastor rose, skirted the desk, and grabbed her arm, pulling her to him.

"Kyra, this does not change anything about the souls trapped in Hell." His voice carried enough concern that she looked at him.

She softened for a moment, then she grew suspicious. "That could be lies too."

His face hardened and his eyes flickered from brown to hard, shiny black. Tightening his grip on her arm, he dragged her over to the mirror hanging on the wall.

"Look at your aura, darling. You are one of us now, there is no turning back. If I am not able to finish what I started, you shall be trapped in Hell forever."

A gray fog surrounded her reflection. Her eyes widened. Alastor stroked the skin on her arm with his fingertips. She let out a sigh and her eyes met his in the mirror. The heartache in her chest intensified when he grinned. The sour taste of defeat tainted her mouth as he softly kissed her neck.

Chapter Twenty-Six

"Alexis, I can't help you. It could get me fired and probably killed," Nathan said, his blue eyes serious.

She loved his stubbornness. He wasn't a pushover like most of the men in her life. She knew she had a weakness for men in uniform with an aura of authority about them—like cops, enlisted men, FBI agents, basically any courageous fighter who knew his way around firearms—but she had an extra weakness for Nathan. She liked him; he was interesting, fun, and thoughtful without smothering her. If he were a witch, he would have been the perfect man for her.

"There's no job to get fired from anymore." She reached across the table and took his hand. "And soon there won't be a world to save, if we don't stop them."

Axel rummaged through the kitchen cupboards while Jez stood in the corner, watching Alexis and Nathan bicker across the table. Xavier was off wandering through the house.

"Why would you?" He pulled his hand away. "You're one of them."

Axel looked over his shoulder and snorted.

"What are you looking for?" Nathan asked, annoyed.

"Food. Don't you have anything good to eat?"

"Sorry, I wasn't expecting company," Nathan replied coldly.

"What do you plan to survive on during the apocalypse?" Axel went back to his searching.

"Nate." His attention returned to Alexis. "I'm not one of them. Neither is Kyra. She was taken by the demon because of her power. If we can get her back, this will all be over." She smiled reassuringly, hoping that he would be able to understand. He was an open-minded kind of guy—another quality she liked about him—but she wasn't sure how open he was to the idea of witches with real magic.

"She didn't seem like she was an unwilling victim at the press conference," he said, tapping his fingers on the table.

"She's under his control, but we think we can save her," Alexis said. Jez nodded vigorous agreement, taking a couple steps toward them before hesitating and stepping aside, giving them their space. "We can stop them and end all of this."

"Have you ever used magic on me?" He lowered his head, his eyes locked on Alexis.

"Well... some," she said carefully. "But nothing major," she added quickly. "Witches use their powers all the time. There are some aspects that we can't turn off. It's just a reflex, like yawning."

"What did you do to me?" His eyes went wide with horror.

"Nothing bad!" she blurted. "Sometimes I gently persuaded you to do what I needed. But I can't do that at the moment." She lowered her head and mumbled, "Which doesn't make any sense." She shook her head slightly, looked up at him, and sighed. "Please Nate, understand that I'm a good person and I would never hurt you, or anyone."

"I don't know if I trust you. Hell, I don't even know if I know you anymore." He pushed back from the table and crossed his arms.

"I'm still me. I could've had Jez or Axel just make you get on board and saved a bunch of valuable time, but I want you to be help us because you understand what's happening."

He scratched his head, ruffling his blond hair. "I guess I've never done anything for you that I regretted... yet."

Alexis beamed and started bouncing in her chair with excitement. "Well, what do we need to do?"

"Nothing but wait," Nathan replied. "I have to sneak into my office building and snag some things. After I saw what you did at the press conference, I didn't think I would be using it."

"We have a better idea for slipping in and out of the FBI headquarters." She grinned. "Xavier! Come here, please."

"Jez will go with them, and you should come with me to get some supplies," Axel said to Alexis as he sat down with a box of crackers. Xavier came skipping into the kitchen.

"What? No, I have to go with Nathan," Alexis protested. "I got him into this."

"You have no powers." He shoved a handful of crackers into his mouth and mumbled while chewing, "What's your plan if you run into trouble?"

"I can take care of them, Axel." Xavier smiled. "Don't worry, just get the stuff so we can get my mom back."

"His mom? Are you freaking kidding me?" Nathan dropped his face into his hands.

"I told you, she doesn't belong with the demon." Alexis touched his shoulder. "She's one of us, a good witch."

"This is a bad idea," Axel grumbled, shaking his head.

"It's okay, Axel," Xavier interjected. "You *need* to take Jez to get the stuff."

"Okay, little man, but don't let go of Alexis's hand, and if there's trouble, you hightail it out of there." Xavier bobbed his head, smiling. "I hope you know what you're getting yourself into."

Xavier giggled. "You too, buddy."

Xavier grabbed Alexis's hand before reaching out to Nathan. He looked at the innocent little boy with his hand outstretched, waiting for him to take it. Then with a sigh, Nathan took Xavier's hand, muttering something about office numbers.

They vanished.

***

Axel pulled the car into the silent parking lot and drove slowly down a row, scanning the surrounding area. Abandoned cars littered the parking lot, some scorched wrecks after being set on fire, others with smashed windows. There were no signs of people nearby, which was a good thing, he supposed. The military presence had evaporated, allowing the violence to flourish in the streets again—not that there was much danger for a witch on the chaotic streets of Washington.

"What do you suppose I should grab for supplies for invading the hideout? Or should we call it the demon lair, or dungeon, or labyrinth of the damned?" He chuckled and Jez rolled her eyes. He guided Nathan's car around the broken and abandoned cars and pulled up near the stores where they wanted to scavenge.

"So, is there something between you and Kyra, more than just friends?" Jez asked him.

"Why do you ask that?" He looked over at her as he slowed the car to a stop, taking up space in four parking spots.

She shrugged. "You and Hailey seem to butt heads a lot."

"Yeah, she's a pain in the ass sometimes." He threw the shifter into park and cut the engine.

"She's always giving you the death glare. Either Hailey hates your guts or she wants to jump your bones, and she's desperately trying to hide it."

"It's probably both."

"It would be very confusing for her, having a lot of anger toward you but also being drawn to you because you're a witch."

"I can't help that." He opened his door, climbed out, and slid his forearms over the roof of the car, watching Jez as she got out of the car. "I don't usually have to spend so much time with her."

"It's none of my business, but you should probably sort that mess out."

"You're right. It *is* none of your business." He slammed his door shut. "Can you throw a protection spell on this so we have a car to come back to?" he asked, pointing to the car. It sounded more like a statement than a request.

She nodded, closed her eyes, and chanted under her breath, waving her hands slowly over the car. Axel headed for the hardware store before she had finished the spell and opened her eyes.

He glanced back over his shoulder as Jez headed toward the small New Age Wiccan shop to hunt for crystals and herbs. She had a more comprehensive knowledge about crystals and Axel cursed his sister for being right—he should have studied that aspect a little more. Instead, Axel went in search of supplies they might need to infiltrate an underground bunker. Although Jez had told him repeatedly that it was just a huge house in the middle of nowhere and that only the basement was set up like Fort Knox, Axel wasn't taking any chances. He wanted to be prepared for everything and anything. Jez's voice echoed through his mind: *"I don't know, as soon as I was out of that basement I could use my powers again."* He didn't have a clear plan in mind, but if *no one* was able to use their powers inside that house, they could easily overpower Kyra.

Axel was marching toward Nathan's car with a couple bags in his hand when he glimpsed a petite woman in his peripheral vision, striding toward him. He turned his head to look as he continued to the car. Her coppery skin glowed in the sunlight, and long, silvery white hair swayed across her back. Big round sunglasses covered her eyes.

"Hey," she called to him. "Could you help me? I'm a bit lost." Her pouty pink lips formed a sweet smile as she strolled up and stopped next to him.

"I can try, but I'm not sure I'd be much help," he said, eyeing her suspiciously, knowing she was a witch—because he couldn't sense her presence or her aura. There was something... something different about her, though—she felt like Kyra, but darker. *A dark witch?*

"I'm not from around here." He flexed his fingers as she drew closer to him. *That's not it, either.*

"Oh, that much is obvious." She placed her delicate hand on his forearm and stroked gently. "I'm sure you can assist me."

He stepped back from her, pressing up against the car, and tried to jerk his arm away but his muscles didn't obey. Instead he dropped the bags to the pavement. They landed with a soft thud. A tingling sensation spread throughout his body as fog rolled into his mind. His tension eased and she began to seem familiar and safe.

"Do I know you?"

She pulled her dark glasses from her face and rested them in her hair. Her black eyes melted through a range of colors, from black to brown to green to yellow before stopping as an exceptionally bright blue.

"You're about to." She ginned.

Both her hands trailed along his biceps as he unconsciously slid his hands around her waist and pulled her close. She pressed her pelvis against him and tilted her face up to his. Their eyes met again. She made his soul weak. He longed for her like he had longed for Kyra. The image of Kyra smiling at him on her wedding day as she unwrapped the little box he'd given her flashed through his thoughts just before their lips met.

"Come away with me," she whispered in his mind. "Let me take you from this place."

"Axel! Axel, snap out of it," he heard a distant voice shout. Then the voice grew louder: "She's a demon!"

He grabbed the woman's hair and yanked her back from his face before he'd opened his eyes; when he did, he glimpsed the evil in her eyes when they sprang open in shock. They flashed black, devoid of irises, before quickly returning to the bright, innocent blue.

"Axel?" She tightened her grip on his arms. "Take me away from here." Her eyes burned desperately into his.

"Axel! She's the demon from the house!" Jez squealed as her body slammed into the car, ending her sprint.

The woman scowled at her. "If you'd taken a couple more minutes, we'd have been gone forever."

Axel threw her to the pavement.

"Demon, eh?"

He hadn't sensed a demon aura emanating from her—and their auras were strong enough to make you nauseous—but he had recognized the darkness in her for a brief moment. He combed his hair from his eyes and mulled over the possibilities. Maybe she was like Alastor, and not so much like the demons he'd dealt with before—but, on the other hand, she wasn't very intimidating and her powers to influence him had only been mildly stronger than what he'd seen before, and still easy enough to break away from. Alastor wasn't that weak.

He took a few steps away from Nathan's car and shook his head. "You almost had me. That's surprising, actually."

She looked up at him, her expression fierce. "You're an arrogant witch, is all." She picked herself up and brushed herself off. "Your powers are nothing compared to mine. You're still part of the pathetic human race."

Axel continued, ignoring her. "It was an odd sensation. Everything just kind of... clouded over." He focused on Jez. "I wonder if that's how Kyra feels."

He looked to the ground and thought of the pendant—the mahogany obsidian pendant—he'd given Kyra on her wedding day. It would have protected her, or at least given her a better chance of being protected, if she'd been wearing it the day the demon came for her.

Kyra had pulled it from the tiny box and smiled, her big, bright emerald eyes glistening as she held back her tears. She knew even less about crystals than he did—which was why Alexis had helped him pick it out. He had explained that it was a powerful earth crystal that would give her strength and protect her, after he moved away. He hadn't told her that it would help her to balance, grow, and bring clarity into her world. He and Alexis had both hoped it would help heal her of her fear of magic but it was never used as intended; she rarely wore it, or so Alexis had informed him, years ago.

"And you." Celista's voice jerked his attention back into the present. He looked up and watched her icy glare drift to Jezabelle. "I will be putting you back in your cage, momentarily."

Jez cocked her eyebrow at Celista. "Can we *please* kill her now?"

"I'm a fucking demon. A couple stupid witches can't kill me. I've been alive for thousands of years."

"I think we could put that theory to the test." Axel's eyes narrowed.

"Give it your best shot, bad boy."

His hands flared open. He closed his eyes, inhaling deeply; his eyelids twitched.

Celista tapped her fingernails on the roof of the car beside her, impatiently waiting for him to concede defeat. She whipped her hair around and groaned, then her expression went serious. Her breath caught in her chest. She looked down at her feet, which were beginning to smolder.

"Fire—really? I was born from hellfire." She tried to sound calm but her voice quivered.

Celista lunged at Axel. Jez reached out and pulled her off of him, then threw her to the pavement. Celista burst into flames as she hit the ground. The flames grew higher as they engulfed her, until she was a ball of orange and red rolling around on the pavement, shrieking.

The sounds stopped before she collapsed. Her body quickly turned to ash and blew away with the breeze. The flames dissipated once she evaporated into the sky.

Axel shrugged. "So much for her theory."

Chapter Twenty-Seven

Back at the Parker residence, the aroma of hamburgers drifted in the open window from the barbeque outside. Iris and Hailey were in the kitchen making a salad when the witches walked in the front door. Jezabelle followed Alexis over to the sofa and quietly sat down next to her, leaving a space between them. She pulled crystals and candles from one of her bags, handing a few items to Alexis and placing the rest beside her. She knew she had to organize them, or it would drive her crazy.

Axel marched over to the coffee table, turned his bag upside down, and dumped the contents out.

"So what's the plan?" Nick asked, looking over the contents on the coffee table: rolls of duct tape, nylon rope, and a bag of zip ties. "Are you going to try to kidnap her?"

"I don't know." Axel shrugged. "There wasn't much to pick from."

"The kiss thing didn't work." Alexis looked up from the polished crystals in her hands. "Kidnapping her is not a half bad idea—at least it would get her away from the demon, if we can't figure out how to coax her back. But I don't know how we would keep her from using her powers on us."

"I do." Jez felt herself flush with excitement when the others looked at her in surprise. She was finally going to be able to help them—really help them. "My mom taught me about angels and melharas, and their powers."

Alexis swung toward her and scooped her up in a tight embrace.

"We're going to have to teach each other our tricks after this nightmare is over." She laughed, released Jez, and smiled.

"Me too," Xavier said, eyeing the crystals as he climbed onto his Uncle Nick's lap.

Axel grunted. "Talking to Kyra and reminding her of the things she lost sort of worked." He ran his fingers through his hair. "I think it was starting to work until the distraction for the demon ended. Maybe if there had been more time…"

"It didn't even sort of work," Hailey said, walking into the living room drying her hands with a tea towel. "She killed James."

"Maybe the kiss didn't work because it was the wrong man," Nick offered, looking over the faces in the room before his eyes came to rest on his wife's scowl. It was obvious to Jez that Hailey didn't like the idea of Axel being her sister's unbreakable love, and she was pretty sure she knew why.

"Well, it sure did piss off the demon when it happened." Hailey plopped down on the empty loveseat and kicked her feet up to sit cross-legged.

"Is that the plan?" Axel asked as he sat down next to Jez. "I'll corner her and kiss her and hope I don't end up like James, or should we try to kidnap her first?"

"Yeah, you would like to be her hero, wouldn't you," Hailey said bitterly as Iris stepped into the living room.

Jez kicked Axel's foot. His head swiveled toward her and she jerked her head toward Hailey, her eyes wide, silently urging him to resolve the issue with the other woman.

He grunted then said through clenched teeth, "What is your problem, Hailey?" He stole a glance at Jez before adding, "You've been a bitch since this whole thing started."

Iris slowed her pace, looking at Axel, stunned. Jez shook her head, disappointed in his last statement.

"My problem? What's your problem?" She threw her legs down on the floor and leaned toward him. "You're an asshole!" She threw her tea towel at him and he swatted it to the floor.

Iris halted, her head pivoting back and forth between Axel and Hailey, mouth agape.

"How could you have had an affair with my sister; how could you do this to—to James and to Kyra?" She looked away and softly added, "Messing with her head like that." Hailey leaned back in her seat, then jerked her head back to glower at Axel. "This is all your fault. You made her weak, and that's why the demon showed up and was able to turn her."

"Hailey, I didn't make her weak," he said softly, leaning toward her. "No one could make Kyra weak. She joined him to protect us."

"It was my fault," Iris cut in as she sat down next to Hailey. "She said yes because I was dumb and would've given my soul to the demon. I didn't really believe that he was a demon... until it was too late."

"It doesn't matter," Hailey said, shaking her head. "I still think Axel is a shit-disturber and shouldn't have gotten involved with Kyra." Her body stiffened as her eyes met Axel's. She gave him a long, pained look before she broke eye contact, snuck in a quick glance at Nick, and dropped her head.

"I'm sorry. I never meant..." He trailed off. "I never meant to hurt anyone." Axel reached out and placed his hand on her knee, making Hailey flinch. "I love her. I always have."

She bit her lip, her sullen gaze lingering on Axel before she shook his hand off her leg. "It still doesn't give you the right to get involved with someone else's wife."

"Aunty Hailey?"

Her face softened as her eyes drifted to her nephew. She forced a smile.

"Don't be mad at Axel. Dad's not anymore."

"What?" Hailey sighed heavily. "I don't know, it just seems wrong. James and Kyra were happy until Axel moved back into town and messed it up."

"No, they weren't," Alexis interjected. "You haven't been around enough to notice."

"Damnit all to hell," Hailey huffed then cracked a weak smile at Axel. "I do remember her hesitation on her wedding day. She did talk to me about you." She sighed, pressed her hands together, and massaged her palms. "I told her that James was the right choice."

"What's done is done. It's not your fault. I should've stepped up and told her about my feelings, before she married James."

Alexis shifted uncomfortably in her seat. "If we're placing blame, then it's on me. I knew both sides. Neither one of you two actually told me until later, but I just knew and should've said something."

"It's not your fault, sis," Axel said, leaning forward to look around Jezabelle at her.

"There's no point in trying to figure out what could've been," Jez said, looking from Axel and Hailey to Alexis. "The question is, what are we going to do now?"

Alexis smacked her hands together and rose. "Axel, Jez, and I will go to the hideout as soon as we hear from Nathan." She pulled her phone from her pocket.

"No way. She's my daughter. I'm going too."

"Iris, you have no way of defending yourself. It's too risky. There's no way of knowing how many men roam that house."

"You, my dear, don't have any powers either. Don't talk to me like I'm an ignorant, helpless old woman. I'm going and that's final."

Alexis looked to Axel for help. He shrugged.

She sighed, defeated. "Fine," she said, and dropped onto the sofa. "Axel, Jez, Iris, and I will go into the pit of Hell and hope we come back alive."

"Well, that sounds promising," Nick said, overly upbeat.

"We're going." Axel's stomach grumbled. "But after dinner, of course."

"I'm going to call Nathan and see where he's at with tracking her down." Alexis rose and headed out of the living room. "We can't do anything until we know where we're going." She thumped up the stairs, two at a time.

"If we can even locate the tracking device," Axel called after her. "It's been days since she left with it and who knows what happened to it."

***

Jensen Harris had been packing the leftovers into the fridge when Kyra walked in and startled him.

"You're mighty jumpy. What's for lunch?"

"Just leftover bacon and egg salad, so you can make a sandwich if you like," he said, handing her the glass bowl full of crispy bacon. "Would you like me to make you a plate?"

"I'll get it." She eyed him suspiciously as she pulled the dish from his hands and slid it onto the countertop with the others. "Your color is quite a bit off." She made circular motions with her hands, as if she were washing an invisible pane of glass. Then she grabbed a plate from the stack on the counter and started picking at the bacon. "My, my, what have you been up to?" she asked without looking up from the food.

He thought of the woman in the basement—the beautiful Jezabelle—and the stressful interrogation the white-haired chick had put him through. She had asked him if he had let her out of her cell, to which he had said no. It was true; he hadn't actually let her out… he'd merely left the keys and she'd let herself out, locked up behind her, and left them hidden in the grass under the window for him to collect in the morning.

"Sorry ma'am, I don't understand what you mean."

"Your aura is a little... *off*." She turned around to face him, holding a plate of crumbled bacon under a scoop of egg salad. She lifted a forkful and put it in her mouth, then dragged her teeth along the fork.

He winced. "I-I've just been cooking and cleaning." He broke eye contact. "Not much to do around here," he stammered.

"For your sake, I hope so," she said coldly, and left the kitchen with her plate.

Jensen pressed his palm to his heart and breathed a sigh of relief.

***

Alexis listened intently, her iPhone pressed to her ear, as she walked into the living room. She felt the eyes of the group watching her as she slowly wandered around in the small space.

"Well?" Axel prodded. She held up her free hand to silence him and continued pacing, staring at the carpet.

She stopped short. "What are you talking about?" She shook her head. "That can't be right."

"What now?" Axel grumbled.

"Hang on, I'm going to put you on speaker." She pressed the button and gently tossed her phone onto the Parkers' coffee table. "'Kay, go."

Jezabelle slid over on the sofa to make room for Alexis to sit next to her brother.

"I found the tracking device out in a bush in the middle of nowhere. The data shows it hasn't moved for days."

"How do you know it's in a bush?" Iris asked, leaning forward and raising her voice louder than she needed to for him to hear her.

"I can see the location over the satellite."

"What, like Google maps?" Hailey asked hesitantly as she glanced around at the others.

There was a long silent pause before Nathan's voice came from the phone, and Alexis imagined he was rolling his eyes—except he wouldn't do that; he was probably shaking his head.

"Sort of, but the satellites we use have a live feed so I can tell you that there is nothing there. It's just trees and hills. There's no buildings or human activity for miles."

Alexis and Axel exchanged a skeptical look. "We still need to check it out," she insisted. "What's the location?"

"I can give you the coordinates."

"Never mind," Axel interrupted. "Nathan, we're coming over to see you. We'll be there in a minute." He reached forward and hit the *End* button.

"What the hell?" Alexis shot her brother an annoyed look.

"Hey, now that we can travel, why not have this conversation face to face? Then we can see this location and satellite images for ourselves." He flashed a quick smile and winked at her. "Nathan doesn't have quite the understanding of magic tricks that we do."

Alexis looked at Xavier. He jumped up from his chair and nodded with his hands out, ready to go. Axel took his hand and Alexis grabbed Jezabelle's, then Xavier's, and they vanished.

***

Nathan jumped in his chair when they appeared in his living room.

"That's very unnerving, you know," he said, smirking as he stood to greet them. The room was cluttered with computers and electronics, linked by masses of cords and wires that snaked over the floor.

"Sorry." Alexis felt her face flush. "We had to come and see for ourselves."

"The location is up on that monitor." He pointed to a desktop computer and screen that rested on the floor a few feet away. "And I did some research on the land." He pulled some papers from the pile next to the printer and shuffled through them. "The only thing that's a little odd is that the property changed hands back to an original owner."

Jez and Axel sank to their knees in front of the monitor to study its visuals.

"Huh. Who owns it?" Alexis asked, reaching out to take the papers from Nathan.

"It was owned by Derek Sommers from 1982 until it sold to Jed Moot in 2010, then just this past month it was bought by Derek Sommers again. Even odder is that it seems to just be a paper trail. The only financial transaction that I could find is when Derek originally bought the land in 1982. He purchased it from the estate sale of a very recently deceased John Steller. It sold at auction for way under its value."

Alexis stood looking at Nathan. "Kyra and I were born in 1982," she whispered.

"Jed and Derek? Jed and Derek..." Axel repeated the names slowly as he rose to his feet. "'Jed and Derek.' That sounds so familiar..."

"The demon sent for a Jed and Derek when we were all held captive." Alexis bounced on the balls of her feet then lurched forward, wrapping her arms around Nathan's neck. "That's the place! No doubt about it."

She squeezed him tighter when his hands came up to her hips. A wave of euphoria washed over her. They had found the hideout and they were going to find Kyra. She gave him a couple of pecks on the cheek, pulled away, and watched his face redden.

"Yes." Axel punched his fist into his other palm. "Kyra killed the Jed guy; that must be why they changed the land title again."

***

"Vance!" Jensen burst into their room. "We have to get out of here right now."

Vance looked up from his plate. "What's wrong now?" He asked before he shoved another piece of bacon into his mouth.

He scanned the room quickly and rushed over to the couch. "The Kyra chick is onto me," he whispered.

Vance's face scrunched up, and he jerked his head back. "What are you babbling about?"

"She's totally suspicious. She said something about 'my colors' being off and was asking me questions about what I've been up to. Then I said, 'Nothing, just working,' and she said, 'I hope so, for your sake.' We can't stay here anymore."

"You're overreacting. I'm sure it's fine." Vance looked back down to his plate and picked up his soggy bread. "Besides, we have nowhere to go, and the world has gotten a lot worse out there since we've been here," he added, giving Jensen a serious look. "I see that crap all day long in that stupid computer room." His mouth opened wide and he chomped out a quarter of the sandwich; bits of egg goo plopped onto his plate.

"If we stay, I'll end up dead," Jensen said, sitting down.

Vance swallowed his food and wiped his mouth with his sleeve. "Then you go and I'll stay."

"They'll probably kill you because you knew and didn't tell them."

"They won't know I knew." Vance put down his sandwich and grabbed a piece of bacon. "I'll just play dumb." He smiled and shoved the bacon into his mouth.

"Oh, for fuck sakes." Jensen jerked the plate from Vance's lap and slid it to the far end of the coffee table. "You're a moron. They'd kill you anyway because we bunk together. Don't you remember that asshole, Travis, who was killed for spilling his drink on the hot chick? And then she killed his roommate for fun."

He shrugged. "Meh. She's not around anymore," he said, reaching for his plate.

Jensen leaned in front of him, blocking his reach. "The others are worse. This is their house."

"You're probably right." Vance dropped his arm and settled back against the couch. "I don't know what you think we're gonna do once we're outta here." He let out a heavy sigh. "This is some mess you managed to drag me into, and all for some stupid girl you'll never see again."

"What, me? I told you getting into that stupid truck was a bad idea. If we hadn't, we wouldn't be in this mess."

"If you hadn't helped that girl get out of here, we could just enjoy being here," Vance retorted.

"Are you crazy? How could I let a bunch of demons keep her locked up? They might have ate her or something."

They both laughed.

"Yeah, I know your bleeding heart can't mind its own business," Vance joked. "Especially if there's a cute damsel in distress involved." He threw his feet up on the coffee table.

"If you'd seen her you'd have done the same thing," Jensen said.

"Maybe, but I wouldn't be acting like a paranoid schizo every day since."

"Well, it's too late and I wouldn't change what I did, anyway. The only thing I would change is getting in that truck and ending up under the same roof as a bunch of demons."

"We have to sneak out in the middle of the night, not right now, so calm down." He smacked Jensen on the back. "Don't do anything out of the ordinary. I have to get to work or there'll be hell to pay." He snickered and Jensen frowned. "Oh come on, that was funny."

"Not really."

Chapter Twenty-Eight

Jezabelle and Axel finished casting spells and placing crystals around the Parker residence to keep out unwanted visitors before they rushed inside to join the others in the living room. Axel pushed his way past the Majai men, skulking in the area behind the armchair, grunting a belated "Thanks" as they belatedly stepped aside.

Jezabelle took Alexis's outstretched hand and reached for Iris, who was already holding Xavier's hand.

"Remember," Axel said, taking Xavier's free hand and watching his face, "land us somewhere out of sight. We need to be sneaky."

"Argh, I know." Xavier squeezed Axel's hand. "Don't worry, I got this."

"Be careful, you guys, and good luck." Hailey gave a little wave as Nick wrapped his arm around her waist and nodded.

They vanished from the Parker house, reappearing in a cluster of evergreen shrubs fifteen yards from the immense two-story mansion silhouetted against the sun setting behind it. They quickly ducked down and scanned the area.

"It's okay," Xavier assured Axel as he pulled him closer to the ground by his wrist. "No one's outside," he said calmly.

Jez closed her eyes and chanted under her breath. "Okay, we should be invisible to human eyes," she announced when she'd finished the spell.

Axel stood up, looked down at Xavier, and said, "Xavier, you get home." Xavier rolled his eyes and vanished.

Jez stepped away from the shelter of the shrubbery. "This place freaks me out," she said, looking over the building. "I can't believe I came back here."

"You'll be okay. We are all in this together." Alexis squeezed her hand, smiling encouragingly.

Jez flashed a tight smile. "Let's get this over with and get out of here," she said, and started toward the entrance.

As the witches strolled up to the oversized double doors, Iris tiptoed behind them, then crept along the house with her back against the wall, ducking to scurry under a window. Alexis glanced back, then stopped.

"Iris, what are you doing? No one can see you."

"Oh, right." She straightened and brushed her hands self-consciously over her pants. "Are you sure? Because I can see you guys."

Alexis giggled. "It doesn't work like that. Just trust me, no one can see you."

"But, you can see me and I can see you," Iris said, flicking her finger back and forth between them.

"When people are invisible they can see everyone else who is invisible."

"So, does that mean just our group, or could we see if someone else was invisible in the house already? Would they be able to see us too?" Iris asked, pulling on her earlobe.

Axel realized that he should have agreed with Alexis and left Iris behind—they couldn't afford to be distracted by babysitting and magic lessons.

"Only us, as a group, because we are all under the same cast." Alexis waved for her to catch up. "Come on." Iris glanced around nervously as she rushed to join the others.

Jez placed her hand on the wooden door and closed her eyes. "The entry is empty." She reached for the door handle.

Axel put his hand against the door. "Wait. I'll go first and check it out. I'm going to try my powers and see if we're screwed."

"Oh, please. At least you still have your powers," Alexis said bitterly.

He whipped around to face his sister. "Get over it, already. You're still alive, aren't you?"

"I can't." Her shoulders slumped. "I don't even have my passive powers. It's like having long hair your whole life and then some ass shaves your head."

"*What?*"

Iris nodded sympathetically.

"It's a chick thing," Jez explained.

Axel shook his head and slowly pushed the heavy door open, grimacing as it creaked. He peered inside. Empty. He exhaled and realized he'd been holding his breath. He squeezed inside the barely open doorway and opened his palm. Flames grew from his hand. He closed his hand and snuffed them.

"All clear," he whispered. "Magic is working."

Alexis slipped through the entrance, followed by Iris and Jez.

Axel closed his eyes, searching for Kyra's presence.

The door flew open behind them. Everyone jumped. Iris parted her lips, about to speak, but Alexis clamped a hand over her mouth and pulled her to the side.

"They can't see you," she whispered into Iris's ear, "but they can hear us."

Jez and Axel stepped out of the path of the three men as they crossed the foyer, chatting amongst themselves, unaware of the intruders. When they turned down the hall past the staircases, Iris breathed a sigh of relief.

"It's faint, but I think she's upstairs," Axel announced, smiling.

They crept up the stairs, pausing at the top while Axel looked in both directions. The carpeted hallway stretched the length of the mansion. It was empty and quiet.

"This way." Axel pointed to the double doors at one end of the hall. "She's in there."

As they approached the doors, they heard voices coming from another room. Slowing as they neared an open door, Axel held up his hand for the others to wait and peered around the edge of the doorframe into the room. He quickly pulled back and faced the others. "The demon is in there."

"Great. Just great," Jez whispered, shaking her head.

"Can we just sneak past and get into that room?" Alexis pointed to the doors a few yards away.

Axel shrugged and hurried past the doorway, then turned on the far side and motioned for the others to follow him. Tiptoeing across the opening, Jez glanced inside the room, and froze. Alexis hurried past her, pulling Iris along. Axel looked at Jez's face, followed her stare, then grabbed her arm and tugged her across.

They stopped in front of the closed double doors and he whispered to Jez, "What was that about?"

She shook her head. "The guy in there, talking to Alastor, is the one who helped me escape. I'm surprised he's still here."

Alexis and Jez each grabbed hold of a door handle. They looked at each other.

"Same time," Alexis said to Jez, then looked at Axel. "Ready?"

He gave a quick nod, then jerked his head toward the door. She turned to Jez, crouching as if she were about to sprint off the start line in a track race. "One, two… three!"

The doors swung open and Axel walked through. Kyra stood looking out a large picture window; she looked over her shoulder at the doorway. Iris rushed in as Kyra scanned over the group, not giving Axel any indication she could see them.

Jez and Alexis softly closed the doors behind them. Kyra turned fully and took a couple steps toward the door.

Axel glanced around the room. This was a bedroom—Kyra's bedroom. Everything was black: the bed, the blankets, the furniture, the walls, and even the curtains and the carpet. Silver chandeliers and lamps glinted throughout the room. It saddened him a bit—the Kyra he knew would have hated any all-black room, never mind her bedroom. As he looked closer he made out the symbols for spells etched in silver on the walls.

"Clever." Kyra closed her eyes and took a deep breath. "The old lady, eh." Her eyes opened and she put her hands on her hips. "Who else is with you?" she demanded, glaring across the space between them.

Jez and Axel exchanged a glance. She cast the spell that made them visible again.

"Axel, the powerless witch, and the escapee. What a group you guys make." Kyra tipped her head back and released a mocking laugh.

"Kyra," Axel said, stepping forward.

"Shhhh." She cocked her head. "Who's the straggler?"

"What?"

Kyra swept her arms through the air, ripping the crystals Xavier clutched in his hands from his grasp with a jerk. He became visible to everyone and stepped out from the corner of the room.

"Ah, the kid."

"Xavier, get out of here now!" Axel shouted.

"No. You guys need my help and she's my mom." He took Iris's hand.

Axel took another step toward Kyra. She scowled at him and crossed her arms. He took another cautious step, trying to gauge her receptiveness.

She rolled her eyes. "Are you scared? Poor baby."

"Well, you are kind of crazy nowadays, aren't you?" He moved another step.

She stomped her foot. "I can show you crazy," she snarled. She raised her hand over her head.

Axel moved in quickly, reaching her in two strides. He grabbed her by the wrist and pulled her to him. She stopped struggling when he stroked her face with the back of his free hand. She looked up at him and her expression softened. Their bodies pressed up against each other, his hand trailing up her spine to the base of her neck. She gasped. He leaned in, closing his eyes, and their lips met. Kyra relaxed further and let her eyelids drift closed as she returned the kiss. They held the embrace for a moment, then Kyra pushed Axel away from her. She looked into his eyes, her hands still resting on his chest.

The door to the bedroom banged open. Kyra shoved Axel away and he stumbled backward as everyone turned toward the doorway.

The demon stood in the opening, looking pissed.

"How dare you come here," he growled, his eyes darting from face to face. His physical form flickered into a grotesque, black-horned, gray-skinned creature before stabilizing into its human form. His eyes remained black pools. His head turned toward Kyra. "Darling, kill them all for this intrusion of my sanctuary."

Jez looked to Axel and he nodded. He flung his fists open and unleashed fireballs toward Alastor's head. The demon ducked into the room.

Behind him, two of his men were fast approaching. Jez faltered, her eyes locked on one of them.

"Jensen," she murmured as he held out his hands and motioned for her to calm down.

The two men entered the room, quickly surveying the occupants. The man called Jensen looked surprised when he saw young Xavier standing in the room. Alexis lunged at the other man as he entered the room behind Jensen, and they toppled to the floor, grappling.

Axel and Jez circled Alastor. The demon deflected the fire attack as quickly as Axel could hurl balls of flame at him, but when Jez held out her palms toward him, the demon began to cough and sputter out water. Distracted, he missed blocking some of Axel's shots, and flames exploded on his skin.

Kyra moved toward Jez, preparing to strike. Jensen sprinted forward and slammed into Kyra. They hit the floor hard. He rolled away and scrambled to his feet.

She rolled onto her elbows and shot an angry glare up at him. "I knew you were trouble," she hissed. She picked herself up as Jensen headed for the doorway, where his buddy sat on top of Alexis, struggling to keep the wriggling woman pinned to the floor.

"Vance! Stop messing around. We have to stop the demons."

"She attacked me!" His gaze darted over to Jensen.

Alexis's squirming ceased. "Kyra's not a demon." They both looked at Alexis, then to each other, looking bewildered.

Iris squeezed her grandson's hand, then moved toward her daughter. "You don't belong here, sweetheart," she said. "I am still your mother and I love you."

Kyra's face hardened. She flung out her arms, reaching for her mother's throat. With his own arms raised, Xavier stepped between them. "Noooo!"

Kyra froze.

His eyes welled up with tears. "Please, Mom."

She looked upon her son's distraught face and cocked her head. Two conflicting forces struggled within her. She lowered her arms and frowned, locked in a tormented stare with her son.

Alastor saw Kyra backing down, and growled. He crossed his arms over his chest and hunched over. A loud howl escaped his throat. He jerked upright, flinging his arms open, and expelled a burst of energy outward. The shockwave knocked everyone but Kyra and Alastor off their feet.

Kyra turned to Alastor as he marched over to her, scowling. His fangs were bared and his eyes were a solid, angry black.

Iris scrambled backward, pushing herself away with her feet. She reached out to grab Xavier as the demon approached, but he ducked out of her reach. Alastor pushed Kyra aside and glared down at the child and his grandmother.

Xavier picked himself up, unfazed by the demon towering above him. He puffed out his chest and tilted his head back, looking straight up into the soulless demon eyes. Their eyes locked. Xavier defiantly crossed his arms. He raised himself on the balls of his feet, trying to be taller.

"I want my mom back," he said firmly, though his voice quavered.

A low growl gurgled from the demon.

Xavier stuck out his tongue and spat at Alastor, antagonizing him further.

The demon's roar shook the room and made the crystal chandeliers jingle. He whipped his arms above his head, hands balled into fists. His skin turned gray and horns exploded from his skull and spiraled toward the ceiling.

Xavier stepped back as the demon grew taller and wider. He gawked at the creature in front of him with recognition in his eyes. He looked to his mother, whose pensive eyes were locked on her son. She leaned forward, almost as if she were going to reach out to him, then jerked back, straightened, rolled her shoulders back, and dropped her eyes to the floor.

Alastor continued to shift. Fangs, mere white tips protruding between his thin gray lips, elongated; large, bat-like wings burst from his back and fanned open, moving forward and back in jerky sweeps. He gazed down on the child and sneered. His fists uncurled, revealing long, bony fingers tipped with shiny black claws. He splayed his clawed fingers and raised his long gray arm above his head, then swept it down, slashing through the air toward Xavier's head.

His arm slowed to a stop inches from Xavier's face. The boy slumped in relief.

Kyra stepped between them. She placed her hand on Xavier's chest and edged him away. Her eyes bored into the demon. She grabbed his wrist and twisted, releasing him from his petrified state.

His eyes narrowed as he straightened. "What are you doing?" He jerked his hand away.

Fury narrowed her eyes. "Don't ever touch my son."

"He wouldn't have died," Alastor growled, and she recoiled.

Her jaw tightened. "I can't let you hurt him," she said coldly, stepping back from the demon.

"Get these witches out of the manor right now," he ordered. "No more games."

She stood unmoving. The blank stare that had become so customary when she was in the company of the demon was gone. She was back in control of her own thoughts and out of his fog.

His roar of fury boomed throughout the room. Kyra waved her hand and silenced the demon. He closed his mouth and scowled at her. The demon slowly melted back into the young, handsome man with the knowing smile.

"Nice try," Kyra said flatly.

"Kyra, come with me," he ordered as he reached for her hand.

"No." She jerked her hand out of his reach.

He scowled. "I own you."

"Not anymore." She sneered at him. "My guess is that you can't make me do anything now, can you?"

Alastor twisted his hands in the air as if turning invisible doorknobs. The motion sucked the oxygen from the room and everyone dropped to their knees, struggling to breathe.

Kyra dropped her arms down to her sides then flicked her hands open, fingers spread and her palms facing the demon. Rolling her shoulders back, she closed her eyes and pushed her arms inward.

The invisible oxygenless bubble shrank in toward the demon. Alexis and the two ex-cons were the farthest from Alastor and the first to begin gasping as air again filled their lungs. Gradually the others were able to breathe again as the invisible force moved inward.

Alastor began to struggle for breath as Kyra tightened her grip around him. He coughed. She drew her fingers into fists. He coughed without making a sound. His body convulsed. She clenched her fists tighter as he clawed at his neck, pulling at the invisible hands that strangled him.

He slammed his hands together, sending a shockwave through the room. Kyra stumbled back. His rigid body relaxed as the crushing sensation Kyra had been inflicting upon him ceased.

"I cannot die from asphyxiation, darling," he told her calmly. "Demons have no need to breathe."

Axel and Jez sidled over to stand next to Alexis, who moved with Iris to take Xavier's hand. Jensen and Vance slipped in behind them. They all strode over to stand behind Kyra.

"My melhara is lost to me," Alastor murmured, then added more firmly, "for now." His eyes narrowed, focused on Kyra.

And then he was gone.

Chapter Twenty-Nine

Brilliant white light burst from inside Kyra's body. She jerked backward, her arms flung over her head as she was lifted from her feet. She hovered, suspended in midair, as the light engulfed her.

The light faded away and then her body drifted to the floor. She lay there unconscious, her blonde hair, now restored, sprayed over her face.

Xavier rushed to her. Axel dropped to his knees next to her. He swept the tendrils from her face as he lifted her torso onto his lap.

"Kyra, Kyra." He shook her gently and bent over her face, listening to her shallow breaths. "She's still breathing. We need to get her home."

"He should come with us," Jez said, and nodded at Jensen.

"No way." Axel's head shot up to meet Jez's gaze. "He's one of Alastor's minions."

"Not anymore," she said, shaking her head. "He just helped us. And," she flung her arms open, "he's the reason I escaped in the first place." She dropped her arms and smiled at Jensen.

Alexis looked him up and down, then nodded.

"What about him?" Iris asked, pointing to Vance.

Alexis looked over at Vance and raised an eyebrow. "You better not cause any trouble." She crossed her arms.

Vance nodded and smiled. "No worries. I'll be a good boy," he said with a wink.

Kyra stirred. Her eyes popped open and Axel sat back and gusted a sigh of relief when she smiled and sat up. He stood and helped Kyra to her feet. Confused, she looked around the room at the people in it as if she was seeing them for the first time.

Jez took Jensen's hand and lead him over to grab Xavier's. He smiled up at his mother and took her hand.

"You brought them here?" she whispered to her son.

"Yep," he said, his eyes gleaming.

"How? I didn't travel until I was a teenager."

He glanced at Alexis, then back to Kyra. "I've been practicing," he said cautiously, dropping his eyes to the carpet.

She looked at Alexis, concerned. "Can you cast?"

"No, that part doesn't work."

"Can we discuss this elsewhere, please?" Jez urged, her eyes darting around the room.

"She's right," Alexis said. "Let's go."

They tightened their grip on each other's hands and vanished from the black bedroom.

***

They reappeared in the safety of the Parker living room, where Iris guided Kyra to the sofa. Hailey pulled her down to sit beside her, then wrapped her arms around her sister, fighting back tears. She looked over the two newcomers, dismissed them, and directed her attention to Axel.

"I guess I was wrong about you."

Jensen and Vance looked at each other and shrugged. Jensen surveyed the room, then nudged Vance and nodded toward the Majai men standing behind James's armchair. They walked over to stand with them.

Axel shrugged. "It wasn't me. It was Xavier." He tousled Xavier's hair before he dropped down onto the loveseat. Xavier patted his hair back down like he was brushing an infestation of bugs off his head, then hopped up to sit next to Axel.

"There is no love like the love between a mother and her child," Iris said, smiling at Hailey and Kyra.

Kyra sat silently on the couch, staring straight ahead as her sister hugged her. She blocked out the noisy chatter of everyone around her, pushing the excited voices to the back of her mind. Confusion festered in her mind. Everything felt somehow different. The cloud over her had dissipated and her mind flooded with memories that made her skin crawl. She shuddered.

"It wasn't me," she choked out. "I mean, it was me, but it wasn't." She searched their faces for some hint of understanding or forgiveness—maybe both—even though she hadn't allowed herself to do the same. "It was like I was drugged or something; I don't understand what happened. I honestly thought you guys were the bad guys and I was doing the right thing."

"But, he's a demon." Hailey pulled back, looking astonished, as if Kyra had just slapped her. "How could he be the good guy?"

"Yeah, didn't you remember your dreams?" Alexis asked, placing a hand on Kyra's knee as she sat down on the floor at her feet.

"I do remember my dreams, but when I was with Alastor—" Axel grunted; Kyra looked at him and decided to choose her words carefully. "I mean, when I was with the demon, I thought of them differently. They weren't a warning of evil to come. It was like I shouldn't have been afraid of the dreams, or my powers, or anything, because it was my destiny. I remembered the angels in my dreams as the evil beings." She shook her head. "It's not so black and white. Having been on both sides of the spectrum, I see it as a broad range of beliefs concerning what is best for all the worlds and all the souls in them."

She felt their eyes on her and the skepticism—along with suspicion—that radiated from them, and knew she had to explain without making them think she was still with Alastor.

"Death on this Earth is irrelevant. We live on in another plane of existence. The choices we make here determine where that eternal life will be. There are billions of souls trapped in Hell, some for eons." She looked over their faces. "That's what he's trying to change."

"So evil can get into Heaven?" Hailey asked, her voice nearly cracking, tight with fear.

"No, he's trying to unlock the gates of Hell. We can't let that happen. The souls in Hell far exceed the souls in Heaven, and it would be impossible to shift the balance away from evil." She felt her chest tighten and knew she had played a part in the destruction of the world. She pressed her fist against her breastbone and bit the inside of her cheek, pushing her guilt aside—for the moment. She swallowed and dropped her hand. "If he succeeds, Heaven's gates will lock, trapping the good souls there, and evil would run rampant on Earth and the other planes."

"What is all this planes stuff everyone keeps talking about?" Nick asked softly, reaching around Xavier to nudge Axel.

Kyra wriggled to the edge of her seat and leaned forward, distancing herself from her mother and sister and deliberately invading Alexis's space, hoping to get her friend to find another spot to sit. She shook her hand in a little wave at Nick until he met her eyes.

"Okay, so the way I understand it..." she started as Alexis moved from the floor and sat on the coffee table, "...there are seven planes of existence. Earth is one, Atlantis is another—but it's actually Heaven. They are all on a different sort of—of frequency. It's like invisible layers on top of each other, but it's very rare that anyone sees each other unless they cross into that plane."

Alexis shifted her weight and opened her mouth, about to speak.

"And Jez is your half-sister," Xavier added casually, his heels kicking the sofa. "You have the same mom."

Everyone gaped at him. His legs slowed, then stopped, and he shrank back against Axel. Jez and Kyra eyeballed each other in the silence that enveloped the room. The others looked back and forth between the two women.

Jez, perched on the arm of the sofa chair, lowered herself into the seat, her gaze shifting from Kyra to Xavier, her eyes wide. She leaned back and looked at Kyra.

"Is he right? Are we really sisters?" Jezabelle asked.

"I don't know." Kyra fidgeted with her hands. "But it feels true, doesn't it?"

"It does feel…" She trailed off.

"Where's your mom, Jez?" Hailey probed.

"I don't know. She vanished years ago. The police never came up with any leads and I couldn't track her down with magic." She turned to Kyra. "Why *did* you kidnap me and keep me alive?"

"Alastor said we had to. He said you were a powerful witch that could stop us, but we weren't allowed to kill you." Her cheeks burned and she dropped her eyes. "He never told me why, but if you're my sister you'd be protected by the deal I made—or maybe it has something to do with the rules in the prophecy."

"What rules?" Hailey's head jerked from Jezabelle to Kyra.

"There are rules that Alastor has to follow in order to stay on Earth. I don't know what they all are—only Alastor knows every detail of the prophecy—except for the Majai, of course, who are experts on the prophecy." She nodded in their direction.

"You've heard about them?" Axel asked, surprised, then glared at the silent figures across the room. "Why didn't they tell us the rest of the prophecy?"

"They are from Atlantis and only here to witness the events of the prophecy. I don't know why, but I know Alastor fears them, and he isn't afraid of anything."

"Hey, I know I'm changing the subject here," Alexis said, gathering her hair and pulling it over her shoulder, "but were you using my powers at that hideout, or whatever you call it? Did you steal my powers?" She tossed her hair behind her.

Kyra laughed. "Yes, I used them but no, I didn't steal them. I just blocked you from using them. You were attacking me with them, remember?"

Alexis stood up and started to pace. "But you blocked my passive powers too, and that's not even possible; I didn't know anyone could do that, or use someone else's powers—without casting a joint spell, I mean."

"I didn't know it blocked your passive powers too, but I know how we can draw off each other's strengths and abilities, if we let each other."

"How could I have let you when I didn't know you could even do that?"

"You wanted to use your powers to stop the demon from suffocating us, but you couldn't use them and you wanted me to fight him. The combination of those two thoughts let me tap into your magic."

"Can you do that to any witch?" Jez asked, her eyebrows furrowing.

"You guys can too," Kyra said, excited. "I'll teach you. Alastor taught me. I know it sounds bad because he's a demon, but drawing from others is not good or evil, it's power sharing."

"Power sharing?"

Kyra nodded. "Alastor always drew from me when we were out in public."

"Can you fix me, please?" Alexis clasped her hands together. "It's like I've lost a limb, not being able to use them."

"Yes, of course." Kyra rose and walked over to Alexis. She grabbed her friend's hands. The room seemed to swirl around them, everything passing in a blur, their hair dancing in the breeze. Then it was over and their hair gently drifted down over their shoulders.

Kyra's smile switched to a frown when her stomach flipped. She put her hand on her chest, trying to ease the bile rising in her throat. She gagged. Her hand moved to cover her mouth as she charged for the washroom.

Chapter Thirty

Hailey groaned as the sound of Kyra's heaves filtered out to the living room, followed by vomit splashing into the toilet.

"I'll go check on her," Axel offered, and left the room.

The washroom door was open. Kyra knelt hunched over, her head resting on her arms as they hugged the toilet bowl. Her hair fell around her.

"Kyra, are you all right?" Axel asked as he entered the washroom.

She raised her head slightly, looking pale and exhausted. "Yep. Just need a minute."

He closed the door behind him and crouched down on the floor beside her. She rolled her head back into the bowl and heaved again. Axel gathered up her hair and held it back for her.

"Don't. Please don't," she said, her voice echoing into the porcelain bowl.

"Don't what?"

"Don't comfort me. I don't deserve it. I've done horrible things."

"It's over now." He gently rubbed in circles on her back. "We can set things right."

She sat up, her eyes fixed on him, her expression serious. "People are dead. People I killed. And that can't be fixed or set *right*." She pulled her hair from his hand and tossed it behind her.

"It wasn't your fault, babe. You weren't yourself." He reached out to rub her arm but she jerked her shoulder back, as if his hand would burn her.

"It was me. It wasn't the demon or his power over me." Her shoulders slumped and her gaze dropped to the floor. "It was me."

"Part of it might have been you, but that wasn't the real you, Kyra." He sighed, wishing he could find the right words to ease her pain. "I know you, and of all the things you are, heartless is not on the list."

"I went to Colleen's house," she whispered, confessing to the tiles on the floor. "I left her husband in a trance to kill her." She glanced at Axel and quickly looked away. "Alastor had nothing to do with that. It was all me."

He shook his head, refusing to believe that she would kill an innocent person, outside of the demon's influence.

"Maybe your resentment toward her was intensified by the demon's darkness over you."

"Oh God, James." She dropped her head down into her hands. "I don't know what was really me and what was the demon. I can't separate them."

"It doesn't matter now. This is all part of fate or destiny or whatever you want to call it; it was meant to happen this way."

Her head shot up. "What was? That I was meant to kill my husband so we could be together?" Her eyes filled with tears. "I don't think so. That's too terrible."

"I don't know what it means, but what's done is done."

Kyra slumped down further and sobbed. "It's not right. I killed my husband."

"Didn't you say that this life doesn't matter, but where we go after does?" He cupped her chin and lifted her face. "James was a good guy and if anyone can get into Heaven, he will."

She pulled away from his touch. "But it's different, because I'm the one who killed him."

He inched closer. "That wasn't you, Kyra. It was the demon," he reassured her, rubbing her back. He touched her face. "We will get through this together. I'll always be there for you."

She fell forward and threw her arms around him. "I know," she sobbed, her wet cheek pressed up against his. "I-I can't just run into your arms. I think it's wrong—"

"What? Why? How could you feel that it would be wrong for us to be together?"

She gave him a look like that was the stupidest question he could ever have asked. "The fact that I killed my husband earlier this week," she sobbed.

The door creaked open. "Don't cry, Mom," Xavier said softly. "Dad said he's okay."

Kyra quickly pulled away from Axel. "What, honey? He talked to you?"

"Yeah. He tried to talk to you first, but it didn't work." He kicked at the grout in the tiles. "I think you don't see ghosts anymore because of what Grandma Iris did when you were little, like me."

She cocked her head, mulling it over, and Axel knew she was remembering the long eight years she had seen a child psychiatrist, and the ever-changing cocktail of prescription drugs she'd been given during those years, as they tried to "fix" her.

"What did Daddy say?"

"He wants me to tell you he's sorry, and he loves us."

She started crying again. "I'm so sorry, baby. I'm sorry for everything that has happened. I'm sorry Daddy's gone and it's all my fault."

Xavier rushed to her side. "It's okay, Mom. Don't cry." He wrapped his thin arms around her neck. "Dad wants you to stop being sad and go fight the demon."

Axel patted Xavier's back. "Does he know how we kill the demon?"

Xavier shook his head. "But I know you need the power of the four friends."

"Is that what the 'four friends' thing was about? How do you know that?"

"I know lots of things—I'm part angel too, ya know."

Kyra laughed and pulled back, but kept her arms around him as she looked into his face.

"Wow, you've sure changed since I've been gone."

He shrugged. "It's kinda cool, not hiding that I'm different anymore. But sometimes," his eyes shifted to Axel, "you guys are kinda weirded out."

"Nah, just surprised." Axel smiled. "It's odd, how much you seem to know."

The three of them hugged on the bathroom floor before Axel and Xavier rejoined the group in the living room. Kyra remained behind to quickly brush her teeth.

Nail polish, a nail file, pens, lipstick, and other small items from Alexis's purse danced around above her head as she played with her powers. Axel chuckled and Alexis floated the items back into her purse, her face reddening.

Jensen and Vance had relocated to sit on the floor in front of the entertainment unit, presumably to be part of the conversation, or—more likely—have a better view of Alexis's magic show.

Axel looked over the vacant seating and decided to leave the bigger space next to Nick open for Kyra. He squeezed into the space on the sofa between his sister and Hailey, and instantly sensed Hailey's unease as she shuffled over, stealing a glance at Nick.

Kyra entered the room with a renewed glow and Nick eyed her suspiciously.

Jez straightened her dress and said, "Axel killed one of the demons that escaped from Hell this morning. It wasn't any harder than killing a regular demon."

"What?" Kyra stopped short and her head swiveled around the room. "Who? How?"

"Some white-haired chick." Axel shrugged. "She almost had me, but Jez screamed and I snapped out of it."

"Celista," Kyra seethed. "That bitch."

Jensen and Vance turned to each other, looking surprised.

Kyra let out a heavy sigh, turning to Axel. "She went after you to get back at me."

"Why would she try to take revenge on you through me? You were off in the land of evil and didn't seem to care about anyone but that stupid demon. That's who she shoulda taken out, and saved us the trouble."

Kyra stared sorrowfully into his eyes and Hailey shifted uncomfortably, bumping in to Axel. He smirked.

"Aw, you still cared about me, even when you were evil. The demon chick knew it and that's why she was after me." He winked at her.

She scowled back at him.

"What, was that too soon for an *evil* joke?" He smiled.

"You were just easy prey for that demon bitch, Celista." She smirked. "Are you sure she's dead?"

Axel nodded without hesitation. "We definitely killed her."

"Yes, she went up in flames and we left her as a pile of ash blowing away in the parking lot," Jez added.

"That's fantastic." Kyra beamed.

"So, do you think she went back to Hell?" Jez asked, twisting the ring on her finger. "Or maybe to the angel and demon plane? Think she can get back to Earth, or is she like, dead and gone into the oblivion?"

"Who knows? Who cares?" Axel muttered.

"Does that stupid vague prophecy say anything about getting rid of the demon?" Hailey asked. "Why wouldn't he just vanish, now that he doesn't have Kyra?"

Alexis tossed her hair over her shoulder. "We have to send him back to Hell. While Kyra is alive there is always a chance he could get her back on his side."

"I would never join him again," Kyra said flatly. "Not even to save your souls now." Her hard stare swept the room. "Hopefully you all learned the difference between death and getting into Heaven."

Iris nodded, staring down at her feet.

"It's better to accept death now, than give in to evil to save yourself from pain, only to end up in Hell later," Hailey said in understanding, looking for Kyra's approval.

Axel shook his head. "What do we know for sure?" He looked at his sister and raised his eyebrows as high as his forehead would allow. He blinked his wide eyes firmly at her, waiting for her to speak up.

Alexis rolled her eyes and huffed, annoyed by her brother's lack of subtlety.

"I have an enormous collection of grimoires, passed down from our ancestors. After we returned home from being prisoners in that basement, Axel and I hit the books. There are over a hundred of them, and some are as thick as encyclopedias, so it was impossible for me to reread them all. They are sort of like diaries of magical experiences and spells from the witches in our bloodline."

"So, do they have anything on demons?" Jensen asked.

"There's a lot of good spells, but nothing that really helps with this type of demon. It's all related to the low level, mischievous demons that live on Earth in human form."

"Could we alter any of those spells to be stronger and work on Alastor?"

"We could try, but there's no way of knowing if it would work until it's too late." Alexis tapped her chin, then added, "The protection spells that we cast around the house to keep out demons and keep us hidden could be altered to keep a demon captive. If we combined it with crystals and a demon binding spell, it might work on Alastor."

"That's not so bad, I'll just ask the demon to stand still and not fight us while we're chanting," Axel joked.

"I may have an idea," Kyra said softly. "We might be able to block his powers."

"How?" Hailey asked quickly.

"Alastor has some kind of crystals set up in the basement that block my powers, but not his. Colleen had two different ones when she came after me. I don't remember what they were, but I think one blocks witches' powers, and one blocks angels'. Maybe, if we could figure out what blocks demon powers, we could use that against him."

Jez shook her head. "My mother gave me this ring when I was young," she said, holding up her right hand, flashing the ring, "to protect me from demons. She knew a lot about demons and angels…" She looked at Kyra. "I guess now, I know why. Anyway, the point is, it didn't work, but it should have."

"Maybe he's not *just* a demon…" Kyra trailed off and looked at the carpet.

"What do you mean? What else could he be?" Jez tipped her head back. "The prophecy says a demon, or the Antichrist, will come to Earth."

"Alastor told me the story of the first demon—his mother. Lucifer is his father—he was an angel, then a fallen angel, then a demon. His mother, Lilith, was the first witch, then she became a demon and had children with Lucifer." She scratched the base of her neck. "So, Alastor could be a melhara, like me, but the power blocking crystals that work on me didn't work on him, so what would a fallen angel and a demon make?" She paused and tapped her index finger over her lips. "He could be a saharki, if you count Lucifer as a demon and Lilith as a witch, or maybe a witch and a fallen angel, or just all demon but he's too strong for the crystals? He could need demon, angel, and witch crystals to block all of his powers."

Alexis fidgeted with her hair. "But we can't do that, or we'd be powerless too."

"Maybe not. I have an idea that we should test out."

Axel snorted. "I don't like the sound of that."

"Power sharing. The crystals block powers, they don't erase them. It's possible we could still power-share with our witch powers blocked."

"If that even works, it's only useful if Alastor doesn't have angel powers."

"I know he doesn't—well somewhat, because he used mine. But he can travel, which could be tricky. Jez, is there a difference between archangel powers and a fallen angel with regards to the crystals we need to use?"

"I don't know of any archangel crystals, but I know what we need for fallen angels." She smiled.

"A lot of the stuff at the press conference—when I was with Alastor—just happened; I'm not sure if I did it, or he did, or it was just instinct. It's all a blur now; I can't remember the details clearly," Kyra said.

Alexis poked Kyra. Kyra returned the playful poke before she hugged Alexis.

"If all else fails, there is one way to rip him from this world," she said, pulling away from Alexis. "I've seen countless variations in my dreams, which I now know have actually happened in the past."

"Well, what is it?"

"The death of the melhara. My death."

Chapter Thirty-One

Darkness cascaded over the Earth, choking out the light. Hordes of demons ran wild in the streets, guiding the souls with dark auras to attack the light ones. The hospitals had been closed down and all government systems had vanished from the public eye, leaving no one to enforce the laws anymore. Once-good people were now stealing and killing out of fear, darkening their souls with every passing day. The apocalypse was well underway. Evil overran the world—real evil. His plan was coming together faster than he expected and the end would soon be near...

There was just one problem.

"Matt! Get in here right now!" Alastor bellowed at the ceiling.

A gangly runt rushed into the office, tripping over his own feet in his haste. His hair was greasy and his clothes several sizes too large for him. He was a scrawny little boy that couldn't strike fear into the heart of a child, a poor excuse for a soldier in the apocalypse—but he did make up for it in determination infused with pure psychosis.

"We haven't found her yet, but I got calls that her friend's condo in Calgary and the New York place appear to have been vacant for a while," he announced.

"I won't need her anymore—as long as she stays alive, that is. Her friends won't kill her, now that she's out of my influence, and she can handle any attacks from humans."

"So, you want me to call off the search?"

"Yes, you moron," Alastor snapped, annoyed by the constant incompetence and stupidity of humans. "The world is still spiraling into darkness without her here."

"Yes, sir."

Alastor turned his back on the young man and gazed out the picture window into the open fields.

"The humans are to be banished from the manor. Contact all of them and make sure they understand, they are never to return here."

"Yes, sir. What would you like them to do for you out there?"

"It matters not. I have no use for them anymore. Follow this last order, and then you are free to do as you please."

"Yes, sir."

"Send that demon secretary in here."

"Yes, sir. It has been an honor to serve you." Matt inclined his head toward Alastor and left the room.

Alastor heard a woman's light footsteps enter his office. "Contact every demon and half demon on this Earth and have them gather here, immediately."

"Whatever for?"

Alastor recognized the voice and it was not the one he was expecting. He spun around and came face to face with a brilliant beauty smothered in gold. Jet black hair shot straight down her back, stopping just above the floor. Symbols branded the flesh of her entire body.

"My husband is eager to join us and is growing impatient." Her eyes flashed into the golden slitted eyes of a reptile when she blinked.

Alastor dropped to his knee and bowed his head. "My Queen, welcome." He looked up. "I was not expecting your arrival so soon."

She motioned him to rise. "Of course not. You didn't bring me out of that cage."

"Your Majesty, it was not yet time, but soon it shall be." He searched her face. "Things are unraveling faster than anticipated."

Her sandals clicked on the marble as she circled him. "So I've heard." She trailed her index finger along his chest. "I've also heard that you lost the melhara." Their eyes locked.

"I'm afraid I have." He bowed his head. "But no other prince of Hell has ever gotten this far, since Azazel."

"Why didn't you release me, if there were enough evil powers stirring in the air?" She eyed him suspiciously.

"It takes a lot of power to release you, my Queen. The goal is to overrun the Earth with sheer numbers of demons, rather than the more powerful ones, to speed up conditions favorable for freeing our lord."

She lowered her eyes. "Very well, Alastor. I'll assist you." She cocked her head and toyed with the serpent necklace dangling around her neck. "That is what you are saying, isn't it, that you could use my immense power to further *our* goals."

"Yes... yes, it would be much appreciated."

She turned her back on him, sauntering over to the shelves on one wall. She walked along them, trailing her claws along his books. Alastor grimaced at the sound of leather and paper shredding, and the four long, white gouges she left behind.

"May I inquire how you came to be in this plane?" he asked.

"A loyal subject." She shot him a withering look. "More loyal than you, perhaps."

He lowered his eyes. "Does this subject have a name?"

"That is none of your concern! And why would one be so eager to know this name?" She flung a glare over her shoulder as she moved along the bookshelves.

"Sorry, my Queen. Perhaps, this demon is trying to move up the ranks by insinuating that I have not been performing my duties."

"No need to worry, my son. Everything is as it should be."

"Yes, my Queen." He bowed.

"Out with it, already," she screeched in irritation.

"My Queen?" he asked, unsure what she was referring to—not knowing what else she may have seen or been informed of—and distracted with running through the candidates who might have helped her escape Hell, now that he had heard Celista was dead.

"Where is the melhara? She needs to be brought here and locked up, to ensure that we can remain." She threw a heavy leatherbound book at his head. He ducked and the book slammed into the wall behind him. Pages exploded on impact, releasing the musty smell of the old leather cover in a cloud of dust.

"I like it here," she continued, trailing along the wall. "Too long, I've waited and watched this world change from the confines of Hell." She stopped and glared at him. "I am not leaving."

"I have not been able to locate her. She is with the other witches and they are all hidden from me."

"What!" The shelf behind her burst into flames. "You worthless maggot! Hunt them down before they show up to destroy you!"

Several books flew off the shelf and sailed through the air toward Alastor. He held out his hands and they disintegrated before he could be struck.

"Your powers are severely diminished without her."

"The world is on its way to apocalypse, obviously, or you wouldn't have been able to escape Hell," he reminded her bitterly.

"Watch your tongue," she hissed.

"Yes, my Queen."

"Why do you have all of these senseless books? You've grown too accustomed to the human condition."

"The witches will come for me when they think they can defeat me," he said, trying to redirect her. "Before they do, defenses need to be placed in and around this building."

"And how do you intend to accomplish that, with a bunch of rocks and an army of half-breeds? It amazes me, the boundless stupidity that fills that space between your horns, that you call a brain."

"With all due respect, there is a difference between theoretical strategy and the execution of one, and it has been some time since you have—"

"Irrelevant," she snapped. "I've seen their powers, and very few demons will hold up to them. The saharkis don't stand a chance; they have the intelligence of a gnat."

"We have the numbers. They need more than one witch's powers to dispose of higher-level demons. We can separate them and force Kyra to the cells."

"That won't work. You need to attack them, capture the melhara, and kill the rest, not sit around planning."

"We could block all powers throughout the building and have a good old-fashioned bludgeoning with swords, axes, maces, and other weapons of the same nature," he suggested, hopeful that she would be appeased.

"That's not too terrible an idea, if of course you meant, seek them out and block the powers where they are." She toyed with her necklace, smiling as her eyes drifted to the ceiling. "Slaughtering in Hell doesn't quite have the same thrill as cutting down someone who is still alive."

The house began to rumble. The jingling of chandeliers echoed in from the hall. Pens rolled off the desk onto the floor. A few books worked loose from their shelves and tumbled to the floor.

She looked around. "Is that an earthquake?"

"Worse. It's Kyra. They're already here."

"Stupid mortals." She spun on her heel and headed for the exit. "We only need the melhara alive."

"Lilith, we're not prepared to take them on."

"Don't be such a coward."

Lilith disappeared through the doorway. Alastor quickly followed her into the hall. The rumbling dissipated, leaving the house quiet and still.

"Where are they?" she demanded, searching the vacant foyer.

"Outside, but there are more presences than just the melhara out there."

"It matters not. They shall all die."

She stormed toward the doors and they burst open. Sunlight flooded the grand foyer, bringing the cool morning breeze with it. Lilith stepped outside and surveyed the lawn. Partway down the dirt driveway, Kyra stood with her hands on her hips.

"Melhara, I'm so glad you have returned to us." Lilith's lips curled, her eyes glowing.

Alastor walked up beside Lilith, his eyes sweeping over the faces in the group that stood before them: his melhara, the three irritating witches, the appalling Majai, and two of his men whose souls he had overlooked in claiming. No matter now—they were just humans.

"I've returned to end this nightmare." Kyra looked at Lilith. "Who are you, Celista's replacement?"

"Hardly. Neither of you can compare to me."

The Majai men glided around the witches. "Lilith, you are not permitted to be here," said one of them, pointing a finger at her. The witches swung their heads toward them, eyes wide and mouths hanging open.

She laughed. "I do as I please."

"*The* Lilith?" Alexis whispered. "That can't be a good sign."

Jez looked over her shoulder and nodded at Jensen. He nodded back and nudged Vance. They circled around the two demons, giving them a wide berth before disappearing into the mansion.

Lilith and Alastor barely glanced at them as they passed by—they were powerless mortals and not a threat to either of them. Alastor's focus remained with the witches; they were the key to his undoing and as long as he didn't break the rules of the prophecy, the Majai couldn't touch him. But Lilith had broken the rules by leaving Hell early.

Lilith whispered to Alastor, "Get the melhara and kill the others." Then she stomped toward the group and drew her hands together. Her arms swept open, lifting Jez and Axel off their feet and hurling them in one direction as Kyra and Alexis flew in the other.

The two Majai men stood alone. They exchanged glances, though their expressions gave no insight into their thoughts.

Lilith walked up to them and grabbed each man by his throat, lifting them both off the ground, their feet dangling. She squeezed, choking the life out of them.

Jez scrambled to her feet. Kyra and Alexis had already picked themselves up. Alastor headed to intercept them. He grabbed Alexis by her hair and threw her back down. Kyra reached out to stop him but he snatched up her wrist and twisted. She dropped to her knees. He turned and started dragging her to the house.

Axel slammed his fist into the earth. A streak of lightning ripped through the clear sky and struck Lilith in the back of her head. She stumbled forward. The feet of the Majai touched the soil, and they ducked out of the demon's grip, turned, and each took an arm, forcing her to the ground. Her arms began to crystalize, the effect creeping toward her torso as flakes of gold fell off her and floated away.

The sky blackened as swirling dust and debris pulled from the earth, violently rotating overhead. Dense fog formed around the house, blocking Alastor's retreat. He pushed forward and hit a wall, a supernatural barrier of layered fog strengthened by the windstorm. He tried to step through again. It was solid. He waved his free arm at the wall, then pushed against it, to no avail.

He turned and growled before dropping Kyra. His eyes flickered between Jez and Alexis. As he prepared to unleash his wrath on the women, Kyra jumped up and pushed him from behind. He staggered forward. She pushed him again, this time without physically touching him. He stumbled a few more steps. Axel rushed over and the four witches surrounded him.

Alastor straightened and cackled, then his eyes glazed over into shiny black pools.

This time his transformation was violent. His human form ripped away from his bones as his torso and limbs elongated. Gray skin crawled over his musculature as it swelled and hardened into an unnatural physique. Smooth black horns sprouted from his crown, spiraling as they screamed toward the sky. His cheeks sank in, his cheekbones protruding in bony shelves; scythe-like fangs protruded from his mouth; wings sprouted from his back, then folded over his shoulders like a leathery cape.

He stepped forward and then stood, cloven feet wide apart, shoulders pushed back and chest outthrust, towering over them. His head dropped downward and shifted as he ran those black, lifeless eyes over them. Then it stretched back, holding his head high, black eyes still glaring at them over his grossly exaggerated cheekbones.

As one, the four witches held out their arms; the demon dropped to his knees. He fell forward, catching himself with his hands, but he was being forced down, crushed under the weight of intolerable gravity. The earth cracked under the pressure of his knees and hands upon it. Hairline spider cracks grew underneath him and radiated outward.

The wall of fog behind him dissipated to a faint misty curtain, and a scrawny soldier, his clothes too big, his hair greasy, burst out of the manor, looked quickly around, then rushed toward Alastor. Easily passing through the remains of the fog, he stumbled across the rutted dirt driveway and through the long grass. Before he could reach them, Kyra squinted her eyes at him and he was ripped off his course, thrown through the air to land on his back with a thud in the long grass.

Lilith pulled herself free of the Majai men, kicking one to the ground and pulling the other to her. She snapped his neck and dropped the body in time to lunge at the other man as he tried to stand on his broken leg.

The scrawny soldier scrambled back to his feet, pulling a knife from his belt. The blade glimmered in the sunlight as he lifted it high and charged at Axel. Axel broke the circle and turned toward his attacker. The hold over Alastor began to waiver. The demon pulled himself up off the ground.

"Axel! We need you to get back here!" Alexis shouted.

Axel flung his arm at his attacker, knocking him off his feet.

"Some kid is trying to kill me," he replied as he turned back to the demon.

"He can't; he's one of Alastor's men," Alexis assured him, and Alastor grinned.

Even so, Axel tried his best to keep Alastor's lackey—and the knife—in his peripheral vision as the man charged.

Lilith smiled as the knife plunged into Axel's back.

Chapter Thirty-Two

The blade scraped over his ribs as it slid out of Axel's side. He dropped to his knees, instinctively bringing his hands to the hole in his side. Blood oozed out between his fingers. Failing in his struggle to breathe he toppled over, collapsing on his uninjured side. Every breath felt as if the knife was entering his body again. He coughed, sputtering bright red blood. A wave of pain made his body stiffen, and he clutched at the agony in his side with every cough. Gasping for air, he rolled his head toward the others.

Alastor and Lilith had vanished.

Alexis flung Axel's attacker against the wall of the house, then jumped on him before he could recover, strangling him with her bare hands, slamming his head back against the brick wall as hard as she could. Fueled by blind rage, she groped for the knife he had dropped beside him and pressed the blood-slick blade against his neck. A thin red line appeared.

Kyra rushed to Axel and dropped down beside him.

"Axel! Axel, look at me," she sobbed, cradling his head.

His eyes darted around before they focused on her face. He parted his lips and tried to speak, but the words caught in his throat. Kyra pressed her hands against the gaping wound in his side. She closed her eyes and rocked back and forth. A white glow radiated from Kyra's hands and a searing pain speared his side. Axel howled in pain. His back arched as he thrashed around beneath her.

Alexis ran over and dropped to her knees on Axel's other side.

"Stop, you're killing him!" she screamed. She looked desperately from her brother to Kyra. "Kyra, stop!"

Kyra continued, ignoring her—or not hearing her; Axel wasn't sure which. He cried out again, involuntarily, and Alexis jumped on Kyra, pushing her off him. The girls rolled away, stirring up dust as they wrestled in the dirt. Jezabelle stood nearby, watching with a stunned look on her face.

Axel's pain evaporated. Momentarily lightheaded at its blessed absence, he touched the hole in his side to find it nonexistent. The pain had faded to an ache under Kyra's touch, and was now no more than a memory—if it weren't for the blood that soaked his shirt, he would have written it all off as an illusion.

He jumped up and pulled Alexis from Kyra. She spun around, stared at him in momentary shock, then embraced him, struggling to hold back her tears. She pulled back and looked at Kyra.

"You can heal?"

Kyra smiled. "I only recently learned how. I guess it's part of the half-angel package." She looked at Axel and their eyes lingered in a moment of tranquility that felt like the world had faded away.

Jez and Alexis looked to their fallen comrades.

"Lilith took out the Majai. Can you fix them?"

Kyra's eyes moved to the Majais' lifeless bodies. "I can't. They are..." She trailed off as they stirred.

They rose from the dirt, their white robes spotless, and clasped their hands together in front of them, looking at the witches as if nothing had happened. When Kyra and Alexis looked to Axel as if expecting an explanation from him, he shrugged.

"Let's get into that house and finish this," Jez said, and headed for the double doors.

They burst through the doors and skidded to a halt in the marble foyer. Finding no living obstacles, they swung around the corner into a long, wide corridor, where Jensen and Vance waited alone in front of an arched alcove at the end of the hall. A semicircle of colored pillar candles burned in front of the mirror inside the archway. Various crystals had been carefully arranged between the candles, several types between each candle. The colorful display reminded Axel of a rainbow.

"Is everything ready?" he asked the two ex-cons.

Jensen looked over the display on the floor before responding. "Yep. What about the other demon chick?"

"She doesn't change anything."

"The Majai said she's not supposed to be here; what does that even mean?" Vance asked.

Kyra grinned. "That we need to… dispose of her, as well. But first things first." She moved up next to Jensen to look over his work on the floor, then asked Jez and Alexis, "Does this look right?" They looked over the arrangement, glanced at each other, then nodded to Kyra.

Axel moved around the circle of crystals and candles while Jensen hugged Jez and whispered something to her. Then, Vance and Jensen stepped back from the others and shuffled a few yards down the hallway, passing the Majai. Kyra joined the semicircle with Jez on her left and Axel on her right, reaching out for them to take her hands.

"You guys ready for this?"

Jez bobbed her head, staring silently at the floor inside the circle.

"I can't believe this is really happening," Alexis said, shaking her head. "If you would have told me, a year ago, that we'd be doing this, I would have laughed in your face. Axel finally moving home, Kyra using magic so prodigiously and discovering she has a half-sister, the whole world knowing that I'm a witch, and we're fighting demons together with untested, altered spells from my family's grimoires."

"Don't forget the apocalypse from Revelations." Axel tugged on her hand and winked.

"Yeah…" she sighed.

"Let's do this." Kyra bowed her head and chanted, the others joining in as she cast the spell.

Electricity charged the air in the hall. Axel felt the hair on his arms rise as evil seeped around them. Alexis squeezed his hand tighter, as if her grip would keep the evil entity contained. Kyra kept chanting, seemingly unaffected by the change in the atmosphere as they conjured the demon.

The transparent manifestation grew from the center of the rock circle, first shiny black hooves, then more of the demon formed, until his facial features solidified and he moved, his massive horns scraping the eleven-foot-high ceiling.

"What is this? How is this possible?" Alastor bellowed. He tried to step over the circle and bounced back to the center of the circle with a hollow thud that echoed down the hall.

"It's a cage, Alastor," Kyra said calmly, scowling.

"I can't be bound by a witch trap," Alastor said dismissively.

"Technically, it's a saharki demon trap," Alexis said cheerfully, "but we added a little extra just for you."

The demon flipped his hands open and bared his fangs. When nothing happened, he shook his arms and his feet burst into flames. He curled his fingers into his palms, extinguishing the hellfire, and growled, low.

Kyra's pupils dilated. *"Malum vivere. EGO praeceptum infernum ad aperi autem caveam. Vivere malum."*

Nothing happened. She spoke the words again, slower, careful to pronounce them properly as she drew all the power she could from her friends.

The refection in the mirror behind Alastor rippled, as if the glass were melting in waves. Then the reflection gave way to blackness, and flames of red and orange licked up from the bottom of the mirror, dancing around behind the glass without extending into this realm; nevertheless, intense heat seeped into the hallway where they stood. The dark void that festered in the vast space beyond—endless space—smothered the light from the flames, and the offensive odor of burning sulphur streamed into this world.

Kyra pushed the palms of her hands at the demon and his body slid backward, hooves skidding over the floor. He leaned forward, struggling to take a labored step before his hooves slid through the archway.

The floor beneath him ripped open. He dropped in, but caught himself on the edges of the archway with both arms. The demon howled as flames danced over him, climbing up his body to consume him, the sound more like that of a wolf than a human. He gripped the doorway and pulled himself back onto this side of the portal.

Slimy black hands reached out from the flames, clawing at his legs. The chanting witches glimpsed the ground underneath the flames—not ground at all, but a pool of water; a lake of burning sulphur—the lake of fire.

Alastor kicked the hands away and pulled himself farther from the portal.

BANG.

Everyone flinched, looked at the demon—who was just as surprised—glanced at each other, then looked behind them.

As the sound echoed off the walls, the gold-smothered demon suddenly appeared in the hallway, closer to the other archway than to this one. Her black hair stood on end and fanned out across the walls and the ceiling like the threads of a spiderweb. Kyra turned her head and glared at Lilith. She stepped toward her, her friends quickly falling in behind, and they lined up across the hall, blocking her path to Alastor. The Majai started down the long hallway, walking with determination toward her. Jensen and Vance stepped aside, pressing their backs against the wall as the Majai moved past them.

Lilith held up her hand and smiled. "You pathetic fools. You're too late. This world is destroying itself and I will finish pushing it into ruin."

Axel heard hooves shuffling behind him and started to turn his head toward Alastor when Lilith shrieked. He jerked his head back in time to see flaming globes hurtling toward them. His hands flew up and snuffed them out before they made contact with anyone. *That was pathetic, for a supposedly all-powerful witch.*

The Majai picked up their pace, their stride still graceful.

Axel no longer felt the heat from the flames within the mirror behind him. He turned. The mirror had been restored and the demon was stepping through.

"He's escaping!" Axel shouted as he lunged for Alastor.

Kyra bolted after him.

The demon slipped from Axel's grasp and disappeared into the mirror. Axel reached out for Kyra, grabbed her arm, and felt his hand sliding down to her wrist as she merged into her reflection. He tried to follow her, but his hand smacked into the mirror, then his body hit and rebounded, and he lost his grip on Kyra. He looked at his empty hand, then balled up his fists and thumped them on the archway.

"Axel," Alexis said calmly, dispelling his anger.

He hung his head, dropped his fists, and turned to the others. The Majai had stopped and were watching him. Looking past them to Lilith, he felt his body grow hotter as his anger flourished again, and refocused it on her.

Lilith sneered.

He launched into a sprint toward her, only to be abruptly halted by the confines of the demon trap, his body jolting back. Lilith cackled as he slammed to the floor, adding to his anger.

Alexis and Jez crouched, splitting their attention between watching Lilith and helping Axel, as they pulled crystals and candles from the circle. Vance and Jensen rushed over to help them.

Axel stretched out his arm, waved it around above the area where the circle had been, then started to step out. Suddenly, Kyra and Alastor burst through the mirror and crashed into Axel; the three of them fell to the floor and sprawled over the boundaries of the open demon trap.

Jez and Alexis shrank back, their eyes darting over the candles and crystals scattered over the floor. Jez sprang to her feet and Alexis swept an armful of crystals toward her, then jumped up.

Alastor rolled off of Axel, knocking Kyra off his back, and rose to his feet. When the weight lifted off Axel, he pushed himself up off the floor, hesitating when he saw Kyra lying on her back beside him—until her eyes met his, then they both scrambled to get off the floor.

Alastor wrapped his arms around Kyra's waist, lifting her from her feet, and tried to step into the mirror again. Jensen and Vance dove forward and wrapped their arms around his legs as Axel clung to the demon's forearm and jerked him back. Jez and Alexis reached out for Kyra's flailing hands, caught them, and pulled her out of his grasp as he stumbled and fell.

They released the demon as he dropped. The women shifted to surround him, the palms of their hands held out toward him. Axel joined them and Jensen and Vance scrambled to move the crystals and candles back into place while the witches held Alastor down.

He writhed, twisted into a ball and forced his hooved feet underneath his body, resisting the restraint. Before he could push himself fully upright, they finished resetting the trap and stepped back. When the witches dropped their hands, Alastor stood with ease and swung at the invisible wall. His arm rebounded and shot back at him. The demon threw his head back and shrieked his fury.

With Alastor secure, the Majai return their focus to Lilith and started down the hall toward her again.

"You're on your own boy," Lilith called sharply. "I told you, I'm not going back in there. Better luck next time—in about three thousand years." She winked at him and vanished.

He growled, his eyes on the spot where Lilith had been standing.

The witches turned back to Alastor. His eyes darted around their faces.

"Fucking witches."

Kyra ignored him and read the inscription carved into the arch. The portal reopened.

Axel's hands flipped out and the flames grew higher as the demon was sucked back into the abyss. Tar-slicked hands grasped his legs and began to pull him in. The three women held their palms toward him, pushing him through the portal.

He howled and roared as he was pulled under the burning lake. The cries were garbled under the water, but remained audible until the space in the arch rippled back into a mirror.

Kyra and the others stood motionless for a moment, staring at their reflections. Slowly their tense bodies relaxed. Kyra released a sigh of relief.

"He's gone."

Epilogue

The witches stood in the rooftop garden of Alexis's downtown condo building. Alexis and Kyra leaned over the railing and surveyed the damage on the streets below as Jez and Axel joined them.

"So, is it over?" Axel asked, leaning over the railing next to Kyra.

"Hardly. There's a ton of damage control we need to do."

"Yeah, like the rest of the demons you said he brought to Earth," Alexis said, still watching the streets. She looked toward Kyra. "How many are there?"

"He has a list in his office files. We can go back and grab it." Kyra sighed. "But that's not even the worst thing we have to deal with."

"Fantastic!" Axel blurted sarcastically. "What else is there to try to fix in this apocalypse?"

"Alastor and I—" Kyra hesitated at the looks on her friends' faces and changed her choice of words. "I mean, the demon and I may have brought some eggs here from another plane, to hatch."

"What kind of eggs?" Jez squeaked, eyes wide.

"Dragon eggs."

"Crap."

"That can't be good," Axel mumbled, pulling Kyra under his arm and giving her a quick squeeze.

Alexis grimaced at her brother, then flashed a smile at Kyra. "Have they hatched yet?"

"I don't know, it's not like I took Dragon 101 in college." She felt a twinge of guilt. "I can't believe I let all of this happen. I destroyed the world."

"No, you didn't, the demon did," Jez said, leaning around Alexis so Kyra could see her face.

Alexis nodded. "You were just destined to go along for the ride," Alexis assured her. "It was your fate, but Alastor's fault."

Jez nodded and Alexis smiled, but Axel wasn't listening. Squinting at something in the distance, he leaned farther over the railing.

"Hey, that's the redhead from Washington. What's she doing here?"

Kyra followed his gaze to the familiar woman standing in the street, staring up at them. Vibrant red hair swirled down over her shoulders in a cascade of curls, blowing softly in the breeze before she whipped around and marched away.

"That's odd. She looks like one of the melharas from my dreams…"

***

Jez's eyes followed the red-head until she disappeared among the buildings then her head jerked back to Kyra. "We have to get those eggs out of here before they hatch," Jez urged, clamping her hands on the railing.

Kyra looked at her and nodded. "Anyone want to go on a weird-ass road trip with me?"

Acknowledgements

Thank you to all of my friends and family that supported and encouraged me over the years by reading my many versions of my work in progress.

Randina, Dawn, Amanda, and many others.

A very special thanks to Channy, Jenilee, Mary Ann, Sharlyn and Nicole, for providing me with constructive feedback that helped shape the story.

And thank you to the fantastic freelance editors from the Editors' Association of Canada, Vanessa Ricci-Thode and Marg Gilks.

If you enjoyed reading Melhara, please let others know by:

Giving Melhara, your star rating and writing a review on Goodreads, Amazon, and your other favorite review sites.

To learn more about the author and her novels check out the author website:

JocelynTollefson.com

And don't forget to join our mailing list for exclusive access, offers, and giveaways.

Thank you and happy reading :)